THE RECONSTRUCTION

THE RECONSTRUCTION

Karl Wiegers

Agent Q Bookworks
Happy Valley, OR

The Reconstruction

First Agent Q Bookworks edition 2017

Published in the United States by Agent Q Bookworks, an imprint of
Process Impact

Agent Q Bookworks
11491 SE 119th Drive
Happy Valley, OR 97086

Library of Congress Control Number: 2017949258
ISBN: 978-0-9992053-0-3

The Reconstruction is a work of fiction. Names, places, and incidents are
products of the author's imagination or are used fictitiously.

Cover design: Vinnie Kinsella

Printed in the United States of America

For Chris

Prologue

Friday, May 24

FRIDAY NIGHT WAS live music night at the Ruby Slippers Club on the south side of Eugene, Oregon. The volume dropped occasionally when the band ended a set, so you could talk to someone without shouting then, if you found someone worth talking to.

Nikki's eyes caught the kaleidoscope of colors reflecting from her tight silver dress as she walked into the club. She looked at the bouncer on duty. He smiled and winked at her, but Nikki pointedly turned her back. *Not tonight, asshole,* she thought.

The characteristic smells of a nightclub flowed over her. Thank goodness people couldn't smoke in bars anymore, she thought, but that just left more room for the heady aromas of sweat, alcohol, and desire. She waved to her friend behind the bar, sending her silver wrist bangles sparkling. "How are you, Peter?"

"Hey, Nikki, good to see you. Can I get you the usual?" She nodded. Peter van Tassel, part owner of Ruby Slippers, poured a Stoli vanilla vodka, neat, and pushed it across the bar. "First one's on me tonight."

Nikki smiled and nodded her appreciation. The heat of the first sip flowed down her core like lava. As she scanned the room, she spotted a few familiar faces, along with some intriguing new ones. Maybe tonight would be as much fun as she hoped.

At twenty-nine, Nikki was older than most of the student-heavy club crowd, but she knew she looked younger than she was. No one had ever complained about her age at the end of the night. Nikki unconsciously moved to the pounding music. It was hard not to when she felt every thump of the kick drum.

Nikki sipped her drink as she wandered through the crowd. She saw a solidly built man with curly blond hair rise from a chair and walk toward her with a drink in his hand, a woman with scarlet hair following. The man had a stubbly blond beard and a small diamond earring in his left ear.

"Hi. I'm Randy and this is Joy," the man said with a friendly smile. "Are you on your own tonight?"

"Just until my friend shows up. I'm Nikki. I come here pretty often for the music"—she met eyes with Joy—"and the scenery."

Joy took in Nikki's silver eyebrow ring and nose stud. "I like the purple streaks in your black hair and the butterfly," she said, touching the tattoo on Nikki's neck. "They fit your exotic look."

"Thanks, Joy. Your tats are cool too," Nikki replied, running her fingers down Joy's colorful left arm. "It must've hurt like hell to get all that done."

"It wasn't fun," Joy admitted. She extended her arm and rotated it. "It took four sessions. Hated every minute of it. I love how it came out, though."

Both Joy and Randy towered above Nikki as they stood near the club's wall. Randy idly stroked Joy's back, an action both sensual and possessive. Nikki could see solid biceps under his long-sleeved shirt. Randy worked out or worked hard, maybe both.

Joy moistened her crimson lips. "Would you like to dance with us, Nikki? I think this set's almost over." The band launched into a respectable cover of Aerosmith's "Walk This Way."

The three of them finished their drinks and joined the dozens of dancers on the floor, where it was sweaty and loud, erotic and exhilarating. Nikki danced with intensity, pressing up against first Joy, then Randy. They danced together through two more songs and then, when the band took a break, headed to a small table at the top of the stairs. Randy bought a round of drinks, and then another as they got better acquainted.

Randy and Joy exchanged a glance. When Joy nodded, almost imperceptibly, Randy leaned toward Nikki's ear and said, "It looks like your friend isn't going to show. Are you interested in a more private party, maybe? Just the three of us?"

Nikki glanced at Joy, who was looking at her with a small smile. "Sounds fun. Where do you suggest?"

Joy offered, "I'll ride with you to our apartment. Randy can meet us there."

The trio walked downstairs and out the front door. The big bouncer gave them an ominous look as they walked past, but Nikki was fixated on Randy and she didn't notice. Randy climbed into his Chevy Silverado and drove away. The women walked three blocks up Pressman Street and got into Nikki's black Honda Civic. They headed toward the neighborhood just west of the University of Oregon campus.

"Parking's always a nightmare around here. Too damn many students and apartment buildings. I see a space on the right by that streetlight in the middle of the next block." Joy pointed. "It's just two blocks to our apartment."

Joy took Nikki's hand when they stepped over the curb under the streetlight's yellow cone. As they entered the apartment, Randy met them with a bottle of vodka and a smoldering joint. Nikki dropped her clutch on an armchair by the front door and returned Randy's passionate kiss.

The two women followed Randy into the bedroom. Half of their clothes were off by the time they reached the king-sized bed. Nikki's short dress shimmered as it fell to the floor; her thong quickly followed. Her compact body bore no trace of hair, just several tattoos and a gold navel ring bearing a dangling turquoise butterfly.

As Joy shed her clothing, Nikki could see the full extent of her intricate tattoos, extending across her heavy breasts and down onto her belly. A colorful dragon on Randy's forearm had been concealed under his shirt. Now fully nude, Randy kissed Nikki heatedly as Joy nuzzled her neck from behind and reached around to cup her small breasts. "Mmm, you smell delicious, like vanilla sunshine," Joy breathed. They tumbled onto the king-sized bed. "We call this the playpen," Joy said with a wink.

*   *   *

When they stopped to catch their breath twenty minutes later, all three were sweaty and panting. The vodka and joint made another circuit. As Randy walked to the short dresser across the bedroom, he caught both women admiring the view of his broad shoulders and bare ass. He smiled to himself.

He returned to the bed with a pair of handcuffs, a riding crop, and an imposing dildo. Nikki raised her hands in protest. "Not my thing, sorry."

Randy was surprised. None of the other girls they'd brought home had objected to a little friendly S&M.

"No taste for adventure, Nikki?" he asked as he passed the handcuffs to Joy. "It's just for fun. If you try it, I think you'll like it."

Nikki shook her head and stood up. "No way, dude. If you want to play that game, I'm out of here. I'm not into pain."

Quick as a cobra, Joy grabbed Nikki's left wrist with her right hand and latched one of the handcuffs onto it. "Tonight you're into whatever we say you're into!" she snarled.

Nikki tried to pull away, but the larger woman kept a firm grip on the handcuffs. Nikki clawed for Joy's eyes with her right hand but missed. Her sharp nails scraped Joy's arm. Joy punched Nikki in the face with her right fist, drawing a bloody gush from Nikki's nose. Nikki desperately yanked her arm, trying to escape Joy's grasp but only scraping skin off her wrist in the process.

Randy dropped the toys and ran around the bed to grab Nikki. She aimed a kick at his groin, catching his upper thigh instead.

Randy backhanded Nikki hard across the face as the handcuffs, slick with blood from Nikki's abraded wrist, slipped from Joy's left hand. Suddenly off-balance, Nikki lurched backward and fell hard. The side of her head slammed into the sharp corner of a metal nightstand. Her neck snapped sideways. She collapsed onto the floor, her head at an impossible angle. Blood flowing from the hole in her head matted her hair and soaked into the carpet.

Joy and Randy stood naked in shocked silence.

"Fuck!" Randy screamed. "What if she's dead?"

"Shut up! Don't panic!" Joy was holding her hand over her racing heart. She knelt by Nikki's nude body, checked for a pulse, and listened for breathing. Randy could vaguely detect the metallic smell of Nikki's blood; closer to the body, Joy's nostrils flared at the odor. "Nothing," she said. "She's gone."

Nikki's eyes stared up at nothing between long lashes and smeared mascara.

"Oh, shit, I can't believe it." Randy put his shaking hands over his face. He breathed rapidly, practically hyperventilating. "Fuck," he whispered this time.

Randy and Joy sank to the floor together. They had just been looking for a party tonight, like usual. This was beyond anything in their experience.

"Now what?" Randy asked.

"Hell, I don't know. This is my first body." Joy paused, her face ashen. "We can't call 911. Look at her face and her wrist! The cops would know she was handcuffed. Even though it was an accident, we'll be in jail for the fight, at least. People have seen us at Ruby Slippers before, and people saw us walk out with her tonight. If anyone finds her body, we're the obvious suspects."

"What are you saying?"

"I'm not exactly sure. All I can think is that we have to make her disappear completely. We can't just throw her body into a dumpster, you know?"

They were silent until Randy said, "So we need to bury her someplace. Let me think." He paced around the apartment, begging his fogged brain to function. Eventually he said, "I know this isolated area south of Eugene above the Lorane Valley. When I worked for the logging company, we scouted forests around there. There are some little side roads going off into the woods. I think I can find one of those in the dark."

"That might work. It's almost two already. We need to get rid of her now, before it gets light, and worry about the rest later. I'm still shaking. I can't fucking believe this."

Joy and Randy quickly dressed in jeans, dark sweatshirts, and boots. Randy took a flashlight and some work gloves from the closet. He left the apartment and walked around to a small storage shed in the alley behind the building. He took out two shovels and quietly laid them in the bed of his truck.

Returning to the apartment, he saw that Joy had wrapped the dead woman's body in a bedsheet, now splotched with her blood. Nikki's silver bracelets, just costume jewelry, sat on the dresser.

Randy and Joy carried their bundle to the front door. They didn't see anyone outside and only a few lighted apartment windows down the block. Hoisting the body to his shoulder, Randy quickly carried it to the truck and laid it in the bed. While Joy climbed in, he covered Nikki with a tarp, weighing it down with the shovels.

Randy drove south on Sumner Street to the Lorane Highway. The streets were deserted. After another fifteen minutes he took a left onto Peaceful Valley Road, struck by the incongruity of that name. Two and a half miles later, Randy turned onto Redhawk Road and crept along until a narrow side lane came into range of the truck's headlights. He drove as far as he could into the woods and then stopped in a partial clearing when the trail petered out.

Joy and Randy sat in the truck for a moment. This far from city lights, the night sky sparkled with stars. They heard nothing but the slow ticking of the cooling engine and quiet night sounds. Randy and Joy looked at each other, overwhelmed by what they were about to do—and yet they saw no other option if they wanted to stay out of jail.

An hour later Randy and Joy climbed back into the truck, their clothing splattered with mud after digging a shallow forest grave. It began to sprinkle, becoming a steady rain as they headed back to Eugene. Physically and emotionally drained, they drove to the apartment in silence as the windshield wipers thrummed.

* * *

Randy woke on the living room floor early on a wet, gray Saturday morning. Nikki's sightless eyes had haunted his dreams. He surveyed the bloody mess in the bedroom and barely made it to the toilet before his stomach erupted.

Randy brushed his teeth and stared at himself in the mirror for a few moments. He looked like shit; he felt like shit. He returned to the living room to find Joy sitting cross-legged on the carpet. She dumped the contents of Nikki's small purse on the stained faux-wood coffee table. A lipstick tube fell off and rolled beneath the couch. Joy removed the dead woman's driver's license from her wallet.

"Christ, we didn't even know her last name. Briggs. Nicole Marie Briggs. 261 Northwest Richmond Street, Bend, Oregon. Wait, that can't be right. I thought she said she lived in Eugene."

"Maybe that's an old address," Randy said. "Sometimes people don't bother to notify DMV when they move. Shit. I was hoping we could clean out her apartment tonight so it looks like she left town."

"I found her keys. I'll go see if there's something in her car with her current address."

Ten minutes later, Joy returned to the apartment. "Got it!" she said, waving an envelope triumphantly. "This was on the front seat. It looks like it's from an insurance company, sent to Nicole Briggs at 1847 Jasper Street, Apartment 12, in Eugene."

"Great," Randy replied. "We'll go over there late tonight. Now, if we can get into her phone, we can go through her recent texts

and emails to see who she's in touch with. We could text those
people and say, I don't know, there's some kind of emergency and
she has to leave Eugene right away. That might buy us more time."

"Good idea." Joy turned on the phone. The passcode screen
appeared. "Uh-oh, it's locked. We probably have ten guesses before
it bricks. Where do you want to start?"

"Try the obvious ones. We'll get more creative if we need to."

Joy started touching numbers. "Okay, 1234… no good…
0000… nope. Same for 1111." She tried a few more combinations.
"Crap, 2580, 5555, and 1397 all failed too."

"How about her birthday?" Randy suggested.

Joy looked at the license again. "November 25. Nope, 1125
didn't work, either. I'll try her street address, 1847. Shit. We've only
got a couple more tries."

They sat silently for a minute. The phone would lock up soon.
Eventually Randy said, "Maybe try the birthday backwards: 2511?"

"I'm in!"

Joy touched the Facebook icon first. The app was already open
and Nikki was logged in. "I'll post something about an emergency,
but first I'm going to scan her old posts so I can try to sound like
her." Joy scrolled for a few minutes and then she wrote:

> Hey all, just found out I got a friend with an emergency.
> Should be OK but I gotta help out. Gonna be busy so don't
> worry if you don't hear from me for a while. Back ASAP.
> Kisses.

The post popped up in Nikki's Facebook timeline.

"I'll send a text of the same thing to people who look like her
regular contacts. If anyone responds, we'll just ignore it or send
them some vague reply." She typed a few texts and then turned off
the phone so no one could locate it.

Randy and Joy spent the rest of the day cleaning up. They
rented a carpet cleaner from Home Depot. Even after they went
over the bloody carpet three times, a faint stain remained, so they
repositioned the bed to conceal it. The carpets in their apartment

were already covered with stains anyway, so probably no one would ever notice this new one.

Joy suggested, "We might want to think about moving in case anybody here saw us in the middle of the night with her."

"You're probably right. Have we missed anything?" Randy wondered aloud. "We don't want her mail to pile up. That would be a red flag. People can ask the post office to hold their mail. Let me check their website." He navigated to usps.com on his phone. "No problem. I don't even need to prove I'm her. How dumb is that? I just need her address, email, and phone number." Joy gave Randy the information from Nikki's phone and the letter she found in the car. He set up a one-month mail hold.

Shortly after midnight they drove in Randy's truck to Nikki's apartment on Jasper Street. Her second-floor unit was near a dimly lit corner of the apartment building's parking lot. The first key they tried opened the door.

Nikki had been something of a slob. Dirty dishes were piled in the sink, and clothes lay strewn on an ancient green sofa and the unmade bed. The apartment held the musty odor of unwashed clothing.

They went through the closets and dresser hastily, stuffing most of Nikki's clothing and personal items into garbage bags. Joy threw out the perishables from the refrigerator so they wouldn't stink. They had brought the clothing Nikki had been wearing the night before and her wrist bangles over to her apartment in a garbage bag, which they tossed into the dumpster behind her building.

"Now it looks like she just moved out," Joy said. "Let's go home. This is creeping me out."

They heaved the bags into the truck bed and deposited them in several donation boxes on the drive back to their apartment.

Sunday morning Randy and Joy wracked their brains for anything they had overlooked. Notified friends via texts: check. Notified the world through Facebook: check. Cleaned out Nikki's apartment: check. Got rid of the blood: check (well, mostly).

"Her phone," Randy remembered. He pulled the SIM card out of the phone and crushed it into uselessness. Now the phone had effectively disappeared. They took every piece of paper and card from Nikki's purse, cut them into tiny pieces, and flushed them down the toilet, even the laminated driver's license.

Joy suddenly looked alarmed. "What about her car? She didn't have a residential parking permit for this zone."

"Geez, I forgot about that. Where did she park?"

"We found a space two blocks over on Sixteenth."

"We'd better move it. I hope it wasn't ticketed or towed. Get her keys and let's check."

They donned hooded rain jackets and walked to the parking space. The Civic was still there, but a soggy pink parking ticket poked out from under the windshield wiper. Randy stuffed the ticket into his jacket pocket and moved the car several blocks away to get out of the residential permit zone. He made a mental note to keep it parked legally until they could get rid of it. An abandoned car would raise questions they didn't need.

Once Randy had parked the car, Joy rifled around and found the registration and title in the glove compartment. "That girl had no sense, keeping the title in the car," she said.

Randy suggested they try to sell the car on craigslist or by posting notes on bulletin boards. Joy could sign the title with Nikki's name. No buyer would bother to check if she was really Nicole Briggs. Why wouldn't she be? The car was old but in good shape; it ought to move fast. College students were always looking for cheap cars. They walked back to the apartment as water streamed off their rain jackets.

"I think that does it," Randy said as they shut the door behind them. "Now we just have to act like everything's normal and hope nobody saw anything. We might want to stay out of Ruby Slippers for a while."

A glint beneath the living room couch caught Joy's eye. She picked up the lipstick tube—not her shade—and threw it in the trash.

Nicole Marie Briggs had been deleted.

Chapter 1

Five Years Later

Sunday, May 6

JESSICA SANFORD STRETCHED her arms out as she absorbed the spectacular scenery from the Columbia Rim Trail, thirty-five miles east of Portland. "This is why I live in Oregon!" she proclaimed.

There was nothing better to do on a sunny day in May than to go hiking with friends. The view soared above the water sparkling at the bottom of the magnificent Columbia River Gorge. Looking to her right Jessica could see the gorge cliffs receding into the distance in endless shades of gray and blue. Directly in front of her, to the north, loomed the snow-covered mass of Washington's Mount Adams, all 12,281 feet of it. At home, Jessica had a certificate from the Cascaders Mountain Club proving she had summited the truncated peak of Mount St. Helens, off to her half-left and still misshapen after its devastating 1980 eruption. In the distance in between those two peaks lay the grandest mountain of all in the Cascade Range, Rainier.

"I've been hiking in Oregon for six years and this is still my favorite trail," Jessica said.

Jessica's girlfriend, Maria Estrada-Domingo, said, "Stay right there, babe. I'm going to take a selfie of us with the mountains."

Both women set their backpacks down and smiled for the camera. This shot would be a great memento of their four-month anniversary.

They watched the colorful dots of windsurfers skimming on the Columbia River more than 800 feet below. A long freight train paralleled the stream of traffic crawling along on Interstate 84 at the base of the cliff. The last time Jessica had hiked this trail, the air was pungent with smoke from wildfires in southern Washington. Today, though, all she smelled was fresh spring forest. The gorge wind whipped their hair, Jessica's sleek and black, Maria's curly and light brown.

Jessica took a long pull from her water bottle. "How far back are the others?" she asked Maria.

"Just a few minutes, I think. We've been walking quite a bit faster, even with your stubby legs. Besides, they're older than we are. They're probably taking a nap."

"Hey, just because you're the baby of this group, don't go getting cocky."

"Twenty-five's not exactly a 'baby,' baby. Besides, I might be younger, but you're cuter."

Jessica had to smile at that. "Let's go to where we said we'd stop for lunch and wait for them there." The women slipped their arms through the straps of their matching teal-colored day packs, purchased from Great Northwestern Outfitters with the help of Maria's employee discount, and continued down the trail.

Maria said, "I wanted to talk to you alone today anyway, Jess. So, when do I get to meet your parents?"

"Anytime you like, as long as you don't mind going to Boise. They don't travel much these days."

"That's fine. I've never been to Boise. Maybe we can take a week, drive through Walla Walla for some wine tasting and hike around the John Day Fossil Beds on the way home."

Jessica was enthused. "That sounds great. I never get tired of Walla Walla wines. I can go anytime next month. What does your schedule look like?"

"Should be doable. Will your parents be shocked that you're bringing home a woman?"

"Nah, they've known I'm bi for years. They're cool with it," Jessica replied as she climbed over a tree that had fallen across the trail. "Besides, I already told them I have a new girlfriend."

"That's good. But are they going to mind that I'm Latina?"

"That's no problem either, Maria. I'm Chinese, they're both white, and my big sister's Korean. You'll just make us a more colorful family. Especially if you bring your tattoos along."

Looking relieved, Maria smiled at Jessica, who gave her a soft kiss and touched her cheek. "Don't worry about it. They'll love you, just like I do."

They continued to the lunch spot. Maria told Jessica that she was pleased to hear her humming softly to herself as they ambled along the trail. Jessica hummed when she was happy.

Of all the outdoors things they did together, Jessica enjoyed their hikes the most. Hiking was neither competitive nor dangerous. Maria's audacity when rock climbing sometimes made Jessica nervous. Perhaps it was the fearlessness of youth, but the older Jessica felt Maria took too many chances in a sport where one slip could be deadly. On a stroll in the woods like today she could just enjoy the setting and the companionship.

Four other hikers soon came into view, scattering a trio of ground squirrels crossing the trail. Maria and Jessica already had their lunches out. They had waited to start eating out of politeness. With sighs of relief, Gerhard and Susie Schumacher dropped their packs and sat on a fallen fir trunk. Both fifty-four, they were two decades older than Jessica, in great shape for their age. Still, it took a lot of uphill steps to reach the top of the cliff. The other couple, Robin and Jim Whitney, relaxed on a black slab of volcanic basalt, pleasantly warmed by the sunshine.

Jessica and Maria had met the others through the Cascaders Mountain Club, Portland chapter. They all enjoyed hiking, biking, and sometimes rock or mountain climbing with friends in the endless outdoors, rain or shine. In western Oregon, mostly rain. Not today, though.

"Man, that's a trek," said Gerhard. He took off his hat and wiped his sweaty brow with his forearm. "But it's worth it for the views." He gulped water from his bottle.

"I just love the colors this time of year," Robin added. The clearing across the trail from them blazed with mountain wildflowers in pink, lavender, white, and orange. The late-spring air was redolent with rich, fresh forest smells. Fifty-four degrees was perfect for a hike. They all pulled sandwiches, trail mix, and fruit from their packs and negotiated lunch component trades until everyone was happy with the result.

Jim called out, "Hey, Jessica, I saw you on TV a few weeks ago. The Channel 5 news did a story about how your facial reconstruction helped them identify that dead woman whose remains they found in that Portland park. The Portland Police Bureau showed the face you came up with. It was an amazing match to the victim's. Very impressive! How did you get that job, anyway?"

Jessica replied between baby carrots. "I'm registered as a forensic sculptor with several law enforcement agencies. When they find skeletal remains they can't identify, sometimes they hire me to approximate what the person looked like in life so they can see if anybody recognizes them. I got lucky with that young woman. I just guessed at her hairstyle and eye color. They came out pretty close."

Susie and Gerhard pulled insulated vests out of their packs and put them back on. Bodies cool down fast when they aren't working hard. Susie said, "I thought you said you were an artist. I didn't know that was the sort of 'art' you meant. Are there really enough unidentified dead people around here to keep you busy?"

"No, skeletons don't turn up every day in Portland. I work for Washington and Idaho law enforcement too. I'm one of the few freelance forensic sculptors in the Northwest. Most of them work full-time for police departments."

"Do you do other kinds of art work?" Jim asked.

"Yes, I also do commercial art. My work has been used in some of the TV shows and movies shot around Portland. I also paint and draw just for myself when I have time. If you need a seascape for your wall, I'd love to sell you one. I get a few forensic facial reconstruction cases each year. They always get my top priority."

Gerhard made a face. "Isn't it creepy trying to make some poor girl's skull look human again?"

Jessica sipped some water and shook her head. "It's not creepy once you get used to it. I do find it rather sad. Maybe it's just a skull now, but it was a person once. I get a lot of personal satisfaction from helping to find out who those people are."

"They arrested some asshole for killing that woman, right?" Jim asked through half-chewed trail mix. "It's wild to think we actually know the person who made that possible. What are you going to do next, Jessica, discover Amelia Earhart?"

"No," she laughed, wiping her fingers on a paper towel. "I'm going to walk the rest of the trail on this gorgeous day, and then Maria's going to drive us home, where we'll have some Thai takeout and some wine. Then we'll see what's on HBO tonight."

As the six friends hoisted packs back aboard their shoulders, Robin asked, "Thai food, Jessica? Seriously? I thought your background was Chinese."

"It is, but Chinese food is too oily for me. I much prefer Thai, the hotter the better. If I can still talk after I take a bite, it's just not spicy enough."

Fortified for the rest of the hike, the group headed on down the trail. Glacier-covered Mount Hood soon came into view around a bend. It's impossible not to be awed when you see a huge peak up close. Seattle's mountain, Rainier, might have been higher by more than three thousand feet, but Portland's was pointier, like a good mountain should be.

When they reached the parking lot at the trailhead, foot-sore but soul-enriched, the friends split up for their cars. Maria and Jessica threw their packs into the trunk of Maria's fire-engine red Mazda3. Jessica climbed into the passenger seat, and Maria pulled out of the lot and onto the interstate. Jessica turned on her phone. She had one voice mail message from four hours earlier.

"This is Detective Adam Longsdale from the Lorane County Sheriff's Office in Eugene. I don't know if you remember me. We've met before at law-enforcement conferences. We have a case here that might interest you. Somebody found some skeletal remains in a forest, and we haven't made any progress identifying them. I'd like to talk to you about a possible facial reconstruction. Can you please call me back at (458) 555-0191?"

"Looks like I might not be unemployed as long as I thought," she told Maria. "They found something in Eugene that might be a reconstruction case. I'd better call this guy back before I lose the signal in the gorge." As Maria navigated the winding curves on I-84, heading west toward Portland, Jessica returned the call.

"Detective Longsdale, this is Jessica Sanford. I got your voice mail about the reconstruction project. Thanks for thinking of me."

"Hi, Jessica. Please call me Adam. I appreciate your getting back to me so quickly. I know you do good work, so I hope you're available to help us. These remains look to be five to ten years old. The skull should be suitable for a reconstruction, if you're interested."

"I do have some open time coming up. Can this wait until Wednesday? I need to finish an art project for a client."

"Wednesday's fine. I'll set up a meeting with us and Dr. Silvia Miranova, the forensic anthropology professor from the U of O who consults with us on these cases. She examined the remains and has made some preliminary determinations. I'll text you the meeting location in Eugene."

Jessica put her phone away and looked out the car window. The steep cliffs of the gorge gradually flattened out as the freeway approached the eastern Portland suburbs. Rain clouds darkened in the west as the afternoon sank into evening. Just rain, though—Portland rarely experienced thunderstorms.

"You okay, babe?" Jessica heard the concern in Maria's voice.

"Yeah, I'm fine. I always get a little sad when I start a new reconstruction case. This person's body has been lying out in the forest for who knows how long. Someone cared about them. Someone doesn't know what happened to them and has missed them for all these years. And someone else killed them. If I can help with all those unknowns, how can I say no?"

Maria didn't reply, just reached her hand out and rested it gently on Jessica's arm. They rode in silence the rest of the way past the eastern suburbs of Portland, turning south onto I-205. Maria took the exit for the city of Rosemount and drove toward Jessica's house.

Jessica looked at the yard as Maria turned into the driveway. The lawn was getting long again. Things grew so fast this time of year in Portland. Jessica kept meaning to put in flowerbeds because she enjoyed the colors. She just never got around to it. Just a few stray irises and daffodils lingered from the previous owner's gardening efforts. That was fine, she thought; some of her neighbors had lovely landscaping she could enjoy just by looking out her windows. That was much less work for her, and it involved no dirt.

"If you want to be alone tonight, I can go on home," Maria offered softly.

"Hell no," said Jessica, smiling. "We have Thai food to eat, wine to drink, and TV to watch. How about if you go home in the morning instead?"

Chapter 2

Wednesday, May 9

JESSICA'S ALARM JOLTED her awake at 6:30 on Wednesday morning. So far it had not been a perfect week.

Tuesday morning she had finished her art project for the TV show *Desperation*, a thriller set in Philadelphia but shot in Portland. Portland often stood in for other cities in TV series and movies. The art director said he was happy with her work, so that was a good thing. But later on Tuesday, Jessica had learned that one of her favorite Meals on Wheels clients, ninety-three-year-old Irene Stinson, had passed away. Like many Meals drivers at the Rosemount Senior Center, Jessica got attached to her clients, at least the friendly ones who remembered her name and took a moment to chat when she came by each week. You couldn't be too surprised when someone in her nineties died. Still, you never expected it.

She had finished driving her Tuesday route, pleased that she had helped some people who might not otherwise have a square meal or a human contact that day. Her grandfather, a child of the Great Depression, had told Jessica long ago, "I never sent one of my children to bed without dinner as punishment, because I knew what it was like to be three days hungry." That stark phrase—"three days hungry"—had powerfully motivated Jessica to support food causes.

Jessica turned off the alarm and rolled out of bed. She needed to be in Eugene for the meeting at 11:00 a.m. Breakfast was basic today, just mango juice and cold cereal. Her cupboard held at least a dozen boxes of cereal, which she mixed into countless random combinations, no two bowls the same.

After taking a shower, Jessica wiped the condensation from the bathroom mirror. Normally she wore very little makeup, but today she was meeting with some people who might hire her. Today it paid—literally—to look her best.

She studied the face in the mirror. It was a pleasant face, she thought. Dark brown eyes that needed glasses only for close-up work. A hint of smile lines starting to appear around those eyes. *Sigh.* Straight black hair parted off-center, worn loose down below her shoulders except when a ponytail kept it out of trouble. A strong jawline with a slight asymmetry in the chin. The faint hints of acne scars on her cheeks, reminders of a less-than-perfect adolescence. And a world-beating smile. Everyone loved her smile, or so they said, even if it was a bit lopsided. That just added to the charm.

Jessica applied her face and put on tan slacks, a print top, and a short mocha-colored jacket. Professional yet not formal. Any jewelry today? Maybe the fused-glass necklace. That one was her favorite, with so many glittering colors. She brewed a quick cup of coffee and poured it into her travel mug.

She pulled her silver Honda Accord out of the garage for the drive down I-5 to Eugene. Last night's rain had passed through, leaving the fresh smell of a spring shower, some lingering clouds, and the promise of sun later in the day. The streets were still damp; grass glistened in lawns.

Jessica loved western Oregon's greenness. Everything looked and smelled so fresh and alive this time of year. A few colorful clusters still lingered amid the fading spring bulbs. Rhododendrons spewed fountains of magenta, white, red, and the occasional deep purple—her favorite. Jessica waved at her neighbors across the street as they left for their travel agency in Rosemount. *How do travel agencies stay in business these days?* she asked herself. Matt and Kira did seem to keep busy, though. The car's tires hummed as it cruised at a steady sixty-seven miles per hour down the freeway. Jessica blasted a mix of Taylor Swift, Lady Gaga, Van Halen, and Metallica from her phone through the car's sound system. She would listen to almost anything. Except country. No country, ever.

Two hours after leaving home, Jessica turned into the parking lot for the Lorane County Sheriff's Office ten minutes early and parked in a visitor's space by the two-story salmon-red brick structure. She walked past the two flagpoles and gave her name to the deputy at the front desk. In a minute, Detective Longsdale walked into the lobby from the back and shook Jessica's hand.

Jessica recognized the detective immediately from their previous meetings, although she had forgotten how tall he was. She didn't remember the beginnings of a paunch under his belt and the bags under his eyes, either. Adam's wavy graying hair was a bit longer than regulation, curling over his collar and ears. Being a detective, Adam wore a navy sport coat over light gray slacks and a pale-blue dress shirt rather than a deputy's uniform. He guided Jessica down the hall to an interview room for their meeting.

The interview room's sand-colored walls were a welcome departure from the institutional green she was used to seeing in law-enforcement buildings. But it was still just a plain room in a police station, equipped with a metal table, three basic chairs, and humming fluorescent ceiling lights. A row of glass blocks near the top of an outside wall let in some natural light. Jessica's nose crinkled at the pungent memory left behind by previous occupants who had been in the room for less benign conversations.

Adam brought in three cups of coffee. "Let me know if you need cream or sugar," he offered. "Sorry I can't offer anything fancier. Starbucks hasn't opened a branch in our break room yet. Any week now, they tell me." Adam spoke in measured tones, his voice conveying an impression of solidity and quiet confidence.

The two made small talk for a few minutes, recalling their previous interactions.

A short woman in her fifties with a slight limp walked into the room and set her leather briefcase next to the empty chair. Her pewter-colored hair was pulled back into a bun. Several faint scars marked the left side of her face below her wire-rimmed glasses. Adam introduced her as Dr. Silvia Miranova, professor of forensic anthropology at the University of Oregon.

Jessica stood as they shook hands. "I'm pleased to meet you, Dr. Miranova." The professor wore a short-sleeved top in honor of the warm May day. Jessica noticed a three-inch scar on her left forearm, which looked as though someone had swiped a finger through wet clay.

"Silvia," the professor replied in a soft voice that still held the remnants of a Slavic accent. "I've seen your work, Jessica. You have a real eye for facial reconstruction. I'm impressed with how lifelike your renderings look, whether in clay or on the computer."

Jessica tipped her head slightly and smiled. "Thank you very much. I appreciate that, Silvia." They all exchanged business cards. Jessica's was Office Depot basic:

JESSICA SANFORD, FORENSIC SCULPTOR AND COMMERCIAL ARTIST

The text was small capitals, in dark-blue lettering on a plain cream background with her phone and email, no logo or company name.

"So, what can you both tell me about this case?" Jessica asked.

Adam began. "The remains were discovered about three weeks ago by Dr. Terry Engelman, who's also a professor at the University of Oregon. He and his wife own a twenty-one-acre plot of wooded land on Redhawk Road overlooking the Lorane Valley, southwest of Eugene. He was throwing a ball for his dog to chase, and the dog retrieved a piece of bone instead of the ball. Engelman recognized it as part of a rib. Then he spotted the skeleton partially exposed on the forest floor."

Jessica shivered slightly. No one's final resting place should be an unmarked hole in the woods.

Adam continued, "The body was buried in a shallow grave on a slight slope. The covering soil was washed away by the heavy rains last winter. The skeleton was nearly complete, suggesting it was fully buried until recently. It didn't look like any animals had gotten at the body before it skeletonized. Silvia, what did you learn from your forensic examination?"

Silvia unsnapped the latches on her briefcase and removed a thick manila folder. She laid a stack of eight-by-ten color photos on the table and pointed out key features on them as she spoke.

"Few of the bones or teeth are missing. Based on the pelvic structure and the size and shape of the skull, I'm 98 percent confident these are the remains of an adult female. Examination of the epiphyses—the ends of the long bones—and the growth plates indicate that she was likely older than twenty-three at the age of death. I'm putting her age at between twenty-four and thirty-five."

Jessica took notes as Silvia presented her analysis. "Any clues about race?" she asked.

"The skull and facial features are consistent with the Asian, or Mongoloid, racial group." She pulled out another photo. "Here you can see that the cheekbones are fairly wide and flared out, which is typical of Asians. Both the base and the bridge of the nose are also characteristically East Asian. The eye orbits are more rounded than typically found with either Caucasians or Negroids. The hair had all decomposed, so that didn't help with racial identification."

"What are your thoughts about her stature?"

"From standard formulas of bone measurements for Asian women, I estimated her living height at four feet eleven inches to five feet three inches."

Adam asked, "Do you have an estimate for the time of death?"

Silvia didn't look as certain about that. "We didn't have a lot to go on there. All of the soft tissue is gone. Based on the condition of the bones and the properties of the soil, I think she's been there between three and eight years."

Jessica turned to Adam and asked, "Was there anything else in or around the grave that could be useful?"

"Almost nothing. The lab identified a few small fragments of rotted cloth as cotton, perhaps part of a bedsheet. No DNA or blood on them. We also found three pieces of what looks to be body-piercing jewelry." He laid a photo on the table.

Jessica put on her glasses and studied the jewelry photo. "The only one of these that looks distinctive is the dangly one with the butterfly. That might have been a navel ring, or possibly even a fancy earring. These other two are ordinary, a nose stud and probably a lip or eyebrow ring. Silvia, did the remains show any distinctive skeletal features that might help with identification?"

"Two things." Silvia removed two more photos from her pile. "The deceased had a fully healed fracture of the right forearm, both radius and ulna. The dental work was typical, although this crown on one upper central incisor is unusual for someone this young. She might have broken the tooth in a childhood accident. This would all be helpful for comparison if we ever found a candidate for the victim's identity. Our forensic odontologist took X-rays of the teeth for possible future comparison with a known individual."

Jessica observed, "It looks like the skull is in good shape for a reconstruction, except for that big hole in the temporal region." She pointed to a close-up photo of the injury to the left side of the skull. "I'm guessing that's the cause of death?"

Adam popped a fresh stick of gum in his mouth and flipped through his notebook. "The medical examiner described that as a 'penetrating wound caused by an unknown object.' The edges of the hole are triangular, so it doesn't look like a gunshot. The sharp corner of a metal bar or a piece of furniture could cause an injury like that. The ME isn't certain if the object would have penetrated deep enough to be fatal. He also found a fracture in a cervical vertebra.

Based on how the body was buried, he classified this as a homicide, but the exact cause of death remains uncertain."

The fluorescent lights in the interview room flickered. Adam pushed back his chair and stood. "Can I get you ladies some fresh coffee?" They both nodded their thanks.

After he left the room, Silvia leaned forward and rested her hand on the younger woman's arm. "I really hope you can work on this case, Jessica. You'd be a real asset. How did you get into forensic sculpture, anyway?"

Jessica was instantly transported back to her sophomore year at Upper Bench High School in Boise, eighteen years earlier. A classmate, Bobby Livermore, had disappeared on his walk home from school one day. The entire school body was traumatized. His devastated parents appeared on the local television news for weeks, tearfully pleading for anyone who knew anything about Bobby's disappearance to come forward. Nothing. His decomposed body was discovered almost a year later in the desert, a few miles south of Boise. The case remained unsolved.

Ever since then, Jessica had harbored an anxiety that someone might snatch her away from her family and no one would ever see her again. Nothing pained her more than the idea of an innocent victim simply vanishing without explanation or retribution. She wasn't ready to share all this with a new acquaintance, though.

"As a kid I was always drawing, painting, and sculpting," Jessica replied. "In high school I got interested in law enforcement, so I got my degree in criminal justice from Boise State University. I took a lot of art classes on the side. Then I worked for the Boise Police Department for five years, starting as a crime scene technician and gradually moving into investigation and forensic sculpture."

She doodled on the notepad in front of her with the green pen she always carried. "I've always found human anatomy fascinating. I love those posters in the doctor's exam room, showing the details of skin or muscles or bones. When I was twenty, I saw a TV show about a forensic facial reconstruction that was used to identify the remains of a missing hitchhiker. Watching that show motivated me to become certified as a forensic sculptor."

Silvia said, "I know it can be tough dealing with death all the time, but bringing the dead at least partway back to life is a valuable contribution." Jessica was pleased that Silvia understood just how rewarding her job was when it was successful.

When Adam returned with their coffee refills, Jessica asked him, "Do you have any suspects at all?"

He shook his head as he sat down. "None. We found no trace evidence around the grave site after all these years. The first person we considered as a possible suspect was Dr. Engelman." Adam again consulted his notebook. "Engelman owns the land where the remains were found, and he—well, his dog—made the discovery. We ruled him out because he moved here just two years ago from Boston and it looks like the remains are older than that. Also because a professor couldn't possibly be dumb enough to report this if he'd buried the body in the first place, right?" The women chuckled.

Adam sipped his coffee and continued. "Engelman bought the land from the estate of Walter Nussbaum, who died with dementia a little over two years ago at the age of eighty-four. He'd been in a memory-care facility for years before he died. So while we can't eliminate him entirely because of the timing, it seems pretty unlikely that it was him. I'm thinking this was just a dump job, with no real suspects. Yet."

Silvia checked her watch. "I need to get back to campus soon. Adam, did you find any open reports in the missing-persons database that might be a match for this victim?"

"None from Oregon, Washington, or Northern California. More often than not, young female victims are prostitutes. Few of them are ever reported missing. It's possible someone brought this woman from far away and buried her in the Middle of Nowhere, Oregon, but she's probably a local. We have no ideas at this point.

That's why, Jessica, we're asking you to do a facial reconstruction so we can enlist the public to help identify our victim."

Jessica put her glasses back in their case and closed her eyes. She was intrigued by this homicide. Three months had passed since she performed the reconstruction on the dead woman from Portland; she could use the work. More importantly, there was someone who needed a face and a name. She might be able to supply the face. She opened her eyes and said, "I'd like to work on this project, Adam. I want to find out who this woman is and what happened to her."

Adam slapped the table with his hand, startling the two women. "Great! Thank you. I'll coordinate with Silvia to get you everything we have within a few days. A case this old is not going to be easy. We need all your skills, plus some luck."

The three stood and shook hands. Adam escorted the women back to the building's front door.

Jessica climbed into her car and sat for a moment. The Honda was toasty warm from the sun. It was always a big step, committing to do a reconstruction. But she really wanted to know this dead Asian woman.

On the drive back to Portland, Jessica exited I-5 just south of Salem and drove a few miles through Oregon's wine country. She pulled into the parking lot at Willamette Crest Estates, noted for its big reds made from grapes sourced from Southern Oregon. The Willamette Valley south of Portland was known for its world-class Pinot Noir, but Jessica preferred the in-your-face intensity of a Syrah or Cabernet Sauvignon to the more subtle complexity of a Pinot. She walked into the winery's tasting room, looking forward to sampling for a half hour before continuing home.

Chapter 3

FROM HER PREVIOUS projects, Jessica knew that once she began working on the reconstruction it would consume all her energy until it was done. But this time, waiting to receive the anthropological materials from Silvia gave her several days to catch up on some other activities first.

Priority one was to hit the gym. She hadn't had a good workout for a week; her body nagged her about it. Biking, hiking, and climbing kept her in shape, but she also had to stay in shape for biking, hiking, and climbing.

Energized by the workout, Jessica went home and surveyed her domain. The grass was out of control, consuming the landscape beds and threatening the driveway. She took out the electric mower and trimmer and beat the lawn back into submission.

Satisfied that her home presented an acceptable facade to the outside world, she walked through the front door into her living room. The dark hardwood floors she had installed last year provided a rich contrast with the tan—or "Sepia Froth" as the paint store called it—walls. Her living room featured two tall bookcases filled with volumes on art, law enforcement, and forensics; thriller novels; and a complete set of Pearls Before Swine comic collections.

Jessica walked down the hallway to her studio. After she had bought the house four years earlier, she had it remodeled to combine the two largest bedrooms into a spacious studio. Her computer workstation—laptop, twenty-seven-inch high-res monitor, color laser printer—lived on a heavy table to the left of the door. Next to the table sat a large teak desk with each item positioned in its proper place. The desk featured a framed picture of Jessica with her parents, David and Sharon, and her older sister, Megan. The children's Asian faces in the photo were always a contrast with the white faces of their parents. She remembered the blurted question whenever she was introduced to someone as a child: "Oh, is she adopted?"

The studio walls displayed several of Jessica's own paintings along with work by some artist friends. Pride of place went to an original oil by her favorite painter, a gift from her parents. She glanced at the framed certificate of appreciation from the police department in Tacoma, Washington, for a particularly challenging reconstruction she had performed a few years earlier that led to both identification of the victim and conviction of his killer.

This respite before she got into the project also gave her time to do some painting just for pleasure. When Jessica took a personality test once, she registered in the middle of the extroverted–introverted scale. She was a social person and was comfortable in groups; she enjoyed her diverse circle of friends. Doing things alone was also just fine. Painting on her own, for fun, let the real Jessica flow through the brush onto paper or canvas. Yin and yang, inner and outer. One Jessica that people knew, and another one they didn't know as well.

Jessica painted from photographs, from memories, from her vivid dreams, and sometimes from all three together. Her studio contained an easel with an unfinished acrylic painting, half Winslow Homer and half Salvador Dalí. She checked the clock on the wall: not quite four, plenty of time before meeting Maria and two other friends for drinks. She picked up a brush.

An hour later—or so it seemed—she looked up and discovered it was nearly six thirty. Both the beauty and the curse of becoming lost in a project is that you lose track of time. She nuked a frozen dinner, dressed, and grabbed a cookie on the way out the door to meet up with the girls.

Over the weekend, Jessica finally finished her Homer-and-Dalí-influenced surreal seascape. The Oregon coast was endlessly inspiring for her. She delivered the painting to the gallery that exhibited her work. They loved it. Would anyone else? *Who knows?* she thought. *It's art.* Whether it sold tomorrow, hung in the gallery for years, or was returned by the gallery as unsellable, she was happy to have finished it. She'd find another spot on her own walls for it if she had to.

*   *   *

Monday morning the art director at a local advertising agency Jessica had done some previous work for called her. They weren't happy with an ad their regular contractor had just delivered for a local brewery. Could Jessica take a look at it and pump it up with some fresh ideas? The agency emailed her the piece they didn't like.

She worked on this project through Tuesday and sent them some suggested layout and image improvements. The week "off" had turned out to be a busy interlude for Jessica.

On Wednesday, Jessica answered her doorbell to see a UPS deliveryman holding a large package for her. Signing digital clipboards made her nervous. She scribbled something illegible, like always, thinking, *Where exactly does that digital signature go?* The shipping label said the package was from Dr. Silvia Miranova.

She opened the box on her desk, removed a thousand packing peanuts, and carefully lifted out a skull. She could tell it was not the actual skull from the remains found off Redhawk Road. It had a slick plastic feel to it, not the smooth hardness of real bone. Jessica knew the original skull had to be preserved as evidence in the case. Jessica read Silvia's cover letter:

Jessica:

I'm sorry this took longer than I expected. Rather than creating a mold from the original skull and risk damaging it, I sent it to a hospital in Eugene for 3-D CT scanning. The enclosed flash drive contains the scanned image in several graphics formats in case you decide to use facial-reconstruction software.

I then had a 3-D printer create a resin duplicate, which is enclosed in this box. This is an exact replica of the original skull, differing only in color and density. It will serve as a suitable foundation if you do the reconstruction in clay.

I'm excited to see what you come up with. Let me know if I can be of any further assistance.

Silvia

Jessica pensively held the replica skull in her hands. It sobered her to know she bore the responsibility of restoring this woman to her appearance in life, or at least as close as possible.

"You're not just a skull to me," she said aloud. "You're a person. We just don't know who yet. I have to call you something until we learn your real name. May I call you Alice for now? It's a pleasure to meet you, Alice."

She placed the replica skull on a cork ring atop the stand she used for performing clay reconstructions. Because she hadn't known when the reconstruction materials would arrive, Jessica had already planned a date with Maria for that night. Alice would just have to wait until tomorrow morning.

She peered into her closet. What would be just the right outfit for dinner and dancing with her sweetie? Maybe the short, gold-colored dress. That's what she wore when she first met Maria at Portland's Rose Ballroom several months earlier. Jessica was petite at a couple of inches over five feet, but Maria later told her she had been taken with Jessica's taut curves and athletic legs, saying she looked positively delicious in that gold dress. Maria's energy on the dance floor had caught Jessica's eye immediately. Jessica had gone to the club with a man she knew from the gym. He was friendly enough and nice-looking, but she went home with Maria that night. They had been together ever since.

Jessica loved Maria's passion and intensity, which translated into everything she did. Plus Maria really "got" Jessica. She appreciated her girlfriend's artwork, although she admitted that she found the reconstruction work more than a little freaky.

Maria also got off on Jessica's secret side, the wild bits that came to the fore from time to time. Not everyone would guess that Jessica had a butterfly tattoo on her thigh, let alone imagine the secret piercings. All right, it was the sparkly gold one tonight. Jessica finished dressing and put on just enough makeup to look like she was ready for a good time.

Jessica picked up Maria at her apartment fifteen minutes late. "Where have you been?" Maria demanded when she opened the door. She wore a form-fitting cadmium-red dress and matching strappy heels. A sequined long-chained party clutch was looped over her shoulder. "I didn't know if you forgot about our date, or had a wreck, or what. Why didn't you text me you were going to be late?"

"I'm sorry, babe. I lost track of time so I had to rush. Of course, Eighty-Second Avenue was backed up. I'm here now, though. Where do you want to eat?" They settled on Eddie's Grill, which had much better food than the name might suggest.

As they ate, Jessica filled Maria in on her day, including receiving the reconstruction materials from Silvia.

Maria's eyes widened. "So now you have an actual skull in your house?" she asked.

"Not a real skull, an exact copy of the one they found near Eugene. I'm calling her Alice for now, until we learn who she was. I need to decide whether to do the reconstruction in clay on the skull or using the computer. I'll work on that tomorrow."

"I'm sure you'll figure it out. Could we not talk about this when I'm eating, please? You're used to it, but it weirds me out."

"Okay, no more skull talk tonight," Jessica laughed. "Enjoy your dinner. I just want you to know I'm going to be super busy while I work on this reconstruction. So don't sweat it if you don't hear from me for a few days."

After dinner Jessica drove them downtown to the Rose Ballroom. The club was busy for a Wednesday. Maria took Jessica's hand and grinned. "This looks like a good place to be tonight. And I must say, you do look fine in that dress, all goldy and glittery. Isn't that the one you wore the night we met here?"

"It is indeed. You fill out that pretty red dress just fine yourself, especially the top part." Maria slapped Jessica on the butt playfully. The club's energy washed over them.

They ordered drinks, Stoli vanilla vodka with soda for Jessica and a mojito for Maria. Jessica and Maria danced together and then with some other friends they ran into. Then the two women found a table in the back of the club and took a break.

Two men they didn't recognize walked over and offered to buy a round. "Sure, why not?" replied Maria.

"May we join you?" the taller man asked. Receiving smiles and nods from the women, they pulled up two chairs and crowded around the small table.

Shouting over the music, the taller one, a sharp dresser who seemed quite pleased with himself, asked Maria if she wanted to dance. His friend, slightly overweight with lank brown hair, glasses, and a friendly face, raised his eyebrows in query at Jessica. The women exchanged a glance and a wink. They all headed to the dance floor.

After two songs—really long songs—Jessica's dance partner leaned down near her ear. "I'm Dennis. You look amazing. Would you like to go somewhere quieter so we can talk?" he asked with hope in his eyes.

Jessica smiled and replied, "Thanks, Dennis, but you see the woman there I was sitting with? She's my girlfriend, and I don't think she'd be happy if I left with you. So I'll have to say thanks, but not tonight."

Dennis shrugged good-naturedly. "I enjoyed the dance anyway. You ladies have a good night." When they returned to their table, Jessica and Maria shared a little laugh as the men left to search for more promising opportunities.

Jessica knew she had an intense few days coming up, so they made it an early evening, heading back to Rosemount shortly after ten o'clock.

The two women walked into Jessica's house. Since it was still pleasantly warm outdoors, Jessica carried a chilled bottle of Pinot Gris and some outstanding bud from one of Oregon's legal pot shops out to the fire pit in her backyard. It was a lovely way to spend a late-spring evening. Then they spent an even lovelier time indoors, finally drifting into sleep.

Jessica's dreams were filled with images of both Maria and her new friend, Alice.

Chapter 4

Thursday, May 17

MARIA WANDERED OUT of the bedroom wearing a white tank top and red pajama pants with black dogs on them, a mass of brown curls framing her face. She stretched and yawned. "Coffee, I must have coffee!" Coffee appeared, along with scrambled eggs and toast with raspberry preserves. The seeded whole-grain loaves from the local bakery made fantastic toast.

After breakfast, Jessica stroked Maria's hair and said, "Maybe you don't have to work today, but I do. I wish I had more time before beginning the project, so we could enjoy today together. This case has me preoccupied."

"Can't it wait until this afternoon so we can hang together for a while? Why is this particular skull so special?"

"I'm not sure, Maria. Maybe because the victim is Asian, like me. I need to find out who she is." Jessica smiled sweetly and added, "I enjoyed last night so much, babe. More of the same can be my reward after I wrap up this project—extra motivation."

"And when might that be, do you suppose?"

Jessica heard the edge in Maria's voice. She sighed. "I'm not sure, but the sooner I start, the sooner I'll finish, okay? It's nice to know you're nearby, so take your time this morning. Stay as long as you like. I've got to head into the studio now."

Jessica reached out, but Maria evaded her hug and turned back toward the bedroom. Jessica looked after her for a moment and thought, *Maybe a girlfriend isn't easier than a boyfriend.*

Jessica walked into her studio and closed the door. She wore jeans and a turquoise T-shirt bearing the message "All of the Good Chemistry Jokes Argon," a gift from her sister, a high-school chemistry teacher. Jessica also wore a clean artist's smock. Even when she wasn't doing anything messy, the smock made her feel professional and respectful when handling remains, even simulated remains like today's.

She launched iTunes on her laptop and started her favorite playlist for the studio, songs by jazz guitarist Craig Chaquico. Listening to vocals while working distracted her. She found it impossible not to sing along, even mentally. Instrumental guitar was perfect reconstruction music.

Jessica copied the skull scan image files from Silvia's flash drive to her laptop and opened them in a viewer. She turned to the replica skull sitting on its cork ring and said, "Good morning, Alice. Let's get acquainted."

She sat at her desk for almost an hour, studying the skull and referring to the image files as she contemplated the best way to approach this reconstruction. The vicious hole in the left side of the skull continually reminded her she was dealing with a homicide victim. Some object had penetrated the full depth of the temporal bone, among the thinnest skull bones.

"How did a nice Asian girl like you wind up in an Oregon forest?" she asked aloud.

As she examined the skull, she looked for attachment points where muscles and tendons would connect to bones. Those gave her clues as to how large each muscle should be and exactly where it should go.

The muscles, glands, and other tissues of the face were well understood. You could find pictures in any anatomy book. Unfortunately, individual human beings don't look precisely like those pictures. Sometimes people lack certain muscles. A muscle might be duplicated or positioned a little differently than is typical. But lacking other information, she had to go with the averages. Her goal was to create an image that sufficiently approximated the victim's living appearance that a family member or a friend could recognize her.

Facial reconstruction was a mix of science and art. The skull bones gave much information about how a person looked in life. The shapes of the brow ridge and forehead; the size, shape, and position of the eye orbits; the shapes of the jaw, the chin, and the nasal bones—these all dictated surprising precision in a skilled forensic sculptor's hands. For instance, specific measurements of lengths and angles around the nasal bones gave strong clues as to the shape of the external nose.

Reconstructing other features, however, was more art than science. When there was nothing to work with but bones—no personal property with hints about the individual—the sculptor had to make sensible guesses. Eye color, eyelids and eyebrows, hair color, and hairstyle were all uncertain. The height and size of the teeth suggested the width of the mouth and thickness of the lips. A lot of mouth shape variability simply couldn't be discerned from the skull features, though.

Ears were nearly as distinctive as fingerprints, varying widely from one person to another. With no soft tissues for reference, the forensic sculptor had to create generic ears that might not be close to the originals. And skin! So many variables: hue, scars, wrinkles, tattoos, piercings, dimples, cosmetic surgery, blemishes, freckles, moles, and bumps of every description. The sculptor starting with a bare skull had nothing to go on regarding the subject's skin. With the uncertainty regarding those superficial features, three forensic sculptors would produce reconstructions that resembled each other and yet were not identical.

Jessica considered which of the various facial reconstruction approaches was most appropriate in this case. The simplest method involved drawing on a picture of the skull to estimate what Alice's external appearance might have been like. The usual way to do this was with the help of tissue depth markers.

Anthropologists had collected much data about the thickness of muscle, fat, and skin at numerous locations on the skull. These varied from race to race and between men and women. Jessica could look up the average tissue depths for an Asian woman in up to thirty-six specific locations on the skull. Fourteen of these points lay along the midline—chin, mouth area, nose, forehead, and scalp. The others were bilateral, eleven positions each on the left and right sides of the face. Building up the flesh to the average depth in each position should approximate Alice's living face fairly well.

Based on those standard facial measurements, one of Jessica's reconstruction options was to position tissue depth markers on the skull in all those key locations and photograph it from straight ahead. Then she could sketch a face onto a piece of tracing paper placed atop the photograph. She would follow the skull's shape and contours to ensure the skin she drew matched up with the depth markers. The positions and shapes of the nasal bones, teeth, and eye orbits would guide her reconstruction of the missing soft tissues. Such a two-dimensional reconstruction might provide a fair representation of the living person. However, it looked like a drawing, and it showed the person from just a single viewpoint.

For this project, Jessica had the resources available for a three-dimensional reconstruction. She had a replica of the skull itself, as well as the computer images from the CT scan. Again using the tissue depth markers, she could reconstruct the entire head either in clay or on the computer. She had used both techniques before and was fully proficient in both.

Jessica mentally worked through the options available to her. If she were to use clay, she would cut small rubber rods—erasers for mechanical pencils worked well—to the lengths specified for the various facial locations and glue them to the right spots on the skull. Next, she would choose some plastic eyeballs of the appropriate color—likely brown in this case—and position them in the eye sockets using specific bone markers to identify their precise location. Those locations didn't vary much from one individual to another. Then she would shape clay strips to represent various muscles and position them in the appropriate locations on the skull. After the muscles were in place, she would add glands, fatty tissues, and skin with additional clay. She'd stop when the clay matched the depth of all the tissue markers. These tissue depth measurements were not absolutes that fit every case. Rather, they were guides to follow as an approximation. Finally she would texture and paint the smoothed skin to make it look as realistic as possible.

Jessica had generated some eerily lifelike reconstructions using the clay modeling technique on earlier projects. She loved the feel of the pliable clay in her fingers and its earthy smell. The intimacy of physically molding layer after layer on the skull forged a powerful personal bond between her and the victim. However, it was a tedious process that could take a week or more. Given Jessica's drive for perfection in all she did, usually more.

After examining the skull and carefully considering the various alternatives, she decided to perform a computerized 3-D facial reconstruction for Alice. That should only take about two days. The computer images were much easier than clay to tweak if something didn't come out quite right or if she acquired fresh information about the victim later on.

She launched her facial reconstruction software application, called Anthropological Facial Reconstruction and Modeling, or AFRAM. The AFRAM software approach was based on the same principles used for 3-D modeling in clay.

Jessica imported one of the CT scanned images of the skull from Silvia into AFRAM. *But first,* she thought, *I need to make Alice's skull whole again.* The presumed instrument of death had made a clean penetration into the side of the skull, leaving a triangular hole with sides nearly one inch long. Fortunately, the surrounding skull bones were not cracked or depressed. Jessica used a software function to paint in the hole so she could position the overlying tissues properly when she got to the appropriate stage of the facial reconstruction.

Next Jessica selected the software option to overlay depth markers on the skull. The program asked several questions about the skull's anthropological background—race, age, and sex. After she entered those values, numerous small sticks appeared, sprinkled all over the skull image. These were the depth markers in the thirty-six critical positions.

Jessica began to lay in the muscles of the face and scalp atop the skull image, one at a time. She used a digital drawing tablet, a pressure-sensitive interactive pen display that was more precise and more natural to use than a mouse. She could rotate the skull on her monitor to view it from any angle. Jessica chose each appropriate muscle from a menu in turn and marked its two attachment points. The software positioned the muscle right where she indicated. She could control the exact shape of each element she added. The process of building up Alice's face combined painting with sculpting, using the tablet and its electronic pen instead of a paintbrush or clay modeling tools.

AFRAM streamlined the process enormously. She could request that the software mirror anything she drew on one side of the face onto the other side, cutting her work in half. She could add tissues just as she would with clay, precisely adjusting the positioning to make it look right to her experienced eye. The software performed all the necessary measurements around the nasal bones to make sensible judgments about the length, width, angle, and nostril shape for the soft tissues of the nose. Jessica positioned eyeballs in the centers of their orbits and then sculpted eyelids, including the epicanthal folds that gave people of East Asian descent their distinctive eye shape.

As she worked on the reconstruction, Jessica noticed that the shape of the front teeth was quite similar to her own. Perhaps that was just characteristically Asian, as incisors did vary in appearance from one racial group to another. She and Alice shared the same strong jawline, as well. She also observed that Alice had a slight asymmetry in her chin, a little curve to the right, just as Jessica did. This struck her as an odd coincidence, but not unusual.

Jessica knew human beings weren't as symmetrical as people might have thought. She remembered a well-known television news anchor whose face was noticeably skewed, his chin displaced well over from where you would expect it to be. She adjusted the soft tissue positions to reflect the curvature in the victim's chin area.

Jessica worked on the reconstruction for the rest of the day. She paused only for meals and drinks, to return some phone messages, and for an occasional stretch break to loosen up her cramped neck and wrist. If she didn't remember to take those little breaks, she was going to feel it tomorrow. Craig Chaquico played in the background until she switched to a playlist with some of her other favorite jazz musicians. Still all instrumentals, though.

As an atheist, Jessica didn't think this homicide victim's spirit was hanging around, observing or guiding her efforts to rebuild the missing face. Nonetheless, she always felt a connection to her subject on a reconstruction project. She spoke encouragingly to Alice as she worked. "Don't worry, Alice, we're going to find out who you are." "You're looking good, girl." "I think we're getting close." Alice never answered as she gradually took form in the computer.

Facial reconstruction on the computer was more lifelike than in clay. Instead of a neutral gray-brown color, the computer rendering showed muscles and tissues in realistic pinks and reds. Reconstruction in process looked as though a human head had been flayed and partially dissected. If you weren't used to it, it was quite hideous until you added skin to conceal the inner workings. Jessica's previous reconstruction experience had inured her to this grotesque aspect of her work.

By 10:00 p.m., Jessica had done all she could that day. Her eyes burned. The intense concentration at the computer had taken its toll on her shoulders. She saved all her files and backed them up, both to her external hard drive and to her backup account in the cloud. You couldn't have too many backups. She wasn't finished yet, but Alice was gradually coming to life.

It had been an intense and tiring day. Jessica lit her favorite relaxation candle, one smelling of vanilla and spun honey. She sat down in her pajamas with a glass of Merlot and a flow-right-into-your-arteries frosted chocolate brownie she had picked up the day before. In her mouth, the flavors fused into that of chocolate-covered cherries. Jessica turned on the TV to help her relax before she tried to sleep. She didn't care what she watched; an old episode of *Everybody Loves Raymond* was as good as anything else. Before the show ended, her heavy eyes drove her to bed with hopes of completing the reconstruction the next day.

*   *   *

When Jessica woke on Friday morning, her neck and back still ached. Working on Alice had filled her dreams with images of bare skulls, faces under construction, and unseeing eyes. She had the same dream on the first night of every reconstruction project.

She decided to start her day with a run. Get the blood flowing, loosen up stiff muscles, and clear her mind for another intense day of computer work. She looked out the bedroom window to check the weather. The morning sky was a uniform dreary gray, but at least it wasn't raining at the moment. She pulled her silky black hair into a ponytail and put on running clothes.

Twenty-five minutes and three miles later, Jessica was back at the house, sweaty and invigorated. The skies had cleared, as had been forecast. Jessica put a jug of solar tea out to brew on her south-facing front porch, where the sun's rays lasted the longest. Then she showered and dressed. Today's burgundy T-shirt proudly proclaimed "Wine People Are Fine People," a sentiment she heartily believed. She concocted another of her famous cereal combinations, topped with fresh strawberries. Jessica cycled through the local fruits as they came into season: strawberries to blueberries to cherries (her favorite, especially those sweet Rainiers), and so on through autumn. She was a regular patron of Rosemount's extensive Sunday farmers' market.

Hair still damp from her shower, Jessica walked into her studio and picked up where she had left off the night before. Today she listened to Russ Freeman & the Rippingtons as she worked. She continued positioning muscles and tissues with the AFRAM software, rotating and tilting the image on the screen and zooming in to see exactly where to place and how to shape each component. Jessica layered subcutaneous fat across the face to build it up nearly to the level of the tissue depth guides, just as she could by hand were she working in clay.

After reconstructing the facial tissues, Jessica selected a pair of ears from the long list of options AFRAM offered, and then resized them to fit this specific head. Although she couldn't possibly know what Alice's ears had looked like, features in the skull showed just where to position them. Fortunately, a woman's ears might well be covered by hair, so it wasn't essential to get them perfect.

Eventually she had all of the underlying tissues in place. Then it was time to cover her rendering in skin. Only after that would the image she called Alice really look like a human being. Jessica selected a typical Asian skin tone, not knowing if this victim was of Korean, Japanese, Chinese, Vietnamese, or some other background. Dark eyes were a safe bet. She could easily change them later if necessary. She rotated the nearly completed facial image back to the front, experiencing a peculiar sense of unease as she did.

To complete the reconstruction, Jessica picked a hairstyle from among AFRAM's many options. The style she chose had straight black hair parted just off-center, without bangs that would obscure the forehead.

Finished! For nearly two days, Jessica had focused intently on just one element of the reconstruction at a time: a particular muscle, a nose, an eyelid, an ear. The image on the screen was a collection of body parts, not a person. Adding the external features made the image more real, more human. It was time to see just what Alice might have looked like in life.

Before she took a holistic look at the final image, Jessica walked into the kitchen for a fresh bottle of iced tea. She chugged half of it as she stretched out her cramped muscles, closing her tired eyes and rolling her neck to relax the tension in her upper back. Finally ready for the unveiling, Jessica returned to the studio and sat before the computer monitor.

Her own face stared back at her.

Chapter 5

Friday, May 18

THE TEA BOTTLE slipped from Jessica's grasp and thumped to the floor. She stared at the computer screen, paralyzed. Beyond question, the expressionless face she saw there bore a striking resemblance to her own appearance in her late twenties. The match wasn't exact, but it was indisputable.

Jessica mentally retraced her reconstruction process. Could she have subconsciously projected some of her own features onto this unknown victim? She reviewed her notes and the decisions she had made along the way. They were all based on an accurate knowledge of anatomy, sound forensic reconstruction principles, and reasonable artistic choices. Bones, standard tissue-depth measurements for the victim's sex and race, plausible guesses at hair, eyes, and skin—all seemed solid. So how could this image look like her?

Perhaps she was not remembering her own past appearance clearly. Jessica's computer held numerous photos of herself with various friends from a few years earlier. Other than hairstyle and small variations in specific facial features, the similarity between her younger self and her image of Alice was undeniable.

Just how far did this resemblance extend? Jessica consulted her notes from the meeting last week with Adam and Silvia. The anthropologist had classified the victim as a female of East Asian descent; Jessica knew she had been adopted from an orphanage somewhere in China. Silvia had estimated the victim's living height at four feet eleven inches to five feet three inches; Jessica was five feet two. Based on the skeleton's condition, Silvia had judged the woman's age at her death to be in the range of twenty-four to thirty-five, and the time of death as three to eight years ago. If Alice were still alive today she therefore would be somewhere between twenty-seven and forty-three. At thirty-four, Jessica sat in the middle of that range. The coincidences were piling up.

Noticing the fallen tea bottle on the floor, Jessica got up and returned it to the kitchen, her mind roiling. She crunched on an apple as she wandered around the house in a fog. Eventually she found herself back at her desk. She plucked a green pen from the ceramic mug on her desk that had a snake for a handle. She took a notepad and began to list possible explanations.

1. There is no connection between Alice and me. It's all just a bizarre coincidence. They happen.

She smiled wryly at the old racist cliché that "all Asians look alike." Of course they didn't. There were just a lot of them, and occasionally someone might have known of two who did closely resemble each other. Jessica's friend Phil, an average-looking white man, frequently reported that he had visited some store he'd never been to before and the cashier greeted him with, "Welcome back. Good to see you again." He just had one of those faces people thought they recognized even if they had never met him before. Phil described himself sardonically as a "generic person."

2. Time travel is involved. The body I've been working on is my own, somehow transported into the past.

Or maybe sometime in the future someone would invent a time machine and Jessica would travel back in time to when she was (would be?) murdered, but the original Jessica from today still existed to encounter the dead one from several years ago. Or something like that. As far as Jessica knew, though, time travel was not possible. She could rule that out.

3. We are clones. Alice is not me, but Alice and I are exact duplicates of each other.

Jessica knew enough about biology to understand that cloning of animals was achievable, but that no humans had ever been cloned. Even if a clandestine human-cloning project were going on somewhere in the world, she didn't think she and the woman she called Alice could have been the products of such a program nearly thirty-five years ago, long before the first mammal had been cloned successfully.

4. Alice and I are identical twins.

That too was improbable, though it certainly was not out of the question. Twins did appear to be consistent with all the data Jessica had available so far.

5. Alice and I are sisters, but not identical twins.

This was far more likely than the women being identical twins. Fraternal twins would also be in this category, as they were simply siblings who happened to grow in the uterus at the same time from two separate fertilized eggs. Siblings close in age often shared a strong resemblance, particularly as children. Even first cousins sometimes looked remarkably alike. In this case, however, the similarity was closer than would be expected among adult sisters who were not twins.

Siblings—most likely identical twins—and pure coincidence appeared to be the only plausible explanations. Jessica was stunned to think she could have had a twin sister she never knew about. She looked up from her notepad and stared across the room, eyes focused on nothing. For minutes she sat, mind churning as she pondered the implications and tried to process her emotions. A wave of feelings she couldn't even name flooded over her.

Jessica had known from an early age that she was adopted. She just accepted it as a reality that didn't affect her day-to-day life. Jessica loved her parents, she loved her sister, Megan, and she had enjoyed a normal, happy childhood. Her life did hold a blank spot, a period before her earliest memory when she had been a different person in a different land, surrounded by people who looked different and spoke a different language. However, that gap had never overshadowed her status within her adoptive family, whom she considered simply her family.

Sometimes, though, she wondered about her origins, who she had really been intended to be before her unknown birth mother's life went sideways somehow. She was afraid she would never know. But how much did it matter, ultimately? Now she was thirty-four-year-old Jessica Lynn Sanford of Rosemount, Oregon, successful artist, forensic sculptor, and overall decent person. As a pragmatist, she accepted that as good enough most of the time. But this might be a rare instance when she needed to know more.

Jessica paced around her house, thinking furiously. *I need an action plan*, she thought. *Am I in fact related to Alice? How can I find out? If we are twins, how can I discover her real name and locate her family so they know what happened to her?* She didn't know if an adoption agency would try to keep twins together in the same adoptive family. She had never had any reason to contemplate this before. Perhaps her parents knew.

The neighbor's dog started barking frenetically, breaking her concentration. Stopping to look out the window, she watched a squirrel scamper along the top of her back fence and leap into a tree, eluding the dog. Once the squirrel had made it to safety, Jessica walked back to her studio, considering the ultimate questions: *Who killed Alice, why, and how? Can they be brought to justice? How much of this can—or should—I try to do myself?*

Professionally, Jessica's role in a case like this one was only to help identify the victim. But this skull presented so many questions.

Alice stared fixedly at her from the computer screen, silently imploring: *Find me. Bring me peace. Bring me justice.*

Whom do I tell about this? Jessica wondered. Maria hadn't seemed thrilled about this reconstruction project, and she had been acting more possessive of Jessica's time lately. She might not be the best person to start with. Jessica's parents had never said anything to her about being a twin. She didn't want to alarm them about a potentially earth-shaking issue that might turn out to be nothing. She wasn't even sure yet if this was something she should pursue at all. Jessica needed a sounding board.

This sounded like a job for BJ. Brandi Jo Kellerson was Jessica's oldest friend in the Portland area. They had met at a wine-tasting event soon after Jessica moved to Rosemount from Boise six years earlier. Though they had never been romantically connected, BJ being both straight and married with two children, they shared many interests. BJ was levelheaded, intelligent, and mature. Jessica could always count on BJ to be straight with her and—even better— nonjudgmental. Perhaps the two of them could work through this conundrum before she reported her findings to Adam Longsdale.

Jessica called BJ. They hadn't chatted for more than three weeks, so they had last spoken before she got the first call from Adam about the remains.

"Jessica! How *are* you? It's been too long, girl." BJ's nasal Upstate New York accent always served as a reminder that many Portlanders were transplants from other states.

"I know, I know. I'm sorry I haven't called. You won't believe what's been going on in the last few days."

"Talk to me."

"My head is just spinning. I've got a new facial reconstruction case from Eugene, and there's some really weird stuff going on with it. I need somebody to help me work through it and give me some advice. You've always been great for that, BJ. I can't talk to anybody else like I can talk to you, not even Maria."

"Same here. You're like the sister I never had, you know that. How can I help?"

Jessica's throat choked up at "sister." She couldn't speak for a moment.

"Jessica? You still there? Are you all right?" BJ asked, sounding concerned.

"Yeah, I'm here. Funny you should say that about sisters. Listen, I want to talk about this in person. Can you come over tonight, or can I come to your house?"

"Oh, I'm so sorry, I can't. My parents are in town visiting for a few days. They came for Jacob's birthday party tomorrow. They're leaving Sunday morning."

"Well, are you up for a bike ride Sunday afternoon? I can tell you everything then."

"That works. Maybe we can take that ride out past Sandy toward Mount Hood, the one from Ten Eyck Road. That's one of my favorites. It has trees, it has terrain, and it has no cars. If that sounds good, how about I meet you at the fire station at about one o'clock?"

Jessica's composure had returned. "Outstanding, thanks, BJ. I'll buy the frozen yogurt on the way back."

She hung up and went to the garage to check on her bike and get the rack ready to mount on her car.

*   *   *

Maria had texted Jessica while she was immersed in the reconstruction, but Jessica had left her phone off to stay free from distraction. On Saturday, Jessica finally had the time and energy to follow up with Maria by phone. She wasn't quite ready to share her revelation, not knowing how her girlfriend might respond. She wanted to be more certain of her results before bringing up the idea of having had a twin.

Jessica told Maria, "Sorry I couldn't get back to you sooner, sweetie. I had my phone off so I could concentrate on my work."

``` ``

"That's okay; you warned me you'd be busy. I'm really glad you called, Jess. How's it coming? Can you tell who she is yet?"

"Not yet, but I'm making good progress. I should be done in another couple of days." Jessica felt guilty that she wasn't being completely honest, but she needed to chew on the Alice situation with BJ before sharing her results with anyone else.

"Let me know when you're done so we can get together. I'm planning to go rock climbing tomorrow with some of the other young Cascaders. Too bad you can't join us."

"Yeah, that would be fun. Maybe next time. Be careful, okay, Maria? Don't let any of those kids get you into trouble on the cliff."

Maria laughed. "Hey, they'll be lucky if they can keep up with me. Talk to you soon. Love you."

* * *

Just before one o'clock on Sunday, Jessica parked near the fire station in downtown Sandy, a small town that served as the gateway to Mount Hood. BJ was already there in her bicycling garb. She was a tall, athletic woman with an oval face and short, light-brown hair.

Jessica unloaded her bike from the car's rack. She wore Lycra cycling shorts and a T-shirt that proclaimed "Life is Like an Analogy." The two women hugged.

"It's so good to see you, Jessica. I'm dying to know what you're wrestling with. I was ready for a ride anyway."

"Yeah, I need both a mental and a physical health day. Is that a new bike?"

"It is! I got it a few weeks ago. I love it, so much lighter than my old one. I'm planning to do the Seattle to Portland ride this summer, all two hundred miles in one day. I've done it in two days before, but this year I'm going for the full Monty."

"That's impressive as hell, BJ. Even two days would be too much for me."

"I've got six more weeks to train for it. But today's ride is just for fun. Let's get going."
```

It was a perfect day for riding. The cerulean sky was cloudless, save a layer ringing Mount Hood's summit. The women headed out of Sandy on Ten Eyck Road, pedaling easily as they wound their way through the curves in the woods. BJ caught Jessica up on her family news. Then Jessica gave her friend a capsule summary of the reconstruction case.

She finished, "Can you imagine how shocked I was when I saw that Alice looked almost exactly like me? I dropped my tea bottle onto the carpet."

"My God, that is so bizarre!" BJ replied. "It seems unlikely that you, of all the forensic sculptors around, just happened to work with those remains. But are you reading more into it than is there? I mean, she was a short thirtyish Asian woman; you're a short thirty-something Asian woman. That isn't exactly a unique description."

"I considered all that, BJ, and I checked all my work. I think it's solid. That's just how the reconstruction came out. Weird as it is, this dead woman looks like me!"

"There's got to be more than one possible explanation for the resemblance, though. It's a big leap to immediately conclude you're twins."

"Sure, and I worked through all the possibilities I could think of." She summarized her analysis for BJ. "The explanation that makes the most sense is that I had an identical twin sister I never knew about, but some asshole killed her and buried her in the woods like an old dog."

The women had to pedal harder now, being past the downhill stretch out of Sandy. They turned east onto Marmot Road. The narrow paved road wound through a forest of tall conifers. Ferns of every size dominated the undergrowth. They rode in shade, save an occasional sunbreak when they passed through a forest clearing. All Jessica heard was their tires whirring on the asphalt and their breathing. The woods smelled of evergreens, rich soil, and the dampness lingering from yesterday's rain. A doe with a half-grown fawn crossed the road not far ahead, silently disappearing into the bushes.

"All right," BJ finally said, "I'll buy your story. You know what you're doing, you followed the process, and Alice looks like you. What's next?"

"That's what I wanted to talk to you about. Obviously I need to report my findings to the detective who's handling the case. But now I have a personal involvement. Should I try to investigate whether the dead woman and I are twins? If we aren't, fine, it's just a coincidence and another police case. But if we are, then what? I feel like I'd have to find out who she was, find her family, and all that."

"Isn't that still all a police case?" BJ asked, panting for air as they crested a rise.

"Sure, but it's personal for me! The sheriff's office isn't going to put much time into trying to solve one old, cold homicide. I could help with the investigation. I do have a degree and experience in law enforcement. My parents might even know something about this twin situation. I haven't gotten that far yet. I *could* do all that. The question is, should I?"

Before BJ could reply, the women broke out of the woods and into a broad meadow between peaks of the Cascade foothills. "Let's open it up," BJ suggested.

They put their heads down and pumped hard on the open road, slowing only for the sharper curves as the road wound over gentle rises toward Mount Hood's looming presence before them. They coasted to normal cruising speed as the road turned sharply and reentered the woods.

Back to a pace where the demand for oxygen did not preclude conversation, BJ finally answered Jessica's question. "If I had just discovered I had a twin, alive or dead, I would move heaven and earth to find her. You can't help but wonder about her life, her family, and how she ended up dead so young. I would need to know."

"That's where I keep coming out too. I just needed another perspective."

"So if I were you, I would first try to find out for sure if this Alice person really is your twin. That would be such an amazing thing to discover! And if she was, I would drop what I was doing to learn what happened to her."

The women exchanged less weighty thoughts on the leisurely ride back to Sandy, where Jessica made good on her promise of frozen yogurt. Jessica admired BJ's bike again. She wondered whether or not she could afford—or justify—$1,500 for a new bicycle. Not if she was going to interrupt her work with a personal voyage of discovery, she couldn't. The quest for Alice was quickly becoming her top priority.

Before they got back in their cars, BJ put her hands on Jessica's shoulders and searched her eyes intently. "Go find her, Jessica," she urged. "Go find her."

Chapter 6

Monday, May 21

JESSICA TREATED HERSELF to sleeping in on Monday to recover from the strain and exhaustion of the past several days. When she awoke, she thought, *Today is a pancake day.* She pulled out the Bob's Red Mill whole-grain pancake mix from the cupboard. The package said to add milk, oil, and an egg. That just made ordinary pancakes, though. Jessica also threw in some oat bran, flaxseed meal, and soy protein powder, along with applesauce to replace some of the milk. Add a dash of cinnamon and a splash of vanilla. Top them off with pure maple syrup and sliced fresh strawberries, those big Hoods that were already showing up at the farmers' markets. *Now, these are* perfect *pancakes.*

Still in her pajamas and robe, Jessica wandered into her studio, coffee mug in hand. She glanced out the large window at her backyard with its weathered vertical-slat fence. *I need to stain that dingy gray fence this summer,* she mused, *maybe a nice dark bark color.* But not today; it was raining. No surprise there. She turned on the big computer monitor.

And almost spilled the coffee when she saw her own face—or at least a close facsimile of it—staring out from the screen. *I must remember to minimize that application before I quit work for the day,* Jessica thought. Otherwise, Alice would be kick-starting her heart every morning.

She settled into the purple office chair at her workstation and set the coffee mug in a safe place. Jessica reflected on BJ's comments from the day before. Her friend had said one, two, three, go. But go where?

Jessica took inventory. She had a face to search for: her own, apparently. There were the three little pieces of body jewelry from the forest grave. She knew of an approximate location to begin a search—Eugene. She also had a rough time frame, five years, plus or minus a few. That wasn't much to work with.

As she studied the reconstructed image on the screen, Jessica contemplated her next step. *How can I confirm whether or not Alice truly is my twin?* she asked herself. All she had to work with was a skull and her best guess as to how the outside of that skull had once looked.

"Well," she told Alice, "I happen to have a skull myself."

Maybe there was a way to compare Alice's skull to her own and see if the similarities were more than superficial. If she had an X-ray of her own skull, she could try to match it with Alice's. Another option was skull–photo superimposition. This was a standard forensic technique, though she had never done it herself. Normally the method was used to compare an unidentified skull to photographs of a known missing person taken during life. In this case, she lacked a missing person to serve as a candidate for comparison—but she had herself.

For the skull–photo superimposition experiment, she would need a passport-style photo of her own face: shot straight from the front, looking directly ahead, glasses off, neutral expression. She could get a photo like that easily enough and see how well it overlaid an image of Alice's skull. Unfortunately, she didn't happen to have any X-rays of her own skull lying around to match up with the victim's. That was not a service a photo studio normally provided. But then a name came to mind: Chuck Ziegler.

She had been friends with Chuck ever since she broke her left index finger while rock climbing some years earlier. Chuck had been the X-ray technician on duty at the Parkcenter General Hospital emergency room. When he asked how she got hurt, she described the Cascaders Mountain Club outing she'd been on. "That sounds like fun, except for the part about the broken finger," he observed. A few weeks later Chuck joined the club as well. They had gone on some outdoor excursions together since then. But no rock climbing.

Chuck was a fun guy with a great sense of humor. Though he had asked her out a few times, she wasn't romantically attracted to him. She was happy just having him for a biking buddy. However, maybe they were good enough friends that she could convince him to take some X-rays of her head. After all, he was fond of her head.

Chuck's number was in her phone.

"This is Chuck."

"Chuck, this is Jessica Sanford. What are you doing right now?"

"At this very moment? I'm watching a baseball game I don't care about." Jessica always found the native Kansan's distinctive drawl amusing. "If it ever ends, I'm going to wake myself up and go to work. I've got the 4:00 p.m. to midnight shift for people who decide to hurt themselves and spend some quality time in the ER. Why do you ask?"

"I have an amazing story that I promise is more interesting than your baseball game, although I realize that's a low bar to clear. Plus I need your help."

"All right," he said. "Baseball game, go bye-bye." She heard the announcer's voice and crowd noises in the background go silent. "You now have my full attention."

Jessica filled him in on the reconstruction project, wrapping up with her conclusion that this unknown victim from the woods south of Eugene looked remarkably like her. "This is so weird I hardly know what to think. I'm excited, I'm confused, and I'm a little scared. But mostly I'm excited."

The phone was silent for a moment. "So you just finished building your own face on this old skull you found lying around the yard, and it fits perfectly. That's odd. I thought you were still alive."

"I know, crazy, right? But I can't think of any way this woman could look so much like me unless we were pretty damn closely related. Like identical twins."

"Let's say I accept your argument. Dare I inquire about the part where you need my help?"

"I know this is a big favor to ask, Chuck, but please hear me out. I'd like to compare my own skull to Alice's—I mean the reconstruction subject. I call her Alice. So I want some X-rays of my head that I can compare to the images of her skull and see if they match. As it happens, you're an X-ray technician. What do you say?"

Chuck sounded less than enthused. "I say that I enjoy my job and would very much like to keep it. I could get in big trouble if I went around shooting X-rays of every Tom, Dick, and Jessica who wanted one. Plus I'll have you know that I am not a mere X-ray technician, but rather a radiologic technologist."

Jessica rolled her eyes. She looked at the big oil painting of the weather-beaten lighthouse near Cannon Beach, Oregon, hanging on the opposite wall of her studio. That seascape was her favorite of all her originals. She always found it soothing and inspiring. She sensed she would need all her powers of persuasion to get this done.

"Okay, I hate to bring this up, Mr. Radiologic Technologist, but you leave me no choice. Does the name 'Debbie McGarver' mean anything to you?"

"Hey, that was a long time ago," Chuck protested. "And we only had a few dates. Although I must admit they were excellent dates."

"Sorry, but I'm calling in the debt now. I introduced you to my friend Debbie, you had a good time, and now I'm asking you for this one favor—please. All I want is four shots around my head: front, back, and both sides. Is there some way you could do those for me and still keep your job?"

Chuck thought for a moment. He sighed. "It's not impossible. Could you come by the X-ray lab around ten tonight? Monday nights are pretty quiet unless we get a car wreck or something. I can probably sneak you in and take the shots."

Jessica silently pumped her fist in the air. "How long do you think that will take?"

"Just a few minutes. The X-rays are all digital now, no chemical development required. I can give you the digital images on a flash drive and cover my tracks so nobody will notice. You need to bring your own flash drive, though."

"Thank you, Chuck," Jessica enthused. "I can't tell you how important this is to me. If this victim and I are identical twins, it turns my whole life inside out. I'll be there at ten. And I will never bring up Debbie McGarver again, promise. Thank you, thank you, thank you!"

*   *   *

Jessica spent the afternoon working on an art project for another episode of *Desperation*. Normally she enjoyed having multiple projects to work on at the same time, but the reconstruction dominated her thoughts as she painted.

That night she drove to Parkcenter General Hospital and made her way to the X-ray lab. As Chuck had predicted, it was quiet. She greeted him with a big hug, wrapping her arms around his skinny waist as he looked awkwardly down from his lofty six-feet-five-inch perch, long ponytail draping over his shoulder.

After furtively scanning the empty waiting room, Chuck whisked her to the radiology room in the back. The green tile floor clashed with Chuck's maroon scrubs. A small stool sat near the complex-looking X-ray machine.

Jessica said, "I was looking online at some X-ray images of human heads. Sometimes I could see shadows from soft tissues, even brain folds. I only want to compare the skull bones, so can you please use a setting that will minimize the amount of soft tissue that shows?"

Chuck said, "I'll attempt to meet your requirements, my lady. This is my job, you know, being a radiologic technologist and all." He draped Jessica's upper body in a heavy lead apron to minimize her radiation exposure. At Chuck's direction she sat on the stool and rotated ninety degrees at a time while he lined up the digital radiography equipment for the four views she had requested. He copied the radiographic image files onto Jessica's flash drive and then deleted them from the machine's computer. With a little luck, no one else would ever know about them.

Jessica walked out through the still-empty waiting room and drove home. Wanting to have a clear head when she performed the image comparisons, she set the flash drive on her desk and went to bed. Nervous anticipation robbed her of a sound sleep, however. She rose early and headed right to her studio; breakfast could wait.

Jessica copied the radiographic image files from the flash drive to her laptop and launched an image-processing app. She opened the frontal-view photograph of Alice's skull and the corresponding X-ray of her own head. She resized the images so they looked about the same on the screen. She corrected small differences in the tilt angle of the two skulls from the vertical. Then she made her own X-ray 50 percent transparent and dragged it to overlay Alice's skull.

Jessica carefully aligned the bottommost point of the chin on both images. Her own skull image still looked slightly smaller than Alice's. She enlarged it until the peak of her cranium coincided with Alice's. With a tiny additional rotation of her X-ray to get the angle just right, the two images fused into one.

Everything suddenly seemed a little blurry. Jessica realized she had been holding her breath in anticipation and had grown light-headed. Time to exhale again.

She examined the two images for key alignment points. The nasal bridge and bony areas matched perfectly. Jessica traced the eye orbits and found no deviations. The cheekbones were also nearly congruent. The jawlines looked exactly the same, even down to the slight curvature in the chins. The unidentified skull lacked two teeth, apparently lost postmortem. She also spotted some slight differences in tooth positions. Jessica had had orthodontia as a teenager, two of the worst years of her life. That would account for her teeth having moved around a bit. Perhaps Alice's family couldn't afford braces to straighten her still-misaligned teeth. Other than the teeth, the two skull images could have been from the same person.

Jessica repeated the comparison with the three other X-rays Chuck had taken, evaluating the back and both sides. Again the correlations between the two skulls were uncanny. The teeth held different numbers of fillings in different spots—no surprise there. But even zooming in on her monitor, she saw just minor discrepancies in the bones. She noticed a small depression on the upper right part of her own skull, in the parietal bone. She touched that area of her head just below the part in her hair. Sure enough, she felt a small dent she had never noticed before. The dent could have been caused by forceps during a difficult birth, she thought.

Of course, there was one striking distinction between the two skulls: Alice had a big hole in the left temporal bone, the injury that most likely caused her death.

Jessica's stomach growled, and she suddenly realized she was starving. She had been comparing computer images for more than two hours without so much as a morning caffeine hit. She leaned back and rapidly blinked her eyes, which stung from staring at the screen. Jessica shook her hands to relax muscles cramped up from all the precise positioning movements. This might be a good time to treat herself to a massage, she thought, to let the tension accumulated from days of concentration flow into someone else's fingers.

The fact that the skulls weren't completely identical ruled out time travel as the explanation—not that she had thought that was possible anyway. Alice wasn't Jessica from another timeline or a parallel universe. If Alice and Jessica were ordinary siblings, or even fraternal twins, their skulls should not have matched so precisely.

Everything Jessica had seen this morning supported her tentative conclusion that she and the unknown woman she had named Alice were identical twins. It was one thing to look alike on the outside; it was another thing to match on the inside. Her reconstruction of Alice's external appearance was just her best guess as an experienced forensic sculptor. But bones didn't lie.

After a late breakfast, it was time to perform the second part of her experiment, superimposing her own face on the victim's skull image. First Jessica did some research in her extensive collection of forensics books to better understand the specifics of the process and to learn exactly what kind of photo of herself she needed. She threw on some clothes and headed a mile down Ninety-Third Avenue to her local Box It Up store. They took passport photos there, among their many other services.

Because she was always shipping something somewhere, Jessica was friendly with the Box It Up manager, Erik. She walked past the bronze-colored postal boxes and the wall of shipping cartons and packing materials toward the back counter, where Erik was just finishing up with a customer. Whenever she went to Box It Up, Jessica always thought the gangly, long-haired Erik looked too young to be a store manager, but she appreciated that he was efficient, professional, and friendly. She told him she needed a photograph taken just like a passport picture, from straight ahead, but at a high enough resolution that she could enlarge it on her computer. She didn't tell Erik why she needed this picture, and he didn't ask.

Erik agreed to take the photo using the twelve-megapixel camera in Jessica's own phone. At her request, he also took some photos from the side. Jessica pulled her hair back into a ponytail so her head was more visible. As it wasn't an official passport photo and he was using Jessica's own camera, Erik didn't even charge her.

Jessica waved on her way out. "I owe you one, Erik."

Back in her studio, Jessica transferred the new photos to her laptop. Again she used the image-processing app to make the frontal photo of her face semitransparent. Comparing a skull image with an external facial photograph was harder than simply aligning bones. The alignment marker points weren't as obvious because her own skull bones weren't visible. However, her research had educated her about the key facial and skull landmarks to look for.

She went through the same process as she had with the two sets of skull images to overlay her partially transparent face atop Alice's full-frontal skull image, adjusting the size and angle as needed. She found it discomfiting to see her own ghostlike face superimposed on someone else's skull. The exactness of the fit was even eerier. It was as though she had the X-ray vision that every adolescent craved.

She examined key alignment points for any disconnects. Her own eyes were properly centered in the skull's orbits. In both of them, the left eye was a bit higher than the right, an asymmetry that always made it frustratingly hard for Jessica to get her eyeglasses adjusted perfectly. The skull's nasal bones all lay inside the external tissues of her own nose. Her eyebrows were positioned right along the skull's brow ridge. The curve of the mandible—the lower jaw-bone—accounted precisely for the slight asymmetry in her own face. Nowhere did Alice's bones appear to extend outside the image of Jessica's flesh. She came to the same conclusion from the side views of herself and Alice's skull: she saw no significant differences.

Because Jessica hadn't performed this type of comparison before, she would want Silvia to confirm her assessment from a forensic anthropology perspective. Pending that confirmation, though, it looked like her photographic face fit Alice's skull like a glove. It was Alice. It was Jessica. It was both of them. *Both of us.*

Jessica called Chuck to relate how her experiments had turned out. "They match!" she practically shouted. Words poured out as she described how well all the skull and facial images aligned. "This victim and I are carbon copies."

"Way cool," Chuck replied in his understated way. "I can't even imagine what it must be like to think you have—I mean had—an identical twin you never knew. I'm glad I could help. Does this mean you'll finally go out with me now?"

Jessica's indoor voice returned. "Maybe. I do have a girlfriend, you know."

"Doesn't bother me if it doesn't bother you. What are your plans for tonight?"

"Just the usual for a Tuesday alone: stay home and stick my head in the oven."

"I see. So instead of that, how about if we let a chef in some restaurant put food in *his* oven, and we will eat it together tonight?"

"An excellent plan. In fact, I will go you one better. I will pick you up at half past six, drive you to said restaurant, and even pay for your dinner because you are such a good friend. But it's just dinner. Pick a place."

Once she hung up, Jessica reached for one of the various playthings she always kept within arm's reach for when she was just sitting at her desk and thinking. She picked up three foam washers she had saved from an ancient package of blank CD-ROMs. Jessica liked them because they fit softly around her fingers. She would idly twirl them whenever she had to coax her brain to work on a tough problem. This particular problem involved what to do now.

The Lorane County Sheriff's Office would be highly interested in her revelation, as it was the first clue they had about the victim's identity. The next step, then, appeared to be another trip to Eugene.

Concurrently, though, she considered the personal implications. This project had revealed hints of her biological background that she now must explore and understand. Suddenly she was less alone in the world. Because of her adoption and unexplained origins, Jessica had always felt somewhat separated from the rest of the world. The possibility of having a previously unknown familial connection sent tingles down to her very fingertips—she couldn't remember ever being this thrilled before.

The mystery of the victim's face may have been solved, but the police still needed a name and an explanation. Much work remained to be done, she concluded as the foam washers migrated from one finger to the next.

Jessica phoned Adam to set up a meeting with him and Silvia for Thursday.

Chapter 7

WEDNESDAY MORNING JESSICA went back to the computer and pulled up her completed reconstruction. She made several small tweaks, modifying her initial guesses at the uncertain external features to reflect her own facial characteristics when she was several years younger. She darkened the irises of the eyes to match her own deep brown. She thickened Alice's eyebrows slightly and raised the hairline to reflect her own high forehead. The shape of the full lips already looked about right, though she deepened their color a little.

She wasn't surprised the software didn't let her add acne scars. Perhaps her sister had been more fortunate than Jessica during those painful adolescent years of rampaging hormones. Jessica left the basic straight, black hairstyle alone, lacking any evidence to the contrary. The reconstruction process was based on science, overlaid with a dose of artistic judgment. However, she knew she couldn't just make stuff up.

Jessica's artistic tweaks were consistent both with the shape of the victim's skull and with established forensic reconstruction techniques. She hadn't deliberately intended to make the reconstruction look like herself. She was just trying to render a realistic image that could be useful when asking the public for help identifying the victim. Nonetheless, when she viewed the completed reconstruction on her computer screen it gave her chills. Other than the hairstyle, she could have been looking in the mirror. Who *was* this woman?

She needed a mental-health break. Jessica picked her guitar up from its stand in the corner of her studio. She loved the Taylor's rich sound, so much more bass than other acoustics she'd played. Taylors were pricey, yes, but the Guitar Café had given her an incredible trade-in deal on her old Guild. She usually played with a pick, strumming chords from mellow tunes that always lowered her blood pressure. Today, though, her fingers wandered across the strings on their own. Thanks to some Brazilian-style guitar lessons, she knew many interesting chords to set the mood for any situation. Major sevenths, minor ninths, thirteenths, and minor sixths all flowed effortlessly from her fingers. She felt her tensed muscles relax as her mind churned.

Jessica knew she must learn the truth about the woman she called Alice. The journey would be physical as well as metaphorical. At the least it would involve a trip to Boise to explore her own background in more depth. Fortunately, she had no active commercial projects at the moment; she was all caught up on her commitments for the *Desperation* show. The reconstruction job wouldn't pay a lot, but it would cover some travel expenses.

It was also time to tell Maria what she had learned. Jessica couldn't anticipate her reaction. They had been together for less than five months, so there was still a lot to learn about each other—starting tonight. She dialed Maria's number.

"Hi, Maria," Jessica said. "I hope you're not still annoyed with me for neglecting you lately."

"We're cool, Jess. You know I don't stay mad for long. I'm sorry I got snippy with you the other day. I'm happy to hear your voice. I thought you'd been kidnapped by space aliens or something."

"Nothing like that, but something going on with this project has me tied up in knots. Can you come over tonight? I have some stuff to talk to you about that I want to do in person. Don't worry, it's not us."

"Now you have me a little worried. I can be there around five."

"That's great. We can make some chicken parm, and I have a nice bottle of Barbera. Could you please pick up a loaf of that crusty Italian bread we like from the bakery by your apartment?"

"Sure. I hope everything's okay. I'll see you tonight. Love you."

Jessica spent the afternoon making plans and tying up loose ends. She phoned the art director for *Desperation* and told him she couldn't take on any more assignments for at least two weeks. She called her parents to ask if she could come visit this weekend. She had something important to discuss with them—no, nothing was wrong, but she needed their help. She'd drive there on Saturday, arriving in time for dinner. Finally she wrote to Kathleen, coordinator of the Meals on Wheels program at the Rosemount Senior Center, to say she wouldn't be able to drive her usual route on Tuesday.

Before that trip, though, was tomorrow's meeting with Adam and Silvia. Jessica arranged all the reconstruction files on her laptop so she could efficiently demonstrate the results and her interpretations. She copied the files onto a flash drive for Silvia to review.

A quick trip to the supermarket to pick up essentials for dinner left her enough time to relax for a bit in the leather recliner she found so soothing. She had positioned the chair to pick up afternoon sunshine through her living room window whenever the skies cooperated. Jessica sank into its warm embrace. She melted into the smooth jazz of guitarist Joyce Cooling on her headphones and closed her eyes, just for a few minutes.

*   *   *

Next thing she knew, Maria was gently shaking her shoulder. "Are you all right? You didn't answer the door, so I let myself in. You were totally out. I let you sleep while I worked on dinner. What is going on with you?"

Jessica glanced at the clock; she had slept for two hours. The intensity of the past week had taken its toll. Jessica felt refreshed after her little snooze. She smiled up at Maria's round, brown face and forehead that was crinkled with concern.

"It's so good to see you, sweetie. I'm fine, just worn out. Thanks for letting me sleep and for fixing dinner. Everything smells great." She sat up. "I'll show you what I've been working on after we eat. Did you bring the bread?"

"Yes, and it's already toasting in the oven with way too much butter and garlic. I also brought one of those cherry pies you like so much from the bakery."

"Too much butter? On garlic bread? Not possible."

Jessica stood and stretched. The two women hugged, and Maria led the way into the kitchen.

"Ooh, you look so cute in an apron, so domestic!" Jessica grabbed Maria's butt, dodging the wooden spoon that flew around playfully toward her hands.

A frying pan held breaded chicken cutlets drenched in a thick marinara sauce and topped with melted provolone cheese. A pan of whole-wheat linguine awaited draining. Filled salad bowls sat on the table, along with wine glasses containing the promised Barbera. Jessica could almost see the garlic wafting through the air.

Maria said, "You sit down and have some wine. I'll start dishing everything up."

Jessica smiled her thanks and trailed her fingers through Maria's curls as she sat down. The kitchen smelled like an Italian restaurant, lacking only a red-and-white checkered tablecloth and a straw-covered Chianti bottle. Jessica sipped some Barbera and hummed a nameless tune while Maria served the food.

After they finished eating and cleared the table, Maria asked, "Now, can you please tell me what's going on?"

"Come with me." Jessica led the way into her office, through the hallway with her original paintings hanging on the walls. *If somebody would only buy these damn paintings I wouldn't have to keep them on my own walls*, she thought every time she walked by them.

She told Maria, "You might find this a little startling. This is my final rendering on the reconstruction of the woman whose remains they found outside Eugene." She moved the computer mouse to clear the screen saver.

Maria gasped and took a step backward. She pointed at the screen. "But that's you! Except for the hair. I don't get it."

Jessica walked Maria through the reconstruction process, explaining first how she recognized the striking similarity to herself and then the skull comparison experiments she performed.

"I can't explain it, but it sure looks to me like this poor woman was my identical twin. All the evidence is consistent with that; nothing contradicts it. I can hardly believe it, and yet there it is."

Maria looked thunderstruck by the possibility that her girlfriend could have a twin sister she had never known about. "But what does this mean? This is too much."

"This is why I've been so busy and stressed the last few days," Jessica said. "It just blows me away. If Alice really is my twin, I have to find out what the deal is with her. Who was she? Why weren't we adopted together? It's exciting to think I could have had a twin sister, but it's so horrible to find out this way." Jessica pointed at the screen and practically shouted, "This poor woman has been lying dead in a hole for years, for Christ's sake! Where are her parents? They don't even know she's dead. Why would someone want to kill her? There are so many questions, but I don't have any answers." Jessica slumped into her office chair and sobbed.

Maria dropped to her knees and held her. She stroked Jessica's hair and tear-streaked cheeks.

"Baby, I can't imagine what you must be feeling. It's so weird for me to see that computer picture of someone who looks just like you. It's got to be ten times weirder for you." Maria handed Jessica some Kleenex from the box on the desk.

As Jessica's sobs subsided, she and Maria clung to each other. "I don't know how to feel about this or what to do," she began slowly. "It makes me wonder about my birth mother. What happened to her that she had to give up both of us? I have to find my twin. Even if this is just some bizarre coincidence—which I don't believe—somebody still must wonder what happened to this woman." She pointed at the screen.

Maria exhaled loudly with relief as the Alice/Jessica face faded from the computer display and the screen saver kicked in. "So what's your plan, Jess? Can I do anything?"

"First I have to go back to Eugene tomorrow to show the detective who's handling the case my reconstruction and tell him I think Alice could be my identical twin."

"Is there any other way to know for sure? You seem pretty well convinced already."

"Maybe with DNA. I'll ask him about that. The police might not be much help because it's such an old case. I might need to do most of the work myself. I'm driving to Boise this weekend to learn more about my adoption to see if that gives me a starting point."

"Can I go with you?" Maria asked eagerly. "Maybe I can help follow some clues, or at least be there for you."

Jessica took Maria's hands in hers. She smiled sadly. "That's so sweet of you, Maria. This is something I have to do alone, at least for now. I'm confused, I'm excited, and I'm curious. Let me start this myself, all right?" She squeezed Maria's hands.

Maria pulled back a bit. Jessica saw the hurt expression in her crinkled eyes and the beginnings of a pout. Maria said, "Okay, if you're sure you want to go alone. How long will you be gone?"

"Probably four or five days. I'll call you while I'm there and let you know what's going on. I'm sorry, sweetie, I wish I could bring you with me this time but I just can't. Understand?"

"Not really, but I'll respect your decision. Let me know if there's anything I can do."

Jessica smiled and hugged her. "I sure will. Thank you so much for your support, Maria. It means the world to me."

Maria said, "You said you had to go to Eugene tomorrow. Is it okay if I stay tonight?"

"Oh, absolutely. I need you tonight." Jessica kissed Maria and hugged her tightly. "But first we both need pie."

Chapter 8

Thursday, May 24

THE NEXT MORNING, Maria and Jessica prepared to go their separate ways, Maria to her apartment and Jessica to Eugene for her eleven o'clock meeting. Maria tepidly returned Jessica's warm embrace as they parted.

"I know this is confusing, but please try to understand," Jessica pleaded. "I'm not rejecting you at all. You're very important to me, Maria, you know that. I just have to explore this on my own for now. I'll see you next week, okay? I love you."

Maria gave a tight smile. She shrugged her shoulders and simply said, "Good luck." Jessica watched Maria drive away. Was she losing a lover as she gained a sister? She hoped not. Her life had room for both of them.

Jessica collected her laptop and a large manila envelope that contained the printouts and flash drive for Silvia. She steered her car toward I-205 to bypass downtown Portland on her journey south. It turned out to be a good thing she had given herself plenty of time. The Portland freeways were backed up, as was usual for morning rush hour. Courteous Oregon drivers let her migrate into the leftmost lane. *I'm so glad I don't have to commute in the city*, she thought as she crept along. The slow drive did give her time to admire the colorful arrays of rose bushes the city had planted on the slopes of the freeway overpasses. Portland was not called the City of Roses for nothing.

The 120-mile drive through Oregon's flat Willamette Valley was easy, though not particularly interesting. Jessica observed the undulations of the Cascade Range in the distance to her left and the Coastal Range off to her right as she passed farms flourishing on the rich valley soil. Other than the hills south of Salem and some knobby-looking ridges and hills—volcanic in origin, she assumed—that appeared on her left north of Eugene, there wasn't much terrain. She kept the car on cruise control and contemplated how best to present her findings.

When she pulled into the parking lot at the Lorane County Sheriff's Office, Jessica was running fifteen minutes late. The day had warmed quickly, and her car's air conditioning wasn't working right. She peeled her damp shirt from the seatback and dashed into the building.

Silvia and Adam were already seated in the interview room they had used before. Adam stood to shake her hand, and Silvia greeted her warmly.

"I was starting to worry about you," Adam said.

Jessica set her laptop and the manila envelope on the table and her purse on the floor. She tried to catch her breath from her quick run. "Sorry, traffic was worse than usual."

As Jessica set up her laptop and pulled out the printouts, Silvia said, "Adam told me you have some interesting information to share with us. I'm anxious to see what you think our victim looked like and hear what you're thinking."

"'Interesting' is an understatement," said Jessica. "Let me describe how I approached this reconstruction." She took a few moments to compose herself, gratefully accepting and sipping from the coffee cup Adam handed her.

"I can do both clay reconstructions and three-dimensional digital reconstructions on the computer. Because Silvia gave me the high-resolution CT scan, I decided on the digital reconstruction.

The software uses the same tissue-depth marker data I would use if I were working in clay. The computer also lets me render more life-like skin." Jessica's fingers moved over the keyboard as she brought up the images she had created.

"About all we knew from Silvia's assessment was that the victim was a short East Asian female in her twenties or thirties. I used average tissue depth markers because we don't know anything about her build. I gave her a neutral Asian skin tone and stereotypical hair and eyes. And here's what I came up with."

She turned the laptop toward them and revealed the original reconstruction image, the one that had opened a startling door into her own past.

The room was silent, save the fluorescent lights' buzzing in the ceiling. Silvia leaned in for a closer look, glancing up at Jessica and back at the screen several times. She sat back in her chair pensively, brow wrinkled.

"All right, I'm confused," Adam said. "That's an impressively lifelike rendering, but it looks a lot like you. What's the deal?"

Jessica took a deep breath to calm herself. "Now you see why I said I found something important. If this is a surprise to you, imagine how shocked *I* was when I realized this dead woman's face looks almost exactly like mine. I checked my work and everything seems legitimate. This is just how she came out. I call her Alice, by the way. I always name my reconstructions to remind me they were living people once."

Next, Jessica described her skull-comparison experiments. She laid out color printouts that clearly showed the congruence between the skulls with but tiny variations, other than the victim's penetrating skull wound.

The interview room was hot and stuffy. Adam took off his sport coat and hung it on the back of his chair, revealing the 9mm pistol he carried in a shoulder holster.

"How did you get X-rays of your own skull for comparison?" he asked. "Did you find an X-ray photo booth somewhere?"

"Don't ask," Jessica replied. "It's my secret, but they really are legitimate. You can even feel this little indentation on the upper right side of my skull if you want to." She pointed to that spot on her head. "The important thing is the match. By every measure I can think of, these remains look remarkably like...me. The obvious question is, how is that possible since I'm standing right here? I worked through the possibilities, and I'm forced to conclude that the victim and I are most likely identical twins."

"How could you have a twin sister you don't even know about?" Silvia wondered.

"I was about one year old when my parents adopted me from China. They've never said anything about me having a sister, let alone a twin. Unless they just kept that secret my whole life, this will come as a surprise to everyone."

Jessica continued, "Once I concluded that Alice had to be my twin sister, I tweaked the reconstruction slightly to reflect some specifics from my own features." She brought up the final reconstruction image on her laptop. "As you can see, this looks just like I might have looked a few years ago, except maybe for the hairstyle. All the changes I made were small, like eye color and eyebrow thickness. My changes were all consistent with the skull's characteristics."

Silvia and Adam exchanged a glance as Adam methodically chewed his gum. He folded his arms and cleared his throat. "In almost twenty years in law enforcement, I've never heard anything like this before. It just seems incredibly unlikely." The detective's raised eyebrows conveyed his doubt.

Adam's skepticism surprised Jessica. She thought she had built a solid case to justify her interpretation. She looked to Silvia for some reinforcement.

"It's unlikely," Silvia agreed, "but hardly impossible. Numerous cases have been reported of identical twins separated at birth who discovered their connection later in life by various means. I admit this must be the most bizarre way to learn about such a connection. But as Sherlock Holmes once said, 'When you have eliminated the impossible, whatever remains, *however improbable*, must be the truth.' The twin relationship *is* possible."

"Sherlock Holmes was a fine detective," Adam acknowledged, "albeit fictional. I'll grant that Jessica and Alice being identical twins is possible. However, I'm not convinced. Let *me* quote Carl Sagan, who said, 'Extraordinary claims require extraordinary evidence.' I think you'll have to agree Jessica's making an extraordinary claim."

He turned to Jessica. "I acknowledge that you did some clever experiments and impressive analysis. But Jessica, I don't feel I can go to the public with the claim that the woman we're seeking looks exactly like you based on what you've shown us so far."

"But—" Jessica began.

"Hang on. I'm concerned maybe you're projecting your own feelings onto the victim, looking for a connection where there might not be one. Perhaps we should use a different forensic sculptor who can be more objective."

Jessica's pulse rate shot up, and she knew her dismay showed on her face. If she lost this reconstruction job, it could trash her reputation. Nobody was going to hire a forensic sculptor whose work they couldn't rely on, whom they feared might build her own biases into her reconstructions, even subconsciously. She tried to explain again that she did not intentionally skew the reconstruction toward her own face. That was just how it came out.

Adam held up his hand and shook his head. "I understood everything you said the first time. We just can't go public with this facial reconstruction and your claim of twins yet. I need more solid proof first."

Desperate, Jessica turned to her left and asked, "Silvia, could you please take a closer look at my work to see if I've made any mistakes? I put all the files on a flash drive for you."

"I can't get to it for several days, but I would be happy to review it then. The case is fascinating, and your apparent connection could be a great clue to finding the victim." Silvia turned to Adam, eyebrows raised. "It's standard practice for a forensic anthropologist to review a reconstruction. But I'm a consultant, Adam, and it's your money. It's your call."

Adam paced around the small room, riffling his fingers through his thinning hair and chewing furiously. "This is too damn weird. I need more caffeine and to think about this." He stepped out of the interview room with his coffee cup.

Jessica played aimlessly with the ends of her hair, a nervous childhood habit she kept vowing to break. Silvia studied the images on the computer screen. She took off her glasses and peered closely at the skull-overlay printouts.

"I have to say, Jessica, I can't see any other explanation. Your idea to do the skull comparisons was remarkably innovative. I hope Adam lets us pursue this thread."

Adam returned to the interview room in about five minutes, fresh coffee in hand. "Sorry, I didn't think to ask if either of you wanted a refill." He sat across from Jessica. "Here's what we're going to do. I agree to pay Silvia to review the reconstruction for technical accuracy. But before we do anything besides that, Jessica, you'll need to bring me more evidence of this alleged twin connection. I have to know I can trust both your reconstruction work and your analysis of the results."

Jessica decided to go all in. "I'm going to visit my parents in Boise this weekend to look into my own background for any evidence that I might have had a sister. Maybe they know something. I have to believe that if I'm related to Alice, that would help us identify her and maybe solve the mystery of her death. Can you please give me some time to investigate this on my own before you hire another forensic sculptor?"

Adam thought for a moment and then said, "I'll be at a police conference in Denver all next week. I've also just been assigned to work on a complex case in Forest City. A delay on this cold case won't do any harm. I can give you three weeks to come up with more solid evidence before we start over." He looked at the calendar on the wall. "That gives you until Thursday, June 14. Is that fair?"

Grateful for the reprieve, Jessica said, "Yes, fair enough. Thank you, Adam. If I don't get anywhere by then, I don't expect you to pay me for the work I've done." She paused for a beat. "Besides what I showed you today, are there other ways to test whether or not Alice and I are related?"

"The most definitive way to compare identities is with DNA," Silvia replied. "Usually DNA is used to tie a specific person to evidence from a crime, like blood, semen, or body parts. But it can also show if two individuals are related, like in paternity tests."

"Great!" Jessica exclaimed. "So we can just get some DNA from the remains and compare it to mine, right?"

"No, we can't do a full nuclear DNA analysis because all we have to work with are bones and teeth. We found no soft tissue or hair left on the remains. Adam, have you performed mitochondrial DNA testing?"

"The medical examiner did extract some mitochondrial DNA. We had it sequenced."

"Wait, you lost me there," Jessica interjected. "People do DNA analysis on TV all the time, even with mummies and old skeletons that archaeologists dig up. What's this 'mitochondrial DNA'?"

Silvia switched into her forensic-anthropology professor mode. "Mitochondrial DNA and nuclear DNA are different." She picked up a pen and drew a circle on a pad of paper.

"Here's a typical cell." She drew a smaller circle inside the large circle and pointed to it.

"Nuclear DNA is found here in the cell nucleus. Most of the genetic information about a human being is in the nuclear DNA. However, bones and teeth that have been degraded in soil for this long rarely contain any usable nuclear DNA. So we can't do a complete genetic DNA test on these remains."

Silvia drew several small circles inside the largest circle on the page. "These are the mitochondria, little things inside every cell. They contain a different kind of DNA molecule. It's possible to extract mitochondrial DNA, or mtDNA, even from ancient bones.

Mitochondrial DNA is inherited only from the mother. So the good news is that we do have some DNA. The bad news is that it's not nearly as valuable as nuclear DNA for matching related people together."

Jessica's face fell. "So the mitochondrial DNA couldn't prove Alice and I were twins?"

"No, I'm afraid not. It *would* indicate whether or not the two of you have a recent maternal ancestor in common. Even an exact match would only show that you and the deceased woman are at least cousins of some kind."

"And since I'm adopted, we can't get any DNA from my birth mother for comparison with Alice either, to see if they're related. So we're pretty much screwed on the DNA."

Adam stepped in. "We ran the mitochondrial DNA sequence from the remains through all the available DNA databases, looking for any match at all. The FBI manages a national DNA database called CODIS, the Combined DNA Index System." He wrote *CODIS* on his notepad and then tore out the page and handed it to Jessica. She folded it and put it in her purse.

"CODIS contains forensic profiles collected from local, state, and federal laboratories. These profiles include DNA information found at crime scenes as well as from samples taken from convicted offenders and, in some states, from arrestees. It's great for matching evidence from two crimes together, like if you're dealing with a serial killer or other repeat offender."

Jessica was puzzled. "If Alice had never been involved with a crime, how could her DNA get into the database?"

"CODIS also contains DNA profiles from known missing persons. So the software is useful for looking for matches from all these different sources," Adam explained. "Unfortunately, we didn't get any matches on Alice's sample. That tells us her DNA was never found at a crime scene, and she never had a DNA sample taken by law enforcement. Also she probably was not reported as a missing person. If she had been, CODIS would likely have an entry with DNA obtained from some object that belonged to her."

Jessica wondered why no one had reported Alice's disappearance to the police. She was disturbed to think that perhaps her sister had been an invisible person, with no one who cared if she lived or died. All these years later, Jessica certainly cared. And she was going to help Alice; she had to. She put the printouts from the table back in the manila envelope along with the flash drive she had brought along and handed the package to Silvia.

"Thanks for the explanations," Jessica said. She went silent for a moment to think and then said, "I have an idea. Could you compare my mitochondrial DNA with Alice's? If we don't match, then we aren't related and I'll agree my reconstruction is probably not accurate. If that's the case, you should fire me and get a new sculptor. But if we do match exactly, we definitely are related and I could be on the right track."

"Jessica's right," Silvia said. "The mitochondrial DNA could serve as a rule-out test."

"Plus if you have my DNA and we eventually learn Alice's real name and get some of her DNA, then we could do a complete analysis. That could prove whether we're identical twins, right?"

Adam's exasperation showed in his face. "This is all probably premature, given how thin the evidence is for your relationship to the victim. But if you really want to try it, I could get a DNA sample before you leave here today. It's just a simple cheek swab."

"Thank you, Adam. How long will it take to get the mitochondrial DNA comparison results?"

"Up to three weeks, depending on how backed up the lab is. Cold cases aren't high priority. Let me get a test kit."

Adam walked out and returned wearing purple nitrile gloves. He pulled open a sealed package labeled *Buccal Swab Collection Kit*, took out a long cotton swab, and asked Jessica to open her mouth. Adam rubbed the swab on the inside of her cheek, sliding and rolling it back and forth for about twenty seconds. He sealed the swab in a plastic evidence bag and filled in the label printed on the bag.

"That's all there is to it. I'll call you when we get the results, and we'll see if this DNA connects you to Alice. If so, I'd have more confidence in your theory, even though it won't prove you're twins."

Adam stood and put his jacket on. Jessica rose and shook hands with him. Having her professional reputation riding on this one case was nerve-wracking. She had just three weeks to prove herself. If indeed she had blown the reconstruction on a fantasy about having a twin, she was about to lose a lot of time, goodwill, and perhaps even her livelihood. Like many perfectionists, she never felt her work was good enough. This time it had better be.

As Jessica prepared to leave, she looked at the reconstructed Alice/Jessica image on her laptop screen. *I promise you that I am going to devote all my energy to learning your name, discovering our connection, and finding whomever did this to you. Wish me luck.*

Chapter 9

Saturday, May 26

JESSICA WAS HAPPY the Honda dealer had squeezed her in to fix her air conditioning before she left for Boise. The eight-hour drive gave her plenty of time to think. She was motivated by her silent commitment to Alice to determine her identity and solve the crime that left her body discarded in a grave outside Eugene. Jessica's involvement in a case ordinarily terminated after she delivered a facial reconstruction to the responsible police agency, but not this time. Pursuing her personal connection with Alice would demand her best investigative skills.

Unfortunately her bank balance wouldn't subsidize an extended sabbatical from paying work. Looming over everything was the knowledge that her income could be jeopardized well into the future if she didn't find the real Alice before Adam's deadline, less than three weeks away.

Jessica's mind also churned over her relationship with Maria. Her girlfriend's flashes of impatience were becoming tiresome. Jessica's stomach was always tied in knots after one of Maria's outbursts. Lip service to the contrary, Maria obviously resented Jessica for pursuing this quest alone in Boise.

She pushed Maria to the back of her mind. This weekend was about self-discovery, not about shoring up a relationship that might be starting to crumble.

Usually when she drove to Boise, Jessica would swing by some wineries around Caldwell, in southwestern Idaho. Today she just wanted to get there. She reluctantly drove past Caldwell, and then passed Nampa and Meridian. She exited I-84 at Five Mile Road and headed north.

Jessica had grown up in one of the many subdivisions on the west side of Boise. Her parents still owned the same home there, where they had lived for almost thirty-five years now. She made her way through the development's twisting streets until she pulled into the familiar driveway. *No matter how old I am, there's always a special feel to going "home,"* she thought.

Jessica climbed out of the car and stretched her stiff muscles. Before she and her suitcase could reach the porch, her parents hurried out with greetings and broad smiles.

"Jessie, I'm so glad you could come! How was the drive?" asked her father as he embraced her. Though sixty-seven years old, David Sanford was trim and in good condition. Deep-set, intelligent blue eyes sparkled out of a round, friendly face. He was the operations manager at Q&H Industries, a small, high-tech manufacturing company in Meridian, just a few miles west of their home.

"The drive was fine, Dad. The Honda's great on the highway, but I'm happy to stand up," she replied. "You shaved off your beard!" She rubbed his stubbly chin.

"Yeah, too many people asked me what I was bringing them for Christmas. I cut off all that white and just kept the mustache. Think I should dye my hair?"

"No! The silver makes you look distinguished. You might think about some newer glasses, though, Dad. Aviators went out of style when I was about ten."

"Hey, I like these big lenses. I care how I *see*, not how I *look*."

Jessica's mother gave her a big hug and kiss. "It's been too long, honey. I wish we could see each other more often. Do you need help bringing anything in?"

"No thanks. I've got it. You both look great!"

A year younger than her husband, Sharon Sanford had recently retired from the AAA office in Boise, where she had spent nearly twenty years planning trips for AAA members. Each time Jessica saw her, Sharon appeared to have gained a pound or two. Her thick strawberry-blond hair just brushed her shoulders. Idaho's spring sunshine was activating her sea of freckles that faded every winter.

Her mom peered into the car. "Didn't Maria come with you? We've been looking forward to meeting her."

"Not this time. I'll bring her out before long. Something really strange has happened at work. I wanted to talk to you about it alone this weekend." Her parents looked curious, but she said, "We'll discuss it later, after I get settled."

The three walked up the sidewalk into the single-story house where Jessica had spent her childhood and adolescence. She had always liked the way the white bricks juxtaposed with the slate-blue siding. Her father had clearly been busy gardening. The landscape beds exploded with the colors of blooming zinnias, begonias, and marigolds. A row of tall purple foxgloves stood guard. The shrubs around the house were all neatly pruned.

David carried Jessica's suitcase down the hall. "We're still using your old bedroom for the guest room. We finally converted Megan's room into an office. Are you hungry yet? It's almost six. You know us, we eat early."

"I can eat," Jessica replied.

Sharon said, "A new Brazilian steakhouse opened nearby. We haven't been there yet. Would you like to try it out?"

"Sounds great. But can you drive, please? I'm beat." They got into David's car, and he drove them to the restaurant near the giant multiplex theater and the West Boise Mall.

As they ate, they caught one another up on news about family, neighbors, friends, and work. Her parents knew Jessica had something important on her mind, but they patiently waited for her to broach the subject. She would talk when she was ready—not a minute before.

Back at home, the Sanfords convened on the overstuffed couch and loveseat in the family room. Jessica studied the familiar walls, painted in southwestern shades of gold, tan, and rust. "Do you have your vegetable garden in yet, Dad?" she asked.

"Oh yes," he replied, "I planted everything several weeks ago. We're getting salad stuff out of it already. I'm teaching master gardening classes for the county now, as a volunteer. Mom still volunteers at the middle school and the library. She hasn't found it hard to stay busy after retiring. I hope to follow her good example myself next year. Are you still delivering Meals on Wheels?"

"Every Tuesday. I'm one of the youngest drivers. Driving's not much fun on stormy days, but I just ask myself, 'What if it were my father or my grandmother who needed a decent meal?' That's all the motivation I need." Jessica appreciated the example of lifelong volunteering her parents had set for her.

The room fell silent for a moment, except for the slow tick of the clock on the wall. Jessica had always loved the kooky backward-running analog clock. People did a double-take when they glanced at it, checked their own wrists, and then asked, "What time is it, really?" She sipped the Idaho Chardonnay her parents had served.

"You're probably wondering why I'm in Boise on such short notice. I've been working on this forensic facial reconstruction project. Something has happened that just blew my mind. I need to hear your thoughts, and I need your help."

David and Sharon sat quietly, expectantly, encouragingly. Jessica recapped her reconstruction work and showed her parents a printout of the final computerized Alice.

"The resemblance is obvious, right? Between the computer reconstruction and my X-ray comparisons, I'm convinced this woman I call Alice was my twin sister. I'm hoping you can help me figure out if that is even possible. And if so, I have to learn her real name and find her family. Meanwhile, the detective I'm working with doesn't believe this woman could be my twin. I've got less than three weeks to find her or I could be looking for a new career."

David and Sharon looked stunned by Jessica's revelation. David said, "Your reconstruction certainly looks a lot like our Jessie."

"Honey, this is just incredible," Sharon said. "We had no idea you might have a twin. You must be totally shocked."

"I'm overwhelmed and confused, that's for sure. You told me when I was little that I was adopted; I was special. Obviously I didn't look like you. So I knew I had to come from someplace different, and I've always felt kind of different. But I didn't give much thought to my birth family or to China. It just didn't matter much."

David said, "But now it does matter, right? We understand that. If I discovered a brother I never knew, I would want to learn all about him too. How can we help?"

"I feel like I owe it to Alice to discover her identity, and I owe it to myself to determine if we truly are twins. To begin, I need to learn all about my adoption process. I don't remember much of what you told me when I was a kid. I'm just groping around, trying to find some way to get started here." She finished her wine.

Jessica's father stood. "Let me get our old papers so we don't miss something. Does anybody want any dessert while I'm up?"

"No, thanks," the women replied in unison.

Sharon got up and headed for the kitchen to brew some herbal tea. "I bought some of that iced tea you like, Jessie. Do you want one now, or would you prefer coffee or more wine?"

"Coffee would be great—thanks, Mom. I'll come help."

The three returned to the family room with their beverages. Now that the sun had set, cool evening air blew gently in through the open patio door. David pulled a stack of papers from a tattered cardboard box that once contained a pair of cowboy boots. The box was adorned with glued-on sequins and labeled *JESSICA 1985* in faded pink letters. He flipped through the pages and shared the key points from the documents as he and Sharon took turns telling the Story of Jessica.

Instead of having their own children, David and Sharon wanted to help children who needed a family. First, they adopted Megan from South Korea. A few years later, all three Sanfords wanted to enlarge their family. Megan was excited about getting a baby brother or sister.

They approached the Coulter Adoption Agency in Boise, which specialized in international adoptions and had helped Megan join the family. The Coulter people suggested they consider a young girl from China. China had many orphans available for adoption, thanks to the so-called one-child policy the Chinese government had instituted to control their population growth. Because boys were favored culturally, infant girls were much more likely to be abandoned and in need of adoptive families. David and Sharon agreed that a little Chinese girl would be a welcome addition to their home. After going through all the necessary application paperwork and background checks, Coulter notified them that they had been matched with an adorable toddler named Meilin, meaning Plum Jade.

"Meilin?" Jessica echoed. "That was my original name?"

Sharon said, "Meilin was the name the orphanage gave you, honey. No one knows what your birth mother might have named you, because the orphanage never knew who she was. Meilin's a beautiful name, but we wanted you to have a new name as part of your new start in America. That's why you've always been Jessica to us. You were young enough to absorb the new name easily."

All they knew about Meilin was that she had been abandoned by her birth mother and lived the first thirteen months of her life at an orphanage in the city of Chenzhou in Hunan province. Even her exact date of birth was a mystery. The orphanage had assigned December 3 as her birthday based on her apparent age at arrival.

Coulter Adoptions had sent the Sanfords a small photograph of baby Meilin. David pulled it out of the box and passed it around.

Sharon put on the reading glasses she had worn around her neck since her cataract surgery a year earlier. She smiled at the memories as she studied the photo. David and Sharon had immediately fallen in love with their new daughter-to-be. She seemed healthy and normal in all respects. She just needed a home and a new family to care for her.

"How did I get from China to America?" Jessica asked.

"A group of us adoptive parents from all over the West Coast met in Portland and flew to China together, along with some people from Coulter," David said.

Sharon added, "There were about a dozen couples in our group. Coulter told us they sent groups like this to the same orphanage every three or four months to pick up their new children. The people in each group flew back to Portland with their new kids and then went on to their own hometowns."

Jessica asked, "Did you know if two of the girls in your group were twins? Or is it possible there could have been twins who were split up? Wouldn't they have tried to place twins together in the same adoptive family?"

David answered, "We had asked about the possibility of getting two babies. Back then, though, the Chinese government allowed families to adopt only one child at a time. So twins definitely would have been adopted separately. Nobody said anything to us about you having a twin. I suppose it's possible. We just wouldn't know."

It was getting late. Jessica had had a long day. Her head swirled with all she had learned and with still more questions. They decided to resume the conversation the next day. Sharon asked Jessica if she would like to join them for church in the morning.

"No thanks, Mom. I'm still an atheist. You and Dad can go. I'll sleep in."

Her mother laid her hand on Jessica's arm. "Oh, Jessie, I wish you wouldn't talk that way. You know, if you accepted God, you could look forward to meeting Alice in heaven eventually. Wouldn't that be lovely?"

Jessica smiled wistfully. "It's a beautiful thought, Mom. I just don't believe in heaven. The only way I'm going to 'meet' my twin is by finding some leads to learn her real name and what happened to her." She yawned and rubbed her eyes. "I'm going to go to sleep. I love you both. Thank you for being such great parents." She hugged and kissed them both goodnight.

As Jessica left the room, David said, "We love you too, Jessie. You're our favorite younger daughter!" Her father's old joke still made her laugh.

Chapter 10

Sunday, May 27

JESSICA AWOKE AFTER the best sleep she'd had in days. The house was quiet; her parents must have still been at church. Morning light filtered in through the patterned curtains on the window. She looked around the room she had moved into at the age of thirteen months. It still had the same pale-pink walls she had insisted on when she was six. Clusters of thumbtack holes showed where the usual teen posters had hung. Backstreet Boys had given way to Brandy, who yielded to Buffy the Vampire Slayer, only to be replaced in turn by Britney Spears. The same oak dresser and end table were still there, though cleared of her personal mementos. These walls enclosed a wealth of memories. This was where she had kissed her first boy. Her first girl too, for that matter.

As she lay in bed, Jessica contemplated how her childhood might have been different had she shared the room with a twin sister. A real playmate, not an imaginary one. Megan was a great sister, but enough older to not be a reliable playmate. *Would Alice and I have worn the same clothes and done our hair the same way? Would we have pretended to be the other one when one of us got in trouble? Would we have played jokes on people, like switching places to see if our dates noticed?* She would never know. *But maybe I can learn enough to feel like I knew her,* she hoped.

Jessica got dressed and rummaged through the kitchen for some breakfast. Her parents' cereal collection was pitiful compared to that in her own house, but she made do. Then she wandered around the house to see what had changed since her last visit. Not much. Jessica was on her second cup of coffee, checking her messages, when she heard the garage door open. A minute later, her parents walked through the door between the garage and laundry room.

"Good morning," greeted her mother. "How did you sleep?"

"Fantastic! I needed that. How was church?"

"Church was as church always is," David replied. "It's gorgeous outside. After we change clothes, maybe we can sit on the patio and continue our conversation from last night."

As she walked down the hall to the master bedroom, Sharon called out, "I invited Megan for dinner tonight. She said she can't wait to see you."

"Speaking of Megan," Jessica said when Sharon came out of the bedroom wearing nonchurch clothes, "did she ever try to find her birth parents in Korea?"

"Yes, she did. We adopted her five years before we adopted you. She was two. The records from back then had a lot of holes in them. By the time she decided to go looking, she didn't get anywhere."

"Did it bother you that she looked for her birth mother?"

"Not at all. It's natural to want to know where you came from. I felt bad she never got her questions answered. She's okay with it now, though. You move on."

They assembled sandwiches, chips, potato salad, and drinks and carried them out to the picnic table, which was comfortably warm in the shade of the patio's retractable awning.

David said, "I wish we could tell you more, but we have no way to know if you had any siblings, not to mention a twin—let alone know what might have happened to her."

Sharon added, "We knew a few other Chinese kids of different ages around Boise from various Coulter adoption groups. We all got together sometimes for picnics or to celebrate Chinese New Year. Those connections faded away as you kids grew up and some of the families moved away."

David swallowed a bite of turkey sandwich and some Mountain Dew. He picked up the story. "I don't remember any of the other girls looking like you as they got older. So if you did have a twin, she probably wasn't adopted by another family in our group or in this area. Possibly in another group. Maybe the adoption agency could tell you more. Their office is downtown."

Jessica was dismayed. This might be harder than she had hoped. She had a mental image of Adam tapping his finger on his watch impatiently.

"Do you have any information about the other groups Alice might have been in?" she asked. "Or do you have contact information for the other people from my group so we could ask if they know anything? Maybe networking through these Chinese adoption groups would get us somewhere."

"Some parents from your adoption group stayed in touch for several years," David said. "We would mail pictures and updates to each other. We don't know anything at all about the other groups."

Sharon said, "I do have some addresses and phone numbers for the other parents in the group. I could call them and ask for their emails so I can send them pictures of you. Maybe they'd know of another girl who resembled you. Do you have some digital pictures I could send out? Most of my photos of you are prints."

"That would be great, thanks. I have digital photos from my high school graduation when I was eighteen and college graduation at twenty-two. We think Alice was around twenty-five to thirty when she was killed. I'll get you a couple of me from that age range also."

After lunch, Jessica helped carry the dishes to the kitchen and loaded them into the dishwasher.

"I don't think this is going to be easy, Mom," she said quietly to Sharon. "I have to do it, though, however long it takes. I already told the people at the TV show I've been working on that I can't do any more art projects for them right now."

Sharon set a plate of homemade chocolate chip cookies on the dining room table. "Let's sit for a minute," she suggested. Jessica sat at the head of the table, and she and David munched on cookies. Sharon pushed a vase of flowers aside so they could all see each other. She reached across the table and held her daughter's hand.

"Dad and I want to help you in any way we can, of course. We would like to help pay your expenses while you're searching for Alice so you don't have to work or worry about money."

Jessica was overwhelmed. "Are you sure? You've been saving your money for retirement."

Her father took Jessica's other hand in his and stroked it gently. He said, "We have plenty of money, Jessie. This is so important to all of us. Please let us help. Anything you need, for house payments, travel, whatever. Just let us know."

Jessica stood and hugged both of her parents, choked up with gratitude. *This is what it means to have a family who loves you*, she thought. *Was Alice as fortunate?*

That afternoon, Jessica emailed her mother the photos she had requested. Sharon and David both worked their phones, reaching as many people as they could from the original adoption group. They obtained email addresses for some of the other parents and sent them Jessica's photos. No one they spoke to knew anything about the possibility of twins, though all were fascinated by Jessica's search. Her parents never mentioned that the possible twin they sought was dead. Although this initial quest did not yet yield fruit, David and Sharon clearly enjoyed catching up with old friends.

In the meantime, Jessica called her best friend from high school, Gina Silvestri, who was delighted to hear Jessica was in town for a few days. They arranged to meet for drinks at a Boise bar the next night with two other school friends. What a treat it was to have even one special friend you knew your whole life, even if you only saw each other on occasion. Each time she saw Gina it was as though no time at all had passed. Well, maybe time had passed in their faces, but not in their connection.

Jessica's sister Megan arrived about five o'clock for dinner. "Hello, numbnuts," she said to Jessica, who responded as required: "Hello, poopyhead." Slender and attractive, Megan stood four inches taller than Jessica. Her ears stuck out a little, which was apparent only when she tucked her long, dark-brown hair behind them.

"You look fantastic for someone pushing forty," Jessica teased. "How goes the teaching business?"

"Same old, same old. I admit, teaching chemistry is becoming tiresome. I've been at Treasure Valley High for seventeen years now. I'm applying for an assistant principal opening for fall. Moving into administration would give my aging feet a break."

"Good luck. I hope you like going into admin." Jessica lightly punched Megan in the arm. "Thanks for coming over. It's great to see you, and I have some news to share later on. Are those wine bottles I see in your bag?"

Megan held up a green bottle. "I recall that you are fond of New Zealand Sauvignon Blanc. Mom said we were having salmon, so I brought two bottles. I hope it's good. If it's not, maybe you'll forgive me after you see the chocolate cake I brought."

"I'm sure it will be great, thanks. Let's see how Dad is doing with the food." They walked out to the patio, where David had a large sockeye salmon filet grilling. Assorted slices of peppers and squash covered the other side of the big gas grill.

"That smells fabulous, Dad," Megan said, pecking David on the cheek. "What do you have on it there? I'm a chemist; I need to know what I'm eating."

"If you must know, the secret sauce is a fifty-fifty blend of barbecue sauce and maple syrup. We also have some sweet potatoes roasting in the oven and a big salad your mother made. Everything will be ready in about ten minutes."

At dinner, everyone asked about Maria: where's she from, what's she like, what does she do, show us pictures. Jessica told them how much she and Maria enjoyed the Oregon outdoors. She omitted the parts about going out to the dance clubs, as well as their recent tension.

When they sat down in the living room with coffee and the promised chocolate cake, Megan asked, "What is this big news you have, Jessie? Do I need to buy a bridesmaid's dress?"

"No, nothing like that. Maria and I aren't even talking about marriage." Jessica gave her a condensed version of the story about the reconstruction and her urgent quest for the real Alice.

"Unbelievable!" Megan exclaimed. "Imagine, maybe I could have had two little sisters instead of one. I'm excited for you. It's so sad you had to find out about her that way."

"All true, Megan, all true. Mom and Dad said you looked for your birth mother once. How did you feel about all that?"

Megan chewed some cake thoughtfully and sipped her coffee. "I had mixed feelings. At the time, I really wanted to know more about my origins. I think everybody wants to know where they came from and who they are. The Koreans weren't much help, though. Eventually I realized, how much does it matter? I've got a great family, even a great little sister. What else is important, really?"

Jessica pondered this for a moment. "How curious. I have a wonderful family just like yours, even the sister part. But I've always been a little afraid of just disappearing and nobody noticing or caring because I was only an adopted orphan, not a real kid."

Sharon dropped her fork to her plate with a clang, startling the others. Her eyes glistened. "Oh, honey, I had no idea you felt that way. We couldn't love you more if we tried. I'm so sorry if we ever did anything to make you feel like you are less than our perfect daughter. I hope you know that isn't true!"

"It's nothing you said or did, Mom. You and Dad have always been great. I know it's irrational, but I've always had that fear in the back of my mind. I know I'll never find my birth mother. Now my goal is to find Alice. What was her real name, was she my twin, where did she live, who were her parents? And who killed her? If I don't do this, she'll forever be just a pile of bones a dog found in the forest. I couldn't live with that."

The four Sanfords quietly finished their dessert, and Megan got ready to head home. Then David said, "I can't tell you how proud of you I am, Jessie. Not everyone would drop what they're doing to try to solve a mystery like this. I just know you're going to find the real Alice. I feel it."

Chapter 11

Monday, May 28

AFTER DAVID, SHARON, and Jessica ate breakfast together Monday morning, David went to work as usual. Sharon had no specific commitments for the day. She offered to continue to follow up on contacts with the other parents from Jessica's adoption group and with any of the adoptees themselves she could reach.

Jessica phoned the Coulter Adoption Agency in downtown Boise. She explained that she was an adoptee from China and had some questions about her origins. The receptionist she spoke to set up a 10:30 a.m. appointment with the lead adoption agent in the Boise office, Loren McDaniel.

Jessica's phone rang at about nine o'clock while she was reading the *Idaho Statesman* newspaper and drinking coffee. She was surprised to see the call was from Paul English, whom she knew from Portland's Cascaders Mountain Club.

Paul's voice sounded strained. "I'm afraid I have some bad news, Jessica. Maria had an accident yesterday while we were rock climbing. She's going to be okay, but she took a nasty fall."

Jessica froze, heart pounding. This was news she had long feared receiving, knowing how close to the edge Maria liked to push everything. "What happened? How badly was she hurt? Where is she now?"

"She was leading a climb at Cascade Cliffs, on the Washington side of the Columbia River Gorge. She slipped just before she got to the top. Her right leg is broken in several places, her knee's badly torqued, and she's got some cuts and bruises. She's in the orthopedic unit at Parkcenter General Hospital."

"Why didn't anybody call me yesterday?" Jessica demanded.

"This happened late in the afternoon," Paul said. "It took a while for us to get her down safely and to the hospital. We called her parents first. They both drove up from Salem. By the time Maria was out of surgery and stable it was nearly midnight. There was nothing you could do for her, so I decided to wait until today to call you. I apologize if that was the wrong decision."

Jessica's pulse rate drifted back to normal as she understood Maria was out of danger.

"No, it's okay. Do you think I should come home? I'm in the middle of some really important stuff in Boise."

"That's up to you, of course. She'll be in the hospital for one or two more days."

Jessica thought for a moment. Her girlfriend was in good hands. Paul was right; there was nothing Jessica could do for Maria in Portland right now. She had to finish the mission that had brought her to Boise.

"All right, I'm going to drive home on Wednesday. I'll call Maria later when she might be awake. Thanks a lot for calling me, Paul."

Jessica sat down and sighed heavily. She might take some flak from Maria for not dropping everything and dashing back to sit by her bedside, even if Maria was asleep the whole time. However, searching for Alice had become her top priority. She visualized an hourglass holding seventeen more days' worth of sand. Maria just might have to be disappointed for now. Besides, it was time to go to her meeting.

Jessica drove downtown and parked in one of the many garages that had sprung up during Boise's ongoing revitalization. She saw how much the city had changed in just the six years since she had moved away. Though the city center wasn't large, it now boasted numerous trendy restaurants, clubs, shops, and even winery tasting rooms. As she walked past, she peeked into the lobby of the venerable Idanha Hotel, completed in 1901 and among the oldest buildings remaining downtown. Much of the city's architectural history had disappeared as the downtown evolved over the decades.

The Coulter Adoption Agency's offices were on Idaho Street, right in the city center. Jessica introduced herself to the receptionist, a striking young black woman. The nameplate on her desk identified her as Krysta Kendricks. Krysta stood and shook Jessica's hand with both of hers, smiling warmly. She was tall and graceful with delicate bone structure and large, expressive eyes.

"It's such a treat to meet one of our grown adoptees," Krysta said. "We work with small children all the time. Almost none of them come back twenty or thirty years later. Loren will be right with you. Can I get you some coffee?"

Jessica accepted her offer. While she waited for Loren, she gave Krysta the capsule summary of her life. Krysta was fascinated that Jessica had gone into law enforcement and then into forensic sculpture—the work forensic sculptors performed was both intriguing and important. Smiling, Krysta said Jessica's intelligence and accomplishments validated Coulter's mission to place Chinese orphans into stable and loving American families. She also asked Jessica for a business card. Perhaps there would be an opportunity for Jessica to share her success story with potential adoptive parents in the future.

A heavyset, middle-aged man with implausibly dark hair walked into the reception area from the adjacent office. Krysta introduced Jessica to Loren McDaniel. Loren gestured Jessica into his office and closed the door behind them. The wood-paneled walls displayed numerous framed diplomas, certificates, and awards. Several photographs showed Loren with groups of Chinese children of different ages, apparently at an orphanage. Jessica recognized a beaming former congressman in a photo with his wife, two adopted Chinese children, and Loren.

Jessica sat in the chair Loren indicated. She took out a notepad and a green pen. Loren began, "Jessica, when you called this morning you said you had some questions regarding your background. What can I do for you?"

As she had for so many others recently, Jessica recounted the discovery of the skeletal remains outside Eugene and her role in performing a facial reconstruction from the skull. She showed Loren a printout of the reconstructed facial image and noted the similarities with her own face. The results of the skull-comparison X-rays provided even stronger evidence that she and this victim must have a strong familial connection. The police had been unable to match the victim with any missing-persons reports. She remained an unidentified homicide victim, yet one with special significance for Jessica.

"So my mission now, Loren, is to discover who this woman is, our connection—if there really is one—and what happened to her. Because I was adopted from China through Coulter, my parents wondered if you could shed any light on my background that might help. I believe it's likely that the victim, whom I call Alice for now, also was adopted from China, possibly through Coulter as well."

Loren sat back from the edge of his seat and exhaled audibly. "Wow. What a story! Thanks to our rigorous screening process, Coulter has an excellent record of placing adoptees in safe and supportive families. If your Alice was indeed one of our children, I'd be shocked if someone in her family was involved with her death."

Surprised at his defensiveness, Jessica pointed out, "I'm a long way yet from learning how Alice died, Loren. My first step is to discover more about my own background so I know if I possibly had a twin. Would you have any information about that?"

"Let me look at your records." Loren worked the computer keyboard and mouse for a few seconds. He studied the display that appeared. Jessica couldn't see the screen from her chair.

"I've been with Coulter for twenty-four years, so I was not involved with your adoption, let's see, thirty-three years ago. As I'm sure you can appreciate, there's certain information I'm not at liberty to share, to protect the privacy of other individuals involved. Perhaps you should just ask me your questions. I'll tell you anything I'm able to." Loren looked at Jessica expectantly.

Jessica finished her cooling coffee; Loren didn't offer a refill. She recapped the information her parents had provided from the papers in the old cowboy-boots box. Loren nodded, confirming from the computer screen that everything her parents had told her was accurate.

"My parents said the orphanage didn't know who my birth mother was. Is that true?" Jessica asked.

"It is. The orphanage records simply described you as being abandoned and discovered in a public location. There's even a small chance that you had been taken by local family-planning officials who might have claimed the baby was illegal. It could have been the second baby in the family, or perhaps the parents were underage, or the baby—you—might have been born out of wedlock. Occasionally babies were removed from their mothers under such circumstances and delivered to an orphanage. We just have no knowledge about your origins."

"Do you know whether or not I had siblings?" Jessica asked.

Loren looked at his computer screen again. "Your records don't say anything about siblings. If a young mother gave birth to twin girls, she might well have given one or both of them up for adoption. Girl children were not as desirable as boys. Two extra mouths to feed could be an impossible burden for a young, poor mother."

Jessica was disappointed, but not surprised, at the dearth of information. She rose from her chair and began pacing in the spacious office, stroking her chin contemplatively.

"Well, I have this tentative evidence that strongly suggests there *was* a twin. My parents are checking with other members of my adoption group to see if anyone had a daughter who looked like me. So far, nothing. Could she have been adopted from that same orphanage but at another time?"

"That's possible," Loren responded. His eyes tracked Jessica as she paced. "Other outcomes are possible too. Rarely, the mother might come back to retrieve a child if her circumstances change. Another adoption agency might have worked with the same orphanage, though I doubt it. She could have been in another Coulter group or at another orphanage, or maybe she was never adopted at all. That's not uncommon."

"Since it looks like I did have a twin and she did make it to the United States, let's assume for now she would have been in another Coulter group," Jessica proposed. "My parents said you sent groups of around a dozen adoptive parents to that particular orphanage about every three months. Is that correct?"

"Yes."

"What's the age range over which little girls typically would have been adopted by Coulter parents?"

"Most adopted children ranged from eight months to eighteen months old." Loren looked at the screen again. "You were about thirteen months old at adoption."

Jessica jotted some numbers on her notepad and thought for a minute. "So if I had a twin who was adopted, it looks like she could potentially have been in one of five groups. We can rule out my own group, unless the inquiries my parents are making pay off. That leaves the two groups from about three months and six months earlier, and the groups from about three months and six months later. Do I have that right, Loren?"

"Yes, that sounds about right. Where are you going with this, Jessica?"

Jessica sat back down. She leaned forward and placed her hands on Loren's desk. He unconsciously rolled his chair back slightly.

"I believe our best chance for finding the real Alice is to look in those four other groups," Jessica said earnestly. "Can you share with me any information about the adoptive parents from those groups? Then I could ask if any of them have a daughter who looked like me and who might have disappeared several years ago."

Loren shook his head. "I'm sorry, but I cannot disclose such information for privacy reasons. When parents apply to adopt, we promise not to reveal any details about an adoption to any third party without a court order. The parents also agree to maintain privacy regarding any other adoption they know about, such as those of their friends. Of course, parents are free to share information about their own adoption experience with whomever they wish."

"Well, can you contact the parents in those other groups and ask if they're willing to communicate with me about this matter?" Jessica asked, voice rising in frustration.

"I cannot," Loren said through tightened, colorless lips. "If I were to contact families with an unsubstantiated story of twins and homicide—well, that could be highly upsetting to them. I understand how important this is to you, Jessica, and I regret we can't provide more assistance. I hope you find the answers you're looking for." Loren stood to signal the conversation's end.

A crestfallen Jessica put her notepad and pen back in her purse and stood up. She handed Loren her business card. "I understand. If anything changes, please get in touch with me. I would be most grateful for any help you can offer."

Loren and Jessica shook hands before he escorted Jessica back to the office's reception area. Krysta smiled at Jessica and said, "It was great to meet you, Jessica. I hope to see you again."

Nearly in tears, Jessica could not meet Krysta's eyes. She offered a weak smile and left the office.

Jessica walked slowly to her car, disconsolate. It looked like her best possibility for finding Alice had slammed into a brick wall. She drove back to her parents' house and told her mother about the frustrating meeting at Coulter.

Sharon had received some replies from the people to whom she had sent Jessica's photos. None remembered seeing another Chinese girl of that age who resembled Jessica. They agreed to share Jessica's story and photos through their own circles of friends in the Chinese-adoption community. Perhaps these interlocking ripples would lead to someone who knew someone who knew someone who looked like Jessica. That needed to happen soon.

After lunch, Jessica called Maria's cell phone. Her mother, Lupe Domingo, answered. Jessica had met Maria's parents two months earlier when they drove the hour from Salem to Portland to visit their daughter. Lupe said Maria was asleep in her hospital room, floating on serious pain meds, but she assured Jessica that Maria was going to be all right. The hospital expected to release her Tuesday or Wednesday. Lupe would stay in Maria's apartment with her for now.

Two hours later Jessica called again, but Maria was still asleep. She finally reached Maria after dinner on her third try. She was in a daze from the medications, happy to hear from Jessica, but clearly out of it. Jessica said she'd call again the next day. She was glad to hear her girlfriend's voice, however unintelligibly.

*   *   *

At around half past seven, Jessica returned to downtown Boise, to the happening Eighth Street area. She walked into Fireball Fuller's Bar & Bistro. Jessica spied Gina Silvestri's curly chestnut hair at a table near the front.

Gina jumped up and ran over to hug Jessica. "Girl, it is so good to see you!" she squealed. "I thought you'd forgotten all about us, stranded here in the Idaho desert."

Jessica returned the enthusiastic greeting. She and Gina had known each other since preschool. Gina's family lived just two streets over from the Sanfords. The two were inseparable as adolescents, and they had stayed close all through high school and four years at Boise State University. As friends often do, they drifted apart later, immersed in their own lives. Seven years earlier, Gina had married a sweet man they had both known as teenagers. In high school, he was a geeky band nerd with a trumpet. Now he was a popular jazz guitarist, much more attractive without the teen acne and with a few more pounds on his once-scrawny frame. Jessica was happy her old friend's life was going so well.

Jessica and Gina studied each other. Gina had plumped up after her first child, and she plumped up some more after the second. She had a prominent nose and a smooth olive complexion that revealed her family's southern Italian heritage. Jessica couldn't remember a time when Gina wasn't grinning, childhood dimples disappearing as her cheeks filled in over time.

"You never change, Jessica. You still look like you're twenty."

Jessica laughed. "I wish! Last time I looked in the mirror I saw all these little lines around my eyes. I'm glad it's dark in here. Hey, we're not getting older, we're getting better, right?"

"Absolutely! What are you drinking these days?"

"Stoli vanilla vodka with soda sounds good tonight." She caught a waitress's eye and ordered her drink. Gina was halfway through a beer and had an assortment of appetizers sitting on the table.

"Look, there's Jamie and Tish." Jessica waved at her two old friends as they walked toward the table. Hugs and air kisses were exchanged all around.

It was good to have the gang back together. Jessica, Gina, Jamie de Vogue, and Tish Woodhaven had been friends for many years. The four hadn't all gathered together since their tenth high school reunion party six years ago. Jamie had moved to Boise at the beginning of her freshman year of high school and fit right into the tight group with the other three. She had been Jessica's first girlfriend, very quietly. They had long since gone their separate ways romantically, although they'd stayed in touch over the years. Jessica and Tish had been in Girl Scouts together; they had been friends since age eleven.

The appetizers disappeared as glasses were emptied and the conversation flowed.

"What brings you to Boise this time, Jessica?" Tish asked.

The noise level around the table dropped as Jessica once again reiterated the story about the reconstruction project. The story was getting old to her, but it captivated everyone she told about it. When she described how the remains were discovered, everyone fell silent, perhaps remembering Bobby Livermore, their classmate who had disappeared. Some victims never find peace; some parents never get closure; some criminals remain free.

Not wanting to put a damper on the reunion, Jessica moved on quickly. She described the stunning possibility that she might have had an unknown, identical twin.

"One Jessica was enough for me," Jamie teased. "I don't think we could've handled two."

Tish and Gina agreed loudly, as Jessica shook her head in mock dismay. They reassured her they were all impressed with Jessica's self-appointed quest for the real Alice.

The conversation moved to lighter subjects as a new round of drinks materialized. Jessica felt her phone vibrate in her jacket pocket. She recognized the Boise area code but not the number. Puzzled, she walked quickly out to the street where it was much quieter and answered the call.

"Jessica, this is Krysta Kendricks. I met you earlier today at the Coulter Adoption Agency. I'm the receptionist there."

"Of course I remember you, Krysta. I enjoyed our chat. I'm sorry I wasn't very polite on my way out."

"That's why I'm calling. After you left, Loren told me why you had come by. I'm sorry he couldn't give you the information you wanted. Coulter has stringent privacy policies. Your story moved me, though. I have a fraternal twin myself. I couldn't imagine not knowing about her, or not knowing what happened to her if she were found dead. I'd like to help you."

Jessica paused for a beat. "This is very generous of you, Krysta. What do you have in mind?"

"Not to be paranoid, but I'd rather not get into specifics on the phone. Could we meet for lunch tomorrow? There's a cute café called Apricots on West State Street. We won't bump into anyone I know from downtown out there. How about a quarter past twelve?"

"That would be great. I really appreciate your offer, but I don't want you to get in any trouble over this."

Krysta admitted, "It's true—I shouldn't be doing this. It's not against the law, but it is against policy. I'm trusting you to keep this to yourself, please."

"Absolutely! It's our secret. I'll see you tomorrow. Thank you, Krysta."

Jessica clicked off, heartened by the first positive news she'd heard in days. She walked back into the noisy Fireball Fuller's and rejoined her friends.

Gina said, "Wow, you look happy. Did you win the lottery or something?"

Jessica just smiled and said, "Maybe."

Chapter 12

Tuesday, May 29

KRYSTA KENDRICKS WALKED into the Apricots Café shortly after noon. Jessica waved from a booth in the back. She had chosen that spot because it wasn't visible to anyone walking by outside. Krysta slipped into the other side of the booth, sliding along the orange-colored vinyl.

Jessica said eagerly, "Thanks so much for coming, Krysta. I can't wait to hear what you have for me. Shall we order first? Lunch is my treat."

As they waited for their meals, Krysta leaned across the table toward Jessica with a serious expression on her face and quietly cautioned, "Remember, we never had this conversation." Jessica nodded her understanding. "I looked through your adoption records after Loren went home last night. He's right: there's nothing there that would help you. However, I'm willing to give you a list of all of the adoptive parents from the five adoption groups that might have included your sister."

"That would be fantastic, Krysta! How many couples are we talking about?"

"You said your parents were already reaching out to the other eleven couples in your group. I counted a total of forty-six couples in the other four groups, so that makes fifty-seven all told, plus your own family."

"That's a lot, but it's not impossible. How current is your contact information for them?"

"Once the children reach eighteen, we typically don't update our information about the families, so the contact information isn't current. After all these years, some may have divorced, died, moved to Tibet to find themselves, or whatever. The names should at least get you started."

The teenage waitress appeared with Jessica's curry chicken salad and Krysta's ham and smoked Gouda panini.

Between bites, Jessica said, "That information would be a huge help. When can I get it? I've got some real pressure on me here."

Krysta set her fork down, wiped her fingers with a napkin, and reached into her purse. She pulled out a flash drive and slid it across the table to Jessica. "Here's everything we have about each couple, the dates the groups went to China, and the adoptees themselves. Obviously you can eliminate the families that adopted boys. You could narrow the search down by looking at the birthdates for the girls. Remember, though, the birthdates are often just estimates."

Jessica picked up the flash drive almost reverently. "This is so nice of you, Krysta. Why are you helping me like this? It could cost you your job if anyone found out."

"That's a risk I'm willing to take. Remember, I'm a twin myself. I've been working at Coulter Adoptions for three years, ever since I graduated from Upper Bench High School. I'm—"

"That's where I went too," Jessica interrupted.

Krysta smiled and nodded. She continued, "—passionate about the work we do at Coulter. I've been working on my social work degree part-time at Boise State so I can become an adoption agent. Families and adoptions are so important. I feel like we are all connected to each other in ways we don't even realize. So even though it's against policy, I want to help you learn who Alice was."

"Your secret's safe with me, Krysta. Besides, if Alice's parents can learn what happened to her, I don't think they're going to care much how I found them."

When Jessica returned to the house, clutching the precious flash drive, she took a bottle of tea from the refrigerator and a cookie from the jar on the kitchen counter. She carried her laptop into her parents' office and cleared a work area on the desk. She copied the files from Krysta's flash drive onto her laptop and began to look through them.

As Krysta had promised, it was a treasure trove. There was a separate file for each adoption group. Each file listed all the parents, their addresses and phone numbers as of the adoption date, and information about each child: sex, approximate date of birth, name given by the orphanage, and first and middle names given by the adoptive parents. Some records included updates to reflect later moves, divorces, remarriages, and deaths. Jessica believed that somewhere in this data pile was Alice's real identity. But how to find the solitary needle hiding in those five haystacks?

Jessica printed out one page for each family. There were nine couples from the first group, who went to China about six months prior to her own group; fourteen from the group three months earlier than hers; eleven couples plus her own parents from her group; ten from the group three months after hers; and thirteen from the final group, three and a half months later.

She pulled out the pages for the male adoptees in each group. As more than 90 percent of the Chinese children available for adoption were girls, she discarded just five pages for boys. That still left fifty-two girls to consider.

Krysta had suggested that the children's ages might condense the possibilities further. She scanned through the records. None of the other girls had been assigned the same birthday as her, so perhaps Alice and Jessica had been abandoned at different times or places. Because the birthdays provided by the orphanage were not reliable, however, Jessica decided to consider a range of plus or minus one month's uncertainty in the date of birth.

She was about thirteen months old when she was adopted. If Alice was her twin, they would be the same age, of course. Therefore any female child with an assigned birth date from one month earlier than hers to one month later was a candidate for being her twin. That narrowed the possibilities from fifty-two down to twenty-two. Now she was getting somewhere. Still, tracking down that many children based on contact information that was many years old would not be easy.

The desk was covered with stacks of paper. Sitting back and assessing the piles, Jessica wondered which of these girls could be her sister. Was it the one the orphanage called Dandan, or Peijing, or Chuntao? Could it be the girl named Julianna Davis by her adoptive parents, or Emily van Skype, or Amanda Yorke? The obvious approach was to begin contacting the parents from those groups whose children were a possible match. But Jessica had to do that without revealing that someone at Coulter Adoptions had leaked their contact information. She must protect her source.

Jessica's phone rang, startling her. She quickly swallowed her mouthful of tea and answered the call.

"Hi, Jessica. This is Rick Ybarra. Do you remember me?" She was surprised to hear from Rick, an old boyfriend from her college days, some thirteen years earlier.

"Of course I do! No one could forget you, Rick. It's been a long time. How are you?"

"I'm fine. Yes, it has been a while. Gina Silvestri told me you were in town for a few days. She said you're a woman on a mission. I hope you don't mind that she gave me your number."

"Not at all. I'm happy to hear from you. Gina's right. This isn't just a pleasure trip. I'm dealing with an issue that came up from my work in Portland." She didn't feel like getting into the details with a man to whom she hadn't spoken in years.

"I hope everything turns out okay for you. Would you have time to get together for dinner tonight? It would be great to see you and get caught up."

"I do have to eat, so I might as well eat with an old friend. Will your wife be joining us?"

Rick paused and then answered, "No, we've been divorced for almost three years now. We share custody of our two children. We get along pretty well, but it's definitely better that we aren't married."

"I'm sorry to hear that, Rick. These things happen. Do you have a restaurant in mind?"

"I love a Basque place downtown called Benji's. If that's okay, I can meet you there at seven o'clock."

"Sounds fine. I haven't had Basque food in ages. I'll find it and see you then."

Jessica was exhausted from all the activity, stress, and excitement of the past two weeks. A long drive from Portland with the return trip coming up soon; all the revelations about her origins; the strained meeting at Coulter; worry about Maria and her injuries; and now her first tangible leads on her Alice investigation. She made a quick call to Maria's cell, but it rolled over to voice mail. She left a message that she would try again later. Jessica could barely keep her eyes open. She sank into her father's favorite recliner and drifted off to sleep.

David gently shook Jessica awake at about a quarter past five. "And the Papa Bear said, 'Who's been sleeping in my chair?' Are you Goldilocks?"

Jessica floated back to awareness and saw her father's eyes twinkling down at her. "You looked so peaceful there, I hated to wake you," he said. "I thought I should get you up in case you had plans for the evening."

She climbed out of the chair. "Thanks, Dad. Good thing you woke me up. My old boyfriend Rick Ybarra called earlier. I'm meeting him for dinner downtown at seven. I'll catch you up afterward."

*   *   *

Wow, Jessica thought as she hurried back to her car later in the evening, *I certainly dodged a bullet when I decided not to marry Rick back in college.* Dinner at the Basque restaurant was superb, and Rick looked just as handsome as she remembered him. The gray in his salt-and-pepper hair was new since she had seen him last, six years earlier. The gray gave him an air of maturity, but it was an illusion. Rick had kept referring to the drunken once-more-for-old-times'-sake hookup they had enjoyed at their tenth high school reunion. That was clearly all he was interested in for this reunion as well. She deflected his entreaties only by reminding him about her girlfriend in Portland—repeatedly. Finally, he seemed to get the message, but she had still needed to dodge a good-bye kiss.

Jessica navigated through Boise's quiet evening streets back to her parents' house once again, looking forward to returning home to Rosemount tomorrow. The trip had been an emotional roller coaster. Armed with the information from Krysta, for the first time Jessica felt that she had a solid opportunity to connect with the real Alice. Her excitement at being able to confirm whether or not she had a twin was palpable. She thought—she hoped—the answer was right around the corner. First, though, she'd have to see what help Maria needed as she recovered from her nasty accident.

Jessica found David and Sharon sitting together in the family room. "What are you watching?" Jessica asked as she walked in.

"TV," David replied without looking away from the screen.

Sharon rolled her eyes and said, "That's what he says whenever he has the television on because he wants mindless entertainment and doesn't much care what. I'm not watching; I'm coloring."

Sharon had gotten into adult coloring a few months earlier. She owned a tall stack of coloring books and hundreds of felt tips, gel markers, colored pencils, and Sharpies of every hue and thickness. Jessica peeked over Sharon's shoulder to admire her latest creation. Her mother did nice work, with interesting color combinations.

"How was your dinner, honey? How's Rick doing?" Sharon asked.

"He's fine, Mom. He's divorced, but it didn't sound too vicious. We had a nice dinner. I've got to pack so I can leave early tomorrow. But first, I want to tell you both my exciting news." Jessica described her lunch with Krysta Kendricks and the information about the other families from the flash drive.

"I've narrowed it down to twenty-two girls who could possibly be Alice. It's going to be hard to find them so many years later. But there's another problem." She described the need for absolute secrecy regarding the source of this information, feeling guilty that she had just broken her promise to Krysta not to tell anyone.

"So I need some starting point that lets me reach out to people in the other groups to get the ball rolling. That way I'd have an excuse for contacting them without anyone knowing I got their information from Coulter. Have you heard back yet from anyone else in my group?"

Sharon walked into the office and returned with a notepad. "There were eleven families in our group besides us. We reached six of them and left phone messages for two others. Jane Lindsay told me the Bernards and their daughter died in a private plane crash about ten years ago. My contact information for the other two families seems to be out of date."

"How sad about the Bernards," Jessica said. "I guess that reduces my list of possible girls to twenty-one."

Sharon continued, "I got email addresses for five of the people I spoke to and sent them your photos. The ones who use Facebook said they would post the photos and ask anyone who recognizes them to contact you directly. I haven't seen any of them online yet. You know us old folks. We don't spend every minute on social media like your generation does. Give it a few days."

"Thanks for all your help with this, Mom. Something has to connect, I think. I just hope it happens soon. I love being a forensic sculptor. I don't know what I would do if the police didn't trust me to do my job anymore. I'm going to go to bed. I'll see you both at breakfast before I take off." Jessica kissed her parents goodnight and went to her room to prepare for a quick getaway in the morning.

Chapter 13

Wednesday, May 30

JESSICA ATE BREAKFAST, loaded her bags into the car, and bid her parents farewell with heartfelt thanks for all they had done. Sharon promised to update Jessica with any helpful replies she received from others in Jessica's adoption group.

Jessica headed west toward Portland, making good time in light traffic. Interstate 84 largely retraced the old Oregon Trail. Each time she drove this highway, she marveled at how grueling it had been for all the travelers migrating more than two thousand miles from Missouri in ox-drawn wagons. Driving at seventy miles per hour in air-conditioned comfort was far more pleasant. She had good weather clear through the Blue Mountains of Eastern Oregon and into Pendleton.

When Jessica stopped for lunch and gas at midday, she called Maria again. This time Maria herself answered. She sounded alert and energetic, saying, "Hi, babe. Where the hell are you? I miss you like crazy!"

"Maria, it's so good to hear your voice. You were way out of it when we talked before. I'll bet you don't even remember I called. I'm eating lunch at a little restaurant just outside Hermiston. I should be home in four hours. How are you feeling?"

"I'm doing pretty well. I love pain pills! The hospital released me this morning. Mama's still here at the apartment, but she has to go home tonight. I'm not too mobile. Can you come over as soon as you get to Portland? I'll tell you what happened. It was just a stupid fucking accident."

Jessica said, "I need to drop some things off at my house first. Can I bring you anything?"

"We'll figure it out when you get here. Drive safely. We don't need any more traumas this week."

Jessica turned back onto the interstate. The long stretch where it paralleled the Columbia River was a continuously scenic route. The yellow-brown hills along the river wore a coat of heather green from the spring's moisture. That wouldn't last through the summer. Jessica passed numerous wind farms with gigantic turbine blades majestically turning in the steady breezes that blew along the great river even before it entered the gorge.

As she approached The Dalles, she could see dark clouds piling up to the west, straight ahead. The sprinkles that began just east of Hood River intensified into a deluge as she snaked through the gorge toward Portland, wipers thumping frantically.

*   *   *

Jessica pulled into her driveway around half past three. As her parents had so generously offered funds to let her search for Alice, maybe it was time to hire someone to care for the rampaging lawn. She should check with her neighbors Kira and Matt, the travel agents. An efficient team tuned up their lawn every Tuesday afternoon. She could ask about the lawn service when she picked up her mail from them.

Jessica stayed home just long enough to unload the car and check that everything was under control. Then she drove the five miles to Maria's apartment near Southeast Sixtieth Avenue and Burnside Street. Every time she returned home from Boise she was reminded how bad the Portland traffic was, especially around rush hour. She never regretted moving to Portland, though. Boise was so miserably hot and arid in the summers. The phrase "It's a dry heat" only described how your skin felt. It didn't account for how Idaho's high-altitude desert air desiccated your nose and throat. By contrast, Portland's weather—albeit too often wet—was moderate and comfortable year round, other than the occasional hundred-degree day.

She knocked on Maria's apartment door, not knowing if anyone else was there. Maria's mother, Lupe, answered the door. "Oh, Jessica, we are glad you are here now," she said in greeting. "Maria has missed you so much."

Maria lay in the queen bed that filled most of the apartment's single bedroom. The bulky purple cast on her right leg was propped up on a pillow. She looked pale and tired, her brown curls flowing everywhere. Maria beamed and reached her arms up as Jessica walked to the bed.

"Careful, babe, I'm sore all over," Maria cautioned. Jessica hugged her gingerly.

Jessica held Maria's hands and stepped back to examine the damage. Maria's face and arms were scraped, bruised, and swollen. A string of stitches closed an inch-long cut near the corner of her left eyebrow.

"Poor baby," Jessica said. "You must have really bounced down that cliff. I thought *I* had a crazy few days. I admit, though, yours were worse."

"Yep, they sucked," Maria agreed. "You got here just in time. Mama has to drive home and go to work. She drove Papa back to Salem yesterday and came right back. Can you stay the night? I need help anytime I get out of bed. They said I can use crutches, but I'm still wobbly on them. Maybe you can help me practice tomorrow."

"Sure. I can sleep on the couch for a few nights. I'll get anything else I need from home tomorrow. I want to hear all about the accident. But first, do you want some dinner? How about a chicken and vegetable stir-fry?" Although Jessica had never picked up much Chinese culture, she did know her way around a wok.

Jessica walked two blocks to the supermarket. When she returned to the apartment, Lupe said she needed to head back to Salem. "Take good care of my poor Maria," she implored.

"I will, Lupe. She's my Maria too. Say hello to Roberto for me."

The women chatted as Jessica got some brown rice steaming, chopped vegetables, and diced the chicken breasts. They wouldn't be drinking any wine tonight, not with Maria still taking heavy-duty painkillers. Jessica set up a little table for herself next to Maria's bed and helped Maria navigate the stir-fry on her plate. As they sipped hot green tea after dinner, Jessica asked Maria to describe what had gone wrong at Cascade Cliffs.

"I was leading the climb," Maria began. "We decided to try a route rated 5.10b." Jessica remembered that the difficulty of a climb was rated on a scale from 1 for simple hiking to 5 for serious climbs. Class 5 climbs were further subdivided on a decimal scale, with the real challenges beginning around 5.10. Leading a climb required greater proficiency than being a following member of the party.

"I thought you were about a 5.9 leader. You've never led a climb at 5.10-anything before, have you?"

"No, but I honestly believed I could lead this one. I've done that route before with ropes already in place, so I had an idea of how it would go. Everything was great until I got close to the top, about four hundred feet above the base. There were four people in my group. Paul—he's the one who called you in Boise, right?—was belaying me from the ground. I had slipped a little bit twice and tore a fingernail. I was about ten feet above the last bolt. There are hardly any good holds near the top there. My finger hurt like hell, and I was really tired. I didn't remember how exhausting that climb was."

"Yeah, that's why it's a 5.10b, not an 8 or a 9."

Maria's eyes flashed at Jessica's dig. "Anyway, I just slipped. It happened so fast! I fell past the top bolt, about twenty feet all told. The other climbers said I twisted in midair and my leg slammed into the cliff when I was upside down. I don't remember any of this.

Then I must have spun some more, because I hit the cliff with my face on the next bounce. If I hadn't been wearing my helmet..."

"Oh, babe, how horrible! I'm so glad everything held. What did you do?"

"Shit, I just dangled in midair in a daze, didn't know what was going on. My right leg was screaming at me. The rest of the group saw I had a big problem. They lowered me to the ground, trying not to bang me into the cliff too much."

"How did they get you to the hospital?"

"The group would have had to carry me clear back to the parking lot to get an ambulance to meet us. My head was bleeding all over, so the 911 dispatcher sent a helicopter. Paul and the others performed first aid to control the bleeding and keep me from going into shock. By then I was pretty much aware but in a lot of pain. That was my first helicopter flight. They took me to Parkcenter General. After that it's a blur again until I woke up after the surgery."

"Wow, what a story." Jessica exhaled and leaned back in her chair. "I've always wanted to fly in a helicopter, but not like that. Your face doesn't look too bad. What's the deal with your leg?"

"The leg's not so good. They said I have closed tib-fib fractures. Both lower right leg bones are broken in several places. At least it wasn't compound, nothing sticking through the skin. The orthopedic surgeon put pins and screws in both bones. I've got quite a few staples from the incisions."

"How long will you be in the cast?"

"At least six weeks. I can't put any weight at all on it until the cast comes off. My knee's badly sprained too. I'm going to need a lot of physical therapy, maybe knee surgery later on. I won't be hiking or biking for a while, that's for sure."

"Don't worry; we'll find some fun things to do while you're an invalid," Jessica said. She added soberly, "I'm really relieved you're going to be okay, Maria. But it scares me to see you take these chances. I'm afraid someday you're going to get killed, not just hurt."

"You should know me by now, Jess. I like it close to the edge. Yes, this was a little too close. But back off, will you? I dig the rush. I know I screwed up, so I don't need a lecture. What took you so long to get here, anyway?"

"I was in a panic when Paul called, but it didn't sound like there was any point in coming home right away. You were going to be in the hospital for a couple of days. You were zoned out on the pain meds, and your parents were here. I still had some things I had to do in Boise. So I decided to stay and come back today."

Maria smiled weakly. The exhaustion and the medication showed in her dimming eyes.

"How did it go in Boise?" she asked.

Jessica began to explain the trip highlights: what she had learned about her own origins, the seeming dead end at Coulter Adoptions, her elation at receiving the contact list from Krysta Kendricks. Before she could finish, Maria's eyes were closed.

Jessica trailed off. She watched Maria's chest rise and fall steadily in her slumber. Jessica stroked her girlfriend's unbruised cheek and tangled hair. *I'll have to wash that for her tomorrow*, she thought. Jessica tucked the bed covers around Maria and kissed her gently on the forehead. She turned off the light and walked into the living room to catch some much-needed sleep herself.

Chapter 14

Thursday, May 31

JESSICA AWOKE THURSDAY morning, disoriented. Too many days had passed since she had last slept in her own bed. She remembered where she was when she heard Maria calling to her. She rolled off the couch in her underwear and walked into the bedroom.

"Morning, babe," she said, rubbing her eyes and yawning. "How are you feeling today?"

"Like I really, really have to pee. I've been calling you, but you were totally out. Can you help me get to the bathroom, super-fast? I shouldn't have said no to the bedpan."

Jessica carefully helped Maria out of bed and onto her crutches, apologizing for not hearing her calls for help. She steadied Maria as they made their way to the bathroom, just ten feet away. Maria peed forever and sighed with relief. Jessica helped her back to a chair in the dinette area.

"What would you like for breakfast? I don't know what you have. I can run out if we need something."

Maria said, "First I need coffee. I'm pretty hungry. Maybe a couple of eggs and some cereal. But no Jell-O. Two days of hospital Jell-O was enough for a lifetime."

Jessica assembled the requested breakfast and made the same for herself, sighing at Maria's meager cereal options. She would go out later for food supplies. Maria's refrigerator was always stocked just above minimum survivability.

"What are your medical plans for the day?" Jessica asked. "Do you already have an appointment for physical therapy?"

"No, I can't start PT until the cast comes off. I do have a follow-up with the surgeon today, though. I wrote that down. Why do they always tell you about follow-up care while you're still woozy from the anesthesia or the pain pills? Stupid doctors." She rummaged through a messy pile of papers on the table. "Here it is, one thirty this afternoon, right by Parkcenter General. Let's practice with the crutches before then so I don't feel so shaky on them."

They walked around the little apartment with Maria on crutches until she felt confident she wouldn't collapse. She grimaced with the exertion. Maria's hospital discharge papers said she should be careful not to bang the purple-casted leg into anything, lest excruciating pain result. However they also directed her to move as much as she could tolerate, to accelerate healing and rehabilitation.

Maria gingerly sat down on the couch that had come with the furnished apartment, with its faded stripes and sagging seat cushions. Jessica propped the injured leg on the coffee table for her. Maria began to catch up on her mail and phone messages. She had been out of contact for several days, and numerous people wanted to know how she was doing.

Jessica set up her laptop on the dinette table. She pulled out her papers with the information about the twenty-one remaining candidates for the real Alice. One of those pages must bear the name of the person she sought. She would have to do some serious internet searching to try to track them all down. First, though, she should announce the search on her own Facebook page. She uploaded three photos she had selected of herself, at ages eighteen, twenty-two, and twenty-eight. Then she wrote a post:

Do You Know This Woman?

Yes, this is me. But, it might also look like someone else. I just
learned that I might have an identical twin I never knew about!
We would have been separated as infants because we were
both adopted from an orphanage in China, about 33 years
ago. I'm trying to locate this woman or her family.

If any of you know, or once knew, someone who looks like me
but *isn't* me, please contact me ASAP. (Strange, huh?).
Please share this through all your social media channels so
we can reach as many people as possible. The quest begins!
Thanks for your help.

Jessica added her personal email address and her cell phone
number. She posted similar content on her other social media
accounts. She didn't expect much from this initial campaign. People
who were already connected to her would probably already know if
they had ever met a Jessica duplicate. At least it was a start.

Without any other idea regarding how to proceed, Jessica began
searching online for the names in her pile of candidates. She
searched for both parents as well as the adopted girl on each page.
The searching was a tedious process. Some names were common,
others less so. Ages and middle initials helped narrow the possibilities down. Many of the daughters could have been married and
changed their last names by now, perhaps more than once, leaving
dead ends.

Her searches often led to websites offering copious information
drawn from public records—for a price. She signed up for two of
those services, hoping they could reveal current phone numbers and
addresses that a general public search might not find. Gradually she
began to fill in the blanks with contact information for people who
were possible matches for those in the Coulter records. Many blanks
still remained.

*   *   *

After lunch, Jessica drove Maria to her doctor's appointment. They took X-rays to make sure the bones were properly aligned, checked for infection, and assessed her overall condition. Everything looked as good as could be expected. When the women returned to the apartment Maria crashed from pain and exhaustion.

Jessica used the downtime to do some grocery shopping and stop by her house for fresh clothes. Her neighbor, Kira, looked to be home, so she walked over to pick up her mail. She also got a phone number for the lawn service company Matt and Kira used. When Jessica got back to her house, she opened a letter from her parents and stared at a check for $1,000. She took out her phone and called her mother.

"Mom, I can't believe you sent me this check. I haven't even asked you for anything yet. This is so nice of you and Dad!"

Sharon said, "We told you we wanted to help, and we meant it. What are parents for if they can't help their children when they need it? I hope it's enough to get you started."

"It's a huge help. Tell Dad how much I appreciate it. I'll pay you back when I can."

"Honey, this is a gift, not a loan. Let us know if you need more. Your search for Alice is important to us too, you know. To think our daughter had an identical twin? How exciting! Hey, how is Maria doing?"

"She's okay. She broke her leg pretty badly and wrenched her knee. I'm staying at her apartment for now."

Sharon made a sympathetic noise.

Jessica said, "Today I started trying to locate the families who might potentially know Alice."

Sharon said, "I'm still getting replies from people in your group. Do you remember the Hardwicks? They moved to Spokane, Washington, when you were eight. They adopted a girl from your group they named Rebecca. Phyllis Hardwick and I have stayed in touch, at least with Christmas cards and a letter occasionally. She called me back after she got my voice mail."

"Did she know anything about a twin?"

"No, but Phyllis said that when they moved to Spokane they connected with several other Chinese adoptees and their parents. Rebecca met a boy from another Coulter group in that same year. Rebecca and this Tony Gallo boy eventually got married. Phyllis gave me Rebecca's number. Maybe you could call her and see if Tony knows someone who looks like you from his group."

Jessica wrote down Rebecca Gallo's contact information and paged through the information from Krysta. She finally found the Hardwicks listed in her own group, as well as the Gallos in the previous group. At last she had an entry point into the world of the twenty-one Alice candidates she could exploit without compromising Krysta. One group down, three more to go.

Soon after she hung up with her mother, her phone pinged with an incoming email. The message was from Silvia, addressed to both her and Adam:

> I reviewed Jessica's reconstruction on the female remains from Redhawk Road, as well as her skull-comparison experiments. I don't see any problems from a forensic anthropology perspective. The work and the analysis appear solid.

> Jessica, I agree with your conclusion that you and this victim could be identical twins. I hope you are making progress with your investigation and that we can eventually obtain some DNA from the victim to verify your relationship to her.

Jessica breathed an audible sigh of relief. At least her work was validated in Silvia's mind. She still needed to convince Adam. Jessica had exactly two more weeks to pursue the elusive Alice before the bottom dropped out of her career.

She drove back to Maria's apartment for some leftover chicken stir-fry. Maria clearly felt much better after her nap. She was able to maneuver around the apartment by herself on the crutches now.

Maria and Jessica enjoyed a pleasant evening together for the first time in eight days. Jessica had brought her guitar over from her house. Neither woman could sing well, but they didn't let that minor limitation stop them from joining in with the guitar. It was a treat to laugh together after all the previous week's serious business.

*   *   *

Friday morning after she and Maria ate breakfast, Jessica phoned Rebecca Gallo in Spokane. She barely remembered Rebecca from when they were little girls.

"Hello, Rebecca, this is Jessica Sanford. My parents, David and Sharon, were good friends with your parents a long time ago when we all lived in Boise. You and I both were adopted from the same orphanage in China."

"I remember you, Jessica. My mother said she talked to yours recently. You're trying to find another adoptee or something?"

"Yes. I won't bore you with all the details, but I have reason to believe I might have had an identical twin. She might have been in the same orphanage we were. I'm trying to locate her, if she really exists. My parents were helping by contacting some other parents, which is why she called your mother."

"Holy cow," Rebecca said. "I guess there'd be no way any of us would ever know if we had a twin. The Chinese only let families adopt one child at a time back then."

"I've just been learning about all that. Anyway, I'm trying to find people in any of the other adoption groups around the same time as ours, in case my twin was in one of those. The lead agent at the Coulter Adoption Agency in Boise wouldn't tell me anything. My mom says you married another Chinese adoptee."

"I did, four years ago. We grew up together here in Spokane. His name is Tony Gallo. His parents are Italian. Tony Gallo's a funny name for a Chinese man, right?" Rebecca laughed. "He was in the group before ours."

"If I sent you some pictures of myself, could you please ask Tony to circulate those to anybody he knows from his group to see if they recognize her? Obviously I'm assuming my twin and I look a lot alike. I guess that's what 'identical' means." They both laughed.

Rebecca said, "Tony won't mind at all. His parents could help spread the word too. They're still friends with some of the other Chinese adoptee families around Spokane. We can all post the photos on our Facebook pages. Sometimes one link leads to another." Rebecca and Jessica exchanged contact information.

Jessica asked, "Do you or Tony know any Chinese adoptees or parents who might be from Coulter groups other than our two?"

"Tony once told me he met a man at church who had adopted a Chinese girl about our age. This other guy had an Italian name also. I've never met him. Let me check with Tony and get back to you."

Right after the call, Jessica went to her laptop and sent the three photographs of herself at various ages to Rebecca, along with the link to her original query on Facebook. She was excited to finally get some traction.

Rebecca Gallo called back around lunchtime. "Tony said the man he knows from church is Giorgio Iacovangelo." She spelled the last name for Jessica. "Giorgio adopted a girl named Melissa six or seven months after you and I were adopted. He's been divorced a long time. His ex-wife and Melissa moved to Florida."

The name was familiar. Jessica looked through her records. A Giorgio Iacovangelo was in what she had come to think of as group number five. That was the final group in her potential time range, which held four possible candidates for Alice. She had already found Giorgio's current address, email, and phone number through the online sources she had subscribed to. Rebecca didn't need to know that though.

"That's great, Rebecca. Please tell Tony thanks for me. I'll try to reach Giorgio Iacovangelo to see if he knows anything about the woman I'm looking for."

Jessica was thrilled to have an entry point into yet another of the adoption groups. She sent her photos to Giorgio and explained what she was doing, mentioning that Tony Gallo had given her his name. Giorgio replied within an hour. Some people in her parents' generation could not spell Facebook; others lived on the computer, continually connected with the rest of the world. Giorgio seemed to be among the latter.

Giorgio said he did not know of any girls in his daughter's group who looked like Jessica. He hadn't seen most of them in many years, though, not since his divorce. He offered to repost the information from Jessica's Facebook page on his own page, and also to write to the few people from his group for whom he still had contact information. He named some of the other parents from his group. Jessica figured that was enough for her to reach out to them directly, using the old addresses from Krysta and the updated information she had acquired through her online searches. Jessica's net was widening.

She still had two groups to go.

Chapter 15

Friday, June 1

FRIDAY AND SATURDAY blurred together. Jessica stayed with Maria and prepared her favorite meals. The apartment filled with the familiar and comforting aromas of Mexican and Asian seasonings. They played some games for diversion and went outside for short walks around the neighborhood to enjoy the sunny days and get some exercise. They tried to walk a little further each time, aiming to eventually make it to the park nine blocks away. Fortunately Portland had short blocks. Their return route sometimes included a stop for ice cream at the local convenience store, Maria's reward for making good progress.

Jessica watched the tension in Maria's face ease as the pain did. She gradually weaned herself off the serious pain pills, using just ibuprofen now except at night. Maria continued to field calls from people wanting to know how she was doing.

Jessica's phone rang late Friday afternoon. She was delighted to hear from BJ, who wondered how the trip to Boise had gone and if she was making any progress on her quest.

"The trip was a whirlwind," Jessica told her. "I got some really useful information I'll tell you about, and I saw some friends. I came back on Wednesday to help Maria."

"What's wrong with Maria?" BJ asked, sounding puzzled.

"Oh, I guess there's no way you would have known. She broke her leg pretty badly while rock climbing last Sunday. She's home now and doing okay, but she can't move around much. I've been staying at her apartment since I got back on Wednesday."

"What a shame. I hope she recovers quickly." BJ gave a little laugh. "I was going to ask if you wanted to do something outdoors this weekend, like a hike or some easy rock climbing, but now I don't know if I should."

"A month ago I would have said yes to a climb. Not anymore," Jessica replied. "After seeing Maria's condition, rock climbing seems too dangerous for me now. A bike ride would be great, though. I'll tell you all about Boise."

Before getting off the phone, they arranged to meet Sunday afternoon in Newberg, twenty miles southwest of Portland, for a leisurely ride through the gentle hills of Oregon's scenic wine country. Jessica knew she could leave Maria on her own now for several hours at a time.

Jessica continued her online search for the current addresses of her Alice candidates through the weekend. Some people seemed to have disappeared entirely. She knew of one who had literally disappeared, until a dog rediscovered her several weeks ago. Perhaps one of those absent names was the one she sought. She fervently hoped not, as that would make it nearly impossible to identify her sister. The odds were long, but she was still in the early stages of the exploration.

Jessica monitored the responses to her Facebook and other social media posts, as well as responses to Rebecca's, Tony's, and Giorgio's posts. They were getting some replies and some reposts. A few people suggested possible matches from adopted girls they knew, posting photos of Chinese girls and young women of all ages. Jessica eagerly studied each image. Could she have found her sister at last? Her disappointment deepened with each false alarm. She knew exactly the face she sought. She hadn't seen it yet.

*   *   *

On Sunday Jessica got ready to leave the apartment for her bike ride with BJ. Maria looked up from her crossword puzzle and asked, "Where are you off to now?"

"I told you earlier, I'm going for a ride with BJ. I want to tell her about Boise and how my search is going."

"I thought you were going to stay with me today, Jess. With all the time you've spent on the computer and the phone, it seems like I've hardly talked to you lately. I'm sick of reading, doing puzzles, and watching TV by myself."

"I know, Maria, I'm sorry. You know how important this search is to me. I feel like I'm getting close to a breakthrough. If I can just keep pushing, something has to pay off soon. I've got exactly eleven days left to find Alice, or I lose this reconstruction job and maybe my whole career!"

"But when is enough, enough?" Maria asked, her voice rising. "I'm glad you're making progress, but are you going to spend your whole life on this? Are you just going to ignore me while you chase down this mysterious Alice?"

"Ignore you?" Jessica retorted. "Hell, I've been here for days, dropping everything else to be with you. Who else has helped you get to the bathroom and to the doctor and kept you fed? Nobody, right? I haven't even been to the gym in weeks. So don't give me any shit about going on a bike ride with my old friend. Jesus!"

Maria looked surprised and chastened by Jessica's pushback; Jessica didn't lose her temper often. Jessica stalked out of the apartment and drove off to pick up her bike at home and head out to Newberg.

As always, she found the ride and conversation with BJ to be a perfect combination of invigorating, relaxing, and enlightening. After being friends for so long, they could talk about anything without getting upset or judgmental. BJ was a rock. Her steady friendship and good judgment kept Jessica sane and centered.

BJ offered a supportive ear as Jessica described her progress—and her frustrations—on the search for the real Alice. She offered a sympathetic ear as Jessica related her argument with Maria. And she offered an encouraging ear regarding Jessica's personal commitment to discovering her sister's identity, family, and killer.

The countryside around Newberg was a mix of rolling hills and flat valleys. They found plenty of side roads with little traffic and enough contours in the land to make for fun biking. They agreed that you can't go through wine country without stopping for at least a sample or two at one of the many small wineries there. But one tasting stop was enough. No one wanted to be wobbly on her bike on those curvy roads.

On her drive home, a refreshed Jessica concluded that this ride with BJ was her best idea in a long time. By the time she got home, Jessica felt much more mellow. She was sorry about the clash with Maria. She didn't know why it was so hard for Maria to understand why the search for Alice was so important to her.

After she dropped her bike off and showered at home, Jessica went back to the apartment and let herself in. Maria was asleep on the couch but woke as Jessica walked in. She smiled and reached out for a hug. It was as though Jessica's outburst had never happened. At least for the moment.

*   *   *

Monday and Tuesday proceeded much like the previous days. Emails and social media posts continued to trickle in with possible Alice leads. None went anywhere. Jessica crossed several names off her candidate list as she saw photos of more adoptees who didn't resemble her. She was down to sixteen possibilities now.

Jessica did hear from someone in one of the two adoption groups she had not yet broken into. Following up with him yielded some updated contacts and justification for directly contacting several more people on her list of candidates. Jessica was relieved that her plan of "infiltrating" all of the Coulter adoption groups without anyone suspecting Krysta as the source appeared to be a success.

Shortly before eleven on Tuesday morning, Jessica went to the Rosemount Senior Center and picked up sixteen meals for her Meals on Wheels route. Today her clients were getting stuffed cabbage, mixed vegetables, cornbread, wheat-berry salad, and peaches, plus a small carton of milk if they requested it. The meals looked and smelled delicious. She hoped one of the clients wouldn't answer the door, as the senior center let drivers take home any leftover meals.

As always, her clients were happy to see her. They appreciated the daily human contact as well as the hot food. The ninety minutes she spent delivering the meals always gave Jessica a sense of accomplishment for the day. All of her clients were home, so she didn't get to take a leftover meal for herself.

Jessica observed that Maria was gaining independence and strength daily. She would still be using crutches for several weeks. At least she could fix a meal for herself when she was alone. Jessica decided to start sleeping at her own house so they could both be as comfortable as possible. She needed some time alone anyway.

Shortly before eight o'clock that evening, Maria was napping and Jessica was working on her laptop in the apartment's living room when her phone rang. She didn't recognize the number; the caller ID did not show a name.

Chapter 16

"**HELLO, JESSICA, MY** name is Angela Montgomery," said the caller. The name didn't sound familiar. "You don't know me. I got your phone number from my mother's Facebook page. She reposted an item about you that she got from a man named Giorgio something. Montgomery's my married name. My mother is Madeleine Stark."

That *did* ring a bell: a family in group five was named Stark. Angela Stark was one of the adoptees from that group, which went to China about six months after Jessica's parents did.

Angela continued, "You're looking for a Chinese woman who you think might be your twin sister, right?"

Barely suppressing her excitement, Jessica said, "Yes, I am. Thank you for calling, Angela. Do you know something about this?"

"I believe so. I recognized your photos from my mother's Facebook page. You look almost exactly like an old friend of mine named Nicole Briggs. She and I were in the same adoption group. We grew up in Billings, Montana, together."

Jessica sank to the floor of Maria's apartment, speechless. She hadn't been prepared for the emotional impact of Angela's words, words she had been waiting to hear for weeks.

"Jessica? Are you still there?" she heard from the phone.

Jessica tried to compose herself. "Yes, I'm here," she croaked through the lump in her throat. "I'm sorry, this is stunning news. Good stunning, but still stunning. Can you tell me more, please?"

Angela said, "Nikki—Nicole—and I were good friends from as far back as I can remember. She moved away from Billings not long after we graduated from high school. I haven't seen her for about fifteen years. But back then she looked almost exactly like your high school graduation picture. She was short, only about five-one or five-two."

While Angela was explaining, Jessica had walked over to the dinette table and frantically flipped through her papers until she found the Briggs family in group five. Parents: Mark and Suzanne Briggs. Hometown: Billings, Montana. Daughter: Nicole, named Chuntao by the orphanage. Birthday: November 25. Approximate age at adoption: nineteen months. All definitely plausible as a match for the mysterious twin. The Briggses were one of the families she had not yet located. They apparently had no online presence at all. "Do you know when her birthday was?" Jessica asked.

"It was sometime in late November. I don't remember the exact date. She complained whenever Thanksgiving fell on her birthday because nobody wanted to go to a birthday party after a big turkey dinner. Do you think this could be the right girl?"

Jessica took a deep breath and willed her racing heart to slow down. "It sure sounds like it, Angela. This is the best lead I've had so far. Do you have any idea where she or her parents might be living now?"

"No, when she left Billings, she was gone for good. Her parents moved away a few years later. I don't know where they went."

"Where do you live now? Maybe we could get together so I could learn more about Nicole."

"I live in Richland, Washington, with my husband."

"I'm in Portland, only a few hours from Richland. Is there any chance I could drive to Richland soon and meet you?"

"I'm not working tomorrow if you want to drive out. If that isn't good for you, I'll have to wait until Sunday."

Jessica said eagerly, "Tomorrow's fantastic. I've got something of a time crunch here. I can be there by lunchtime. Could you text me a good place to meet? I can't tell you how much I appreciate your call, Angela. I'm overwhelmed."

Angela replied, "I can imagine. I'll tell you everything I know tomorrow. I'll find some old pictures of Nikki to show you too."

Jessica hung up. She sat in a chair and stared into space. *Could Alice's real name be Nicole Briggs? Am I really this close to finding my twin?* She had to tell some people, and she had to get ready to drive to Richland tomorrow. She looked for Maria to share her excitement but found her snoring gently in the bedroom. Maria needed her rest; Jessica didn't want to wake her, even for this news flash.

Jessica called BJ and excitedly shared Angela's report. BJ offered to accompany Jessica to Richland. She could take a personal day off from work. Her husband did have to work tomorrow, but she could ask her parents to watch the kids. Jessica was happy to have her best friend join her. It would be nice to have some time to talk when they weren't panting on their bicycles. They decided BJ should drive to Jessica's house in the morning and leave her car there.

Next Jessica called her parents to tell them about this vital lead. If it panned out, she would let them know so they could stop working on the search themselves.

Maria called sleepily from the bedroom, "What's all the noise out there? Who are you talking to?"

Jessica danced into the bedroom and described Angela's call. She told Maria she'd be leaving the next morning with BJ for Richland, returning sometime on Thursday.

Maria seemed to be trying to absorb all this input, her brain fuzzy with slumber. "Wow, that's quite the news. Maybe your grand quest is at an end. But what about my doctor's appointment on Friday? You said you'd take me."

Jessica paused, remembering the commitment. "Yes, I'll be home to take you to the doctor on Friday, and I'll make sure you have enough food for the two days I'm gone. You can always call a Cascader or a neighbor if you desperately need something. Now, I have to get home and pack."

"What time are you leaving tomorrow?"

"Early. BJ and I are supposed to meet Angela for lunch. I'll come back in a little while to make sure you're set for the night. Do you mind if I sleep at my house so I don't bother you when I get up?"

"No problem. Thanks for thinking of that. I should be fine by myself in the morning. Be careful driving. I'll see you later on, babe. If I'm asleep, wake me up and give me a kiss before you go."

Chapter 17

Wednesday, June 6

BJ PULLED INTO Jessica's driveway early Wednesday morning and handed her friend a steaming sixteen-ounce Starbucks cup. She transferred a small overnight bag into Jessica's car.

They headed toward the Columbia River Gorge for the nearly four-hour drive to Richland. Kennewick, Richland, and Pasco constituted the Tri-Cities in southeastern Washington State. Jessica retraced her recent drive on I-84, departing the freeway near Hermiston, source of the best melons in the Northwest. She drove past the little cafe where she had eaten lunch on her return from Boise just one week earlier. It seemed like a month, with all that had happened since then.

Angela had suggested they meet for lunch at Nuclear Brew, a popular brewpub whose name played on the fact that the Tri-Cities were home to one of America's largest nuclear-weapons manufacturing facilities. Dating back to World War II's Manhattan Project, large quantities of plutonium had been made at the enormous Hanford Site nearby. The radioactive-waste cleanup at this heavily contaminated site would likely go on for decades.

BJ and Jessica pulled into the crowded parking lot just before noon and walked into Nuclear Brew. Jessica felt so filled with nervous anticipation that she wanted to hide behind BJ.

A tall Asian woman with neatly styled, dark-brown hair rose from her seat in the waiting area by the front door. She looked at the two women walking in and gasped.

"My God, I would have sworn you were Nikki if I hadn't been expecting you, Jessica. You look just like her, only older. I can believe you're identical twins. This is so exciting! I would love to see the expression on her face when you finally meet her."

Jessica shot a glance at BJ but said nothing. Explanations could wait for later.

Jessica introduced BJ to Angela. The three women took a booth next to the red brick wall toward the back; it was quieter there than in the bustling main seating area. A glassed-off area with two large copper brewing tanks occupied the restaurant's center. Jessica recognized the typical smell of a brewpub, with aromas of yeast and hops overlaying those of sizzling burgers and hot oil in the fryer.

The three made small talk as they studied the menu. Jessica pointed out they might as well sample the local wares while they were there, so they all ordered some beer flights with their meals.

Angela kept looking curiously at Jessica, who had anticipated that reaction. Angela said, "I'm sorry to keep staring, Jessica. It's just so strange to see someone who looks and sounds and acts like someone else I used to know. I feel like I dived down the rabbit hole into the past, but we're all grown-ups now. I did find some photos of Nikki from when we were kids."

She pulled several pictures from her purse and laid them on the table. Jessica could see the striking resemblance between Nicole Briggs and herself. Those photos could have been taken during her own childhood. She picked up one showing Nikki and Angela as teenagers. She said, "We look so much alike it's spooky. I have to believe we're twins, even though I can't totally prove it yet."

"How did you find out you had a twin, anyway?" Angela asked.

Jessica looked down at the table, and then at BJ, who nodded and squeezed Jessica's arm in support. She had been dreading this moment. She took a deep breath.

"I'm afraid I have some sad news, Angela." She described how she came to be acquainted with the remains discovered above the Lorane Valley, and how she concluded that the dead woman must have been her twin. Angela sat immobile, staring at Jessica the whole time. "As far as I can tell, the remains found near Eugene are Nicole's. And your pictures make me certain she's…" Jessica choked up. She couldn't say more.

Tears pooled in Angela's dark eyes and streaked down her cheeks. Jessica reached across and took both of Angela's hands in hers. She began to weep too.

When she could talk again, Jessica said, "This has all been a huge shock to me as well. To discover that I have a twin, to see pictures of her, and yet to know I'll never meet her. Maybe I can get to know her through you, Angela. Can you help me with that, please?" Angela slowly nodded. The women dried their eyes as the waiter brought their beer samplers and entrees.

As they dug into their meals, BJ broke the awkward silence. She asked Angela to fill them in on what she remembered about Nicole Briggs. BJ and Jessica leaned in attentively toward Angela.

Angela chewed thoughtfully as she seemed to consider how best to begin the story. "My parents and Nikki's parents both lived in Billings. They didn't know each other until they both decided to adopt children from China through the Coulter Adoption Agency. They wound up in the same group of adoptive parents and traveled on the same flight to China, along with others from throughout the West, to pick up their babies. They became close friends. Billings isn't a big city, so we saw each other a lot as Nikki and I grew up."

Jessica asked, "Did you and Nikki go to the same schools?"

"Not elementary school, but we were in the same class at Billings Centennial High School. We stayed good friends all along. Our older brothers became friends too. Our families went on picnics and camping together."

"What was Nikki like?" Jessica asked, wondering how deep the resemblance went.

"Oh, she was a hoot. Tons of energy, smart, always getting into trouble. She loved to draw. She was good at it too. After high school she attended Montana State University Billings for a year. Then she moved away and I never heard from her again. I don't know why. I thought it was strange that she didn't tell me where she was heading. She just said she wanted to 'see the world.'"

"It sounds like maybe she was trying to find herself or start over fresh somewhere else," BJ said. "What other things did Nikki like to do?"

"She loved outdoors activities. She wasn't an athlete or into team sports, but she liked to go hiking and camping in the mountains. She told me she wanted to get into rock climbing also. That sounded too dangerous to me. Nikki said she got off on the danger. I guess she was an adrenaline junkie."

Jessica thought this over for a moment, idly playing with the ends of her hair. Angela sat up and pointed at her.

"There! Nikki was always playing with her hair just like that. Oh, this is too weird." She leaned back in her seat and looked askance at Jessica. "Are you really Nikki, playing some kind of trick on me?"

"No," Jessica replied sadly. "I'm definitely not Nikki. But we have so many similarities that we just have to be twins. I like doing outdoors things too, but I'm not as interested in dangerous thrills as it sounds like Nikki was."

Jessica took some more bites of her barbecued pulled pork sandwich and sipped her Lawrencium Lager sample. She said, "This is a bit awkward, Angela, but do you know whether Nikki dated boys or girls?"

"She liked both. I think she preferred girls, but she went out with boys too. Being bisexual was something you kept quiet in Billings back then, probably even now. It's a conservative city."

"That's one great thing about Portland," Jessica said. "Nobody much cares about someone else's sexuality. I'm also bi. BJ is my best friend in Portland, but she's an old married lady with two kids. Right now I have a girlfriend named Maria."

Angela said, "Nikki hated that she had to sneak around when she had a girlfriend. She liked to go out to dance clubs with a fake ID. Sometimes she would go home with a man, sometimes with a woman. But you know, she never got too close to anyone. It's like she was always holding back emotionally, afraid to really commit."

The salads, sandwiches, and beers were gone. The waiter asked if they were interested in dessert or coffee. BJ and Jessica ordered coffee; Angela requested hot tea. BJ and Jessica couldn't resist splitting the house special dessert, warm apple crisp with a scoop of vanilla bean ice cream.

Jessica said, "This has been quite a conversation, hasn't it? I'm more sure than ever that Nicole Briggs was my twin sister. I'm also virtually certain Nicole's body is the one discovered outside Eugene. I can't quite prove either yet, though. And I don't yet have any idea how she died or who might have killed her."

BJ said, "Jessica, you're experienced in law enforcement. What information do you need to prove Nicole's identity and verify your relationship to her?"

"Dental X-rays could demonstrate if this homicide victim is really Nicole. If we could find her family, we might be able to get some of her DNA and compare it to mine to confirm whether or not we're twins. So I have to locate her parents as quickly as possible. My job's on the line here. Angela, do you have any thoughts about that at all, or would your parents maybe know where the Briggses moved to after Billings?"

Angela sipped some tea and then set the cup down. She stared into the distance for a moment. When her eyes met Jessica's again, she looked somber.

"There's something else I should tell you. My brother, Brian, is two years older than me. He was my parents' natural child, not adopted. Brian liked Nikki a lot. They dated some in high school. The fact that Nikki preferred girls pissed him off. She liked Brian, but she wasn't really *into* him, you know? Brian had always had a hot temper. One night, when he was on a date with Nikki, he got really angry about something and he raped her."

The other women gasped. Angela continued, "She didn't tell anyone except me about it initially. Nikki soon learned she was pregnant and had an abortion on her own. She was only sixteen. Her parents eventually found out about the rape and the abortion."

Jessica and BJ sat silently, absorbing this shock. Such a traumatic experience could scar someone for life, affecting her self-image, her relationships, and her behavior.

"Nikki's father was furious, of course. He had Brian arrested for rape. This incident caused a permanent rift between our families. Nikki's parents never spoke to mine again. Nikki and I stayed friends, but she wouldn't come to our house, and our relationship was never the same. I was humiliated and really angry that my brother could do that to my friend."

"What happened with Brian?" BJ asked.

Angela said, "The rape charges were dropped eventually because he convinced the judge the sex was consensual. That was bullshit, but he got away with it. He moved away from Billings not long after that. He's been in and out of trouble over the years, just small stuff as far as I know. He just bounced around. I couldn't guess where he is now. We don't hear from him anymore.

"So, as a result of all this," she continued, "I have no idea where Nikki's parents might be. As I said, Nikki left Billings after one year of college. Her parents moved somewhat later. And that's it, pretty much everything I know about Nicole Briggs."

Hesitantly, Jessica asked, "I'm sorry to have to ask this, Angela, but do you think there's any chance Brian could have been involved in Nikki's death?"

Angela reluctantly admitted, "It's not totally impossible. He harbored a grudge that Nikki had ruined his life, as though *she* had attacked *him*. True, Brian had anger issues and a history of fighting. I don't think he'd ever kill someone, but who knows?"

No one said anything for a minute. Then Jessica asked, "Maybe you don't know, but would you be afraid of Brian? Is he likely to still be dangerous to others, or is he more the self-destructive type?"

"I just can't say for sure. You should be careful, though. If he *was* involved with Nikki's death and somehow learned you were looking into it, he might not be happy about someone digging up dirty laundry."

It was the middle of the afternoon. Through the course of their conversation, Nuclear Brew had grown quiet and nearly empty. The considerate waiter had kept refilling their drinks and hadn't rushed their departure, but it was time to leave. Jessica paid the bill, leaving a generous tip. The three women walked together to the parking lot.

Jessica said, "Angela, I can't thank you enough for your time and for all this information. I am really happy you called me, and sorry to have to bring you the bad news about Nikki. You've given me a huge breakthrough. Now that I know who this woman I've been calling Alice really is, I can search for her parents and try to get the evidence that might help us solve this case."

"I do hope you can discover who killed Nikki," Angela replied. "I can't believe she's dead. Please let me know how it goes."

After Angela drove away, BJ and Jessica sat in the car and reflected on the extraordinary conversation. Jessica felt she had taken a giant leap forward—so much progress. She could now focus her online search on just two people, Mark and Suzanne Briggs.

Notwithstanding the day's intense discussion, Jessica and BJ thought it had been fun to have a little road trip together. They took a room at the Columbia View Hotel in Richland, right on the riverfront. The Columbia River Gorge lay well to the west; here the river flowed flat and wide through the Tri-Cities. Through their window the women marveled at the moving water's quiet power. The Hanford nuclear manufacturing facility had been situated in this area precisely because the Columbia River afforded such a tremendous amount of water and hydroelectric power.

Jessica felt herself fading out early that evening. Before she dropped off, she called Maria to update her on the lunch with Angela. Not sure what mood Maria might be in, she approached the conversation cautiously. Fortunately, Maria seemed mellow, happy to hear from Jessica, and excited that Jessica had learned Alice's real identity. Maria could be such a delightful companion when she was in a good mood, and yet so unreasonable and exhausting when she was not.

Chapter 18

Thursday, June 7

THE NEXT MORNING Jessica called Adam and excitedly explained that she was quite certain she now knew the identity of the remains from Redhawk Road. She summarized her investigations of the past week, culminating with her meeting the day before.

"The photos Angela showed me, and her reaction to my own appearance and mannerisms, together convince me that Nicole had to be my twin sister. You wouldn't believe how similar we look, Adam. Everything fits. If Nicole was my twin, and the victim from Eugene was my twin, then the victim must be Nicole Briggs."

Adam was silent for a moment. "Your logic makes good sense, provided I buy your assumption that you and the victim are twins. I'll feel better about it if we can get some DNA matches. We're still waiting for the results from the mitochondrial DNA comparison between you and the victim."

Jessica said, "I'll keep searching for her parents to get further corroboration and maybe some of Nicole's DNA to analyze. I still have a week, right?"

"That's correct, I gave you until June 14 to convince me. Today is the seventh. If you'd like, I could help you search for Nicole's parents. We police are good at finding people, you know."

"I saw that on your business card: Finders 'R' Us. That would be a huge help; thank you, Adam. I'll send you what I have about their names, ages, and previous address."

As soon she hung up, Jessica sent Adam the information he needed to begin tracking down Mark and Suzanne Briggs. She could use the assistance. All the dead ends were trying her patience, and the clock kept ticking.

Knowing that Adam would help search for Nikki's parents, BJ and Jessica took their time on the way back to Portland. Rather than retracing their route from the day before, they drove west on Interstate 82 through southern Washington. They stopped in the tiny town of Prosser for some wine tasting. Prosser lay at the southeastern end of the Yakima Valley, a rich agricultural area that yielded diverse fruit crops. That stretch across southern Washington—from Yakima, heading southeast through Prosser, and then east to the Tri-Cities and Walla Walla—was prime grape-growing country. Wineries and tasting rooms abounded along a stretch of some 130 miles: paradise for a wine lover.

Fortified with the fruit of the vine and lunch at a bistro they spotted along the way, the women continued west toward home. They scouted out several possible hiking trails near Washington's giant Mount Adams, perhaps the least-well-known big mountain in the United States. They agreed this would be a fun area to return to with hiking boots or mountain bikes, maybe sometime later in the summer.

Jessica turned into her driveway around five thirty on Thursday evening, tired and swamped with emotions, yet energized to continue her quest. As soon as she walked in the house, she called to check on Maria, who invited her over for dinner, provided Jessica could supply said dinner. Neither of them was up for cooking, so Jessica picked up assorted dishes from a Thai restaurant on the way to Maria's apartment. Take-out Thai was quick, it was cheap, and— most importantly—it was easy.

Maria was looking much better. Her strength was returning, and she was hobbling confidently on the crutches. The swelling in her face had gone down as the discolored bruises faded away. She was clearly on the mend.

Jessica updated Maria on her Richland trip as they ate pad prik with pork and extra-spicy chicken with cashews. Maria was delighted that Jessica had all but confirmed the dead woman's name and her identity as Jessica's twin.

"Does this mean it's over?" she asked hopefully. "Can you just turn this all over to the police now so we can get back to normal?"

"Not quite yet. All the evidence we have is solid. However, we still need to prove it. My next step is to locate Nicole's parents. The Briggses are one of the families I haven't got a lead on yet. Adam's helping me look for them. Besides, we still have no idea who killed her. So no, this case is not over yet. If I don't find her parents by next Thursday, not only is the case over for me, but my career might be over too."

Maria reminded Jessica about her doctor's appointment at 10:20 a.m. the next day. She said she was sleeping more comfortably now and invited Jessica to stay the night. Jessica hesitated. "Do I have to worry about you bashing me with that plaster club on your leg?"

"I've trained myself to sleep on my back. The leg doesn't hurt much in that position, so I'm not thrashing around in the night anymore. If you sleep on the left side of the bed, my cast will be clear over on the right. There's a good chance you'll survive the night without damage." Jessica was happy to curl up next to Maria's soft, warm body again.

*   *   *

Jessica drove Maria to her doctor's appointment midmorning on Friday. The verdict was that everything was healing well. The nurse removed the sutures from the cut by her eye. She would have a nice scar there as a permanent reminder of her adventure at Cascade Cliffs. Otherwise she could only wait for the fractures in her leg to heal and stay as active as possible in the meantime. Maria could start physical therapy when the cast came off in about five weeks. She should recover completely, but it would take a while.

Jessica updated her Facebook page to share the good news that the identical twin sister she sought had been identified as Nicole Briggs. She was now searching for anyone who knew how to reach Nicole or her parents. Jessica didn't want to say Nicole was dead until she had incontrovertible proof. She shuddered to think of the shock Nicole's parents would feel if they learned about her death through an online post or a surprise call from some friend who had heard about it. Jessica also directly contacted those people she could reach from the fifth Coulter adoption group to solicit their help in locating the Briggses.

It suddenly occurred to Jessica to look for the name "Nicole Briggs" on Facebook. She got a handful of hits, including several individuals and a few businesses. None of the cover or profile photos were close. She tried searching for "Nikki Briggs."

And there she was.

Jessica's spine tingled as she viewed a profile picture that could have come from her own collection. This photo was newer than the childhood ones Angela had shown her; Nikki appeared to be in her mid-twenties. Jessica forwarded that image and the Facebook page URL to Adam for their publicity campaign materials.

Nikki must have been camera-shy. The page contained no other pictures of her, just photos of things she liked, food, and some friends engaged in various outdoor activities. Nikki's most recent Facebook post was dated May 25, five years earlier. The post said:

Hey all, just found out I got a friend with an emergency. Should be OK but I gotta help out. Gonna be busy so don't worry if you don't hear from me for a while. Back ASAP.
Kisses.

Some people had replied to this post, wondering who had the emergency and wishing Nikki good luck. She hadn't responded to any of them though.

This Facebook post established the likely earliest date of Nicole's disappearance: May 25. Her page contained several other posts from the weeks before that date. Nothing newer. She hadn't been highly active on Facebook. Nicole could have been alive for some time after posting that message, of course. But, Jessica reasoned, she could not have been dead before it, assuming she had created the post herself.

As she waited for any communication back from her network regarding the Briggses, Jessica continued to search on her own. Her public records searches revealed more than three hundred hits for the name Mark Briggs and about sixty for Suzanne Briggs. She began to pare down the list, eliminating many names based on age. Then she looked for combinations of a Mark and a Suzanne with the same address. There was always the chance that the couple had divorced and Suzanne had changed her name, either back to her maiden name or through remarriage. She couldn't chase down every Suzanne in the United States. The haystack wasn't enormous, but she spent hours sifting through it, to no avail.

Friday evening, several friends from the Cascaders Mountain Club met at Maria's apartment with plenty of wine, weed, and snacks. Everyone wanted to sign Maria's cast. They were also eager to hear how she hurt herself, as no one wished to repeat her harrowing experience. The party took Jessica's mind off her looming investigation deadline for a welcome few hours.

*   *   *

The next morning, Jessica received an email from Adam:

> I've located a Suzanne Briggs, age 69, at 8271 E. Sherman Ave., Mesa, AZ 85204. Phone (480) 555-0136. Previous addresses were in Cheyenne, WY, and before that Billings, MT. No email address found. This might be your girl.
>
> There's no record of a Mark Briggs at that Mesa address. There was one at Suzanne's previous addresses in Billings and Cheyenne. I found a death record for that Mark Briggs

from 4 years ago in Cheyenne. No record of a Nicole Briggs at any of these addresses.

Are you going to contact Suzanne directly?

"Yes!" Jessica shouted.

"What's wrong?" Maria asked, sounding alarmed and wincing as she sat up in bed too fast.

"Oh, sorry I woke you, sweetie," Jessica replied. "I just got fabulous news from the detective working Nikki's case. He thinks he might have located her mother in Mesa, Arizona. That's a suburb of Phoenix."

"That's great, Jess." Maria flopped her head back down on the pillow and pulled the blanket over her face. Jessica heard a muffled "Can I go back to sleep now?" followed shortly by gentle snoring.

Ecstatic at Adam's news, Jessica took a break from her quest for a few hours. She finally got to the gym for the first time in nearly a month. She desperately needed to burn off both some calories and some stress.

When she returned to Maria's apartment, she noticed what a mess it was. Maria wasn't much of a housekeeper in the best of times. Judging from the spilled milk and cereal residue in the bowl on the kitchen counter, Maria had gotten up for breakfast and then returned to bed. The apartment's chaos level had exceeded Jessica's tolerance threshold. She spent some time cleaning the entire apartment, except the bedroom where Maria still slumbered. Finally, she had everything under control.

Jessica heard stirrings in the bedroom. Maria thumped out on her crutches, hair everywhere. "Holy shit, what did you do to the place?" she asked.

Surprised by Maria's reaction, Jessica tried to explain. "Your apartment looked like a bomb hit it. I just straightened up a bit, put things back where they belong."

"It was fine like it was, Jess. Now I'll never find anything. Do you always have to be such a damn perfectionist?"

Jessica held up her hands. "Guilty as charged, Your Honor. I confess to being a repeat perfectionist."

"You might think it's funny, but I find it irritating. How about if you perfect your own house and leave mine the hell alone?"

Chastened, Jessica dropped her hands. "Right. Sorry. It's your place. You have the right for it to be as messy as you like. Should I put everything back where it was?"

"No, that's all right," Maria said with a laugh. "It'll get messy on its own soon enough. Just don't clean in here anymore, okay?"

Chapter 19

Saturday, June 9

WHILE MARIA WAS out for a walk on her crutches after lunch on Saturday, Jessica phoned Suzanne Briggs in Mesa. She identified herself and asked if Suzanne was related to Nicole Briggs.

"I do have a daughter named Nicole," said Suzanne. "Why do you ask?"

"This might sound peculiar, Mrs. Briggs, but please hear me out. I'm thirty-four years old. I was adopted from an orphanage in China in early 1985 and grew up in Boise, Idaho. I live in Portland, Oregon, now. Recently I've been researching my background, and I've come to believe that I have a twin sister I never knew about before. I think your daughter Nicole could be that twin. Do you know anything about that possibility?"

Suzanne Briggs said nothing for a few moments.

Finally she responded, "Oh my, Jessica. This is all news to me. Nicole is also thirty-four. My husband and I adopted her from China in July of 1985. We never had any idea that she might be a twin, though. Are you certain about this?"

"I'm not entirely certain yet, no. I've been working with the Lorane County Sheriff's Office in Eugene, Oregon, on a case for several weeks. To our surprise, we've developed information that strongly suggests Nicole and I are identical twins. When did you last hear from Nicole?"

"We've been estranged for years," Suzanne answered. "I don't know where she is or what she's doing. My heart just broke when she disappeared on us. Is she in some trouble with the police up there? Do you know where she is?"

Jessica spoke as gently as she knew how. "Mrs. Briggs, I'm sorry to have to tell you this: although it's not yet certain, we believe Nicole may have been the victim of a homicide several years ago near Eugene. There's a small chance we are wrong, but honestly, I don't think so."

"A homicide? Oh Lord, no."

Jessica heard quiet sobs on the other end of the line. Then she heard Suzanne blow her nose. "What makes you think that victim is my daughter?" Suzanne asked. "And why do you think she was your twin sister? This is all so hard to understand."

"I could hardly believe it myself. I had no idea I might have a sister." Jessica concisely summarized her facial reconstruction work on the case and the clues that suggested she and the deceased Nicole Briggs were twins.

"I'm calling you for several reasons, Mrs. Briggs. First, I'm sure that as her mother you want to know what happened to your daughter. Also we want to confirm the identity of this victim and to discover what happened to her. Plus, of course, I'm eager to determine whether Nicole and I are twins or not."

"Please call me Suzanne. It sounds like we are almost family somehow. Is there anything I can do to help with all that?"

"Probably, yes. To confirm if we're twins, we need a sample of Nicole's DNA. Would you have any clothing or other personal items that might have her DNA on them, such as a hairbrush or maybe an old toothbrush?"

"Nicole left some clothes with me when she moved out years ago, some sweaters she didn't wear anymore and a few other things.

I still have those stored in a box. I guess I kept hoping she'd come back eventually."

"Those would be perfect," Jessica said excitedly. "Please don't touch those items yet. Is there any chance I could come visit you soon to get that clothing handled properly for DNA testing and also to learn as much as I can from you about Nicole? We can talk more then about verifying whether or not the remains are Nicole's. I'm just desperate to get to know my sister."

Suzanne invited Jessica to join her in Mesa on Monday. Jessica confirmed her current address and got directions to Suzanne's condo from the Phoenix airport. Jessica texted Adam immediately after her conversation with Suzanne:

> It's her! I'm flying to Phoenix on Monday to see her. She might have Nicole DNA available.

She made reservations online to fly to Phoenix on Monday, June 11, on Cascadia Airlines flight 1769, departing Portland at 7:53 a.m. and arriving in Phoenix at 10:36 a.m., returning midafternoon on Tuesday. The last-minute fare of $807.55 would traumatize her credit card. She would have to tap the financial reserves her parents had so kindly provided. Jessica made a quick call to Suzanne to tell her when her flight would arrive. Suzanne did not use email or texts, so Jessica would have to rely on voice phone calls to communicate with her.

Jessica made a rental car reservation online too. She could find a hotel once she was in Mesa; no need to book one in advance. Finally Jessica emailed her supervisor at Meals on Wheels, Kathleen, apologizing that she would once again have to miss her route on Tuesday. She explained that she was enmeshed in an intense personal matter she could not evade. Jessica hated to keep dropping the ball on her personal commitments like this. However, with Adam's June 14 deadline looming, she had no choice.

Maria hobbled back into the apartment from her thrice-daily walk around the block and plopped onto the couch. Jessica saw how her lack of mobility was making the normally energetic and active Maria frustrated and irritable. She wouldn't be able to resume her usual outdoorsy schedule for several months. She was also stressed because she was missing so much work as a sales representative at Great Northwestern Outfitters. Someone on crutches from a rock-climbing accident was not an excellent advertisement for ascenders, ropes, and belay devices.

Jessica excitedly said, "Maria, you won't believe it. I just spoke to Suzanne Briggs, Nicole's mother! It was so hard to tell her Nicole is dead. Suzanne said I could fly down to Phoenix to meet with her. Best of all, she has some of Nicole's old clothes. Maybe we can get a DNA analysis and prove we are twins! Isn't that incredible?"

"Whoa, you're going to Phoenix? When?"

"Monday morning. I'll be back Tuesday afternoon. I just made the reservations."

"Jesus, Jess. What's with all this coming and going?" Maria flung her arms out in exasperation. The skin tightened around her eyes, a sure sign of fireworks to come. "Even when you're here, you're not here. You're just sitting at the table on your laptop or talking to people on the phone. You hardly remember that I'm right here in the next room. Why is this so important to you?"

Jessica rocked back, shocked by the intensity of Maria's outburst. "Why is this so important to me?" she echoed quietly. "Maybe I haven't explained that well enough yet. Let me try. You don't know what it's like to be adopted. My own mother threw me away! I don't know anything about myself, really. Not like you, with all your brothers and sisters and cousins who grew up together."

"Dammit, Jess—"

Jessica held both hands up in front of her and said, "Wait. Listen to me. Please." She paused to collect her thoughts, and then continued. "Recently I've learned I *wasn't* alone in the world. Nicole Briggs started life as the other half of me. We came from the same egg. There's still a part of me in her and a part of her in me. I owe it to Nicole, and to myself, to see this through. I owe it to her family, who doesn't know what happened to their girl. I owe it to society, because some evil bastard killed her and dumped her in the woods. I'm sorry if you don't understand, Maria, but I have to do this."

Maria sat quietly, lips compressed and arms folded across her chest. "I get it. A woman you've never met who's been dead for five years is more important to you than I am. So even though I need your help right now, this cold case takes priority over me, right?"

"Maria, if you hadn't been so cocky about your rock-climbing abilities, you wouldn't need *anybody's* help right now," Jessica said tightly. "It's your own fault. It scares me that you always have to be so close to the edge. Yes, right now 'this cold case,' as you call it, does take priority for me. You're doing pretty well by yourself now. So I'm going to Phoenix on Monday. It's only for two days. I'll talk to you when I get home. I have to leave now."

Jessica snatched her laptop and papers from the table and drove back to her house, leaving a speechless Maria in her wake. She had never been so angry with her girlfriend. True, Maria had a short temper and liked to call the shots. The easygoing Jessica usually rolled with it, compromising when necessary because she enjoyed the time they spent together. Most of it, anyway. Today, though, she was furious that Maria was being so selfish, unable to accept how important this search was to her. The mystery of Nicole Briggs was no longer just another police case to Jessica. And it wasn't just about Jessica saving her own job. It was a quest for family and for justice, a quest she could not abandon.

*   *   *

Several hours later, Jessica was still pissed. She wasn't ordinarily one to stay angry for long. Maria's attitude today stuck in her craw, though. Jessica had to get out for a while: away from the house, away from Maria, and even away from the case that had consumed her for weeks.

She drove to a wine bar she enjoyed on Portland's east side called Wine O'Clock. She coveted the rich-looking wooden shelves filled with hundreds of bottles. Jessica had promised herself long ago that if she ever became a gazillionaire she would indulge in a first-class wine cellar. She enjoyed trying something different with each glass. Jessica wasn't one to buy a case of some wine she liked, as many wine enthusiasts she knew did, because right around each corner another one she would enjoy awaited.

Wine O'Clock had a warm ambience about it. She knew the owner well after her many visits there. Like a good bartender, Bruce remembered her tastes. He suggested she try a new Shiraz he had just picked up from Australia's Barossa Valley. She took a seat at one of the tables and ordered a small plate of vegetables, hummus, and pita bread to munch on as she sipped.

The Shiraz was superb, with intense dark-fruit flavors nicely balanced against soft tannins. As much as she enjoyed wine, even after taking several wine-tasting classes years earlier, Jessica was terrible at putting words to what she smelled or tasted. She believed some people's refined palates could identify the various flavors and aromas in a complex wine, but she didn't care about that. To her it was just a parlor game to try to name all those components. She didn't like a wine, liked a wine, or loved a wine. That was enough information for her. And she loved the Shiraz.

A man she had previously met at Wine O'Clock approached her table. "Hi, Jessica," he said. "I'm Brett. It's nice to see you again. May I join you?"

"Sure, Brett. Have a seat. Have a carrot." She remembered Brett as being interesting and engaging. He was a few years older than her, divorced, an engineering consultant who traveled a lot and always had a funny story about the last place he'd been. Brett stood just over six feet tall with a muscular build, crystal-blue eyes, and wavy light-brown hair.

Jessica gradually unwound as they talked. Brett bought them two more glasses, this time a rich Malbec from Argentina.

After their second glass, Jessica's warm wine glow made her feel more relaxed than she had in a month. She idly tore her cocktail napkin into long strips. She took a breath as though to speak and then paused for a beat. Brett gave her the space. Jessica touched his arm and looked into his eyes.

She said, "I'm really enjoying talking with you, Brett. Would you like to come over to my house for another glass?"

He followed her home in his car. Moments after Brett stepped through her front door, Jessica was in his arms. His coarse whiskers against her face touched a part of her that Maria's soft cheeks could not. Jessica inhaled Brett's aura of subtle aftershave, red wine, and desire. She had almost forgotten the pleasure of feeling a man's solid muscles under her hands, his body above hers.

Brett drove home the next morning. Normally monogamous, Jessica felt only a whisper of guilt about cheating on Maria, and with a man at that. She thought the Maria relationship might be on the way out, anyway. Jessica found it delicious to spend the night with someone who paid attention to her for a change. Brett hadn't complained, either.

Chapter 20

Monday, June 11

JUST BEFORE ELEVEN Jessica walked out of Sky Harbor International Airport to catch the rental car shuttle bus, and 103 degrees of desert heat slammed her in the face. Less than three hours after departing Portland on a pleasantly cool morning, she wasn't prepared for the inferno that was Phoenix in the summer. Dark glasses cut the glare, and buying a sun hat suddenly sounded like a good idea.

She navigated to Suzanne Briggs's condo building on East Sherman Avenue in Mesa, just over twelve miles from the airport. The closer she got, the more nervous she became. *What is Nicole's mother like? What happened to her father? Was Nicole blessed with parents as loving and supportive as mine? How will Suzanne react to seeing someone who looks just like her deceased daughter? Maybe I shouldn't have come.* Too late— she had reached her destination.

Suzanne's condo was on the second floor of a block-sized building that housed a public library branch, a bank, and several shops on the street level. The condo entrance had an intercom system. Jessica scrolled through the display's alphabetical listing until she found an entry for "BRIGGS S." A few seconds after she pressed the buzzer a female voice answered, "Yes?"

"Good morning, Suzanne, it's Jessica Sanford. I made it here from Portland." Jessica heard the interlock trip and opened the door.

She walked up to the second floor and down a brightly-lit carpeted hallway to number 8271.

The woman who answered the doorbell looked older than her sixty-nine years. Her hair was completely white, short and curly above her red-framed eyeglasses. She was thin, just shy of frail. The skin on her face and arms showed the leathery effects of long-term sun exposure. She stared at Jessica through the glass security door, her knees sagging. She hung onto the doorknob for support.

"Hello, Suzanne. I'm sorry to startle you. I'm sure it's a shock to see someone who looks so much like Nicole appear at your door like this."

Suzanne opened the door and motioned for Jessica to enter. She still hadn't said anything, just stared at Jessica's face. Finally she found her voice. "Forgive me, Jessica. Please come in and sit down." Suzanne led Jessica into her condo's living room.

The air conditioning was a blessed relief from the oppressive heat outdoors. Jessica understood why people in Phoenix lived either indoors or in their cars, dashing from building to building to avoid melting. She welcomed Suzanne's offer of iced tea.

"I barely slept the night after your call," Suzanne said. "Frankly I'm not surprised something awful happened to Nicole. She always was a little on the wild side and didn't much care for following rules. Still, as a mother, it's devastating to learn your child is dead."

Jessica nodded in sympathy as she sipped the refreshing tea. She took a notepad and pen from her purse. She said, "As I mentioned on the phone, we are not yet absolutely certain we've found Nicole. All the indications do point to that, though. Thank you for inviting me to your home. I have so many questions for you!"

Suzanne adjusted her glasses and cocked her head at Jessica. "You do look almost exactly like Nicole, just several years older than when I saw her last. It's uncanny. You even have the same little curve in the chin. I see some slight differences, though. Nicole had a mole on her cheek right here," she said, pointing to a spot below her right eye. Jessica made a note. That detail could go into the images used in the public appeal for people who knew Nicole. People often remember identifying features like that.

"Your eyebrows are a little different too, and you have beautiful teeth. We didn't have the money to get braces for Nicole, so her teeth were always kind of crooked. I see you have the same cute, lopsided smile that Nicole does. I mean did. It's going to be hard for me to learn to use the past tense for her."

Jessica looked around the living room. She sat on one of a pair of matching patterned loveseats opposite Suzanne, on its partner. A low, smoked-glass table sat between them. Several framed family photographs were arrayed on a credenza against the hallway wall. Jessica asked if she could look at them. Suzanne nodded. Jessica found it bizarre to see someone who looked just like herself in family photographs with Suzanne, a man who must have been her father, Mark, and another, younger man.

"Is this Nicole's brother?" Jessica asked, pointing to the fourth person in one photograph. "Angela told me that both she and Nicole had brothers."

"Yes, that's our son, Steven. He's three years older than Nicole. Steven is our biological child. When I say 'our,' I'm referring to my late husband, Mark." Jessica sensed this was not yet the right time to inquire about what happened to Mark.

Suzanne glanced at the digital clock on the credenza, which showed that it was nearly noon. "I'm getting hungry," she said. "Would you like some lunch? I can offer you a nice pasta salad I made and some fresh bread, or sandwiches, whichever you prefer."

Jessica opted for the pasta salad. She set the table and refilled their glasses while Suzanne organized the food.

Suzanne spent most of the afternoon telling Jessica about Nicole. Suzanne said she was gradually growing accustomed to looking at not-her-daughter across the table. She said she couldn't help but contrast the poised and accomplished woman in her condo with her memories of Nicole's flightiness, rebelliousness, and thirst for danger and adventure.

Although Jessica and Nicole were the same age, their birthdays were not the same because no one besides their biological mother knew the girls' actual date of birth. Nicole's assigned birthday was November 25; Jessica's was December 3. The two women were both five feet two inches tall. Suzanne said their hair and eyes were exactly the same color, and even their voices sounded the same, although their speech patterns differed a bit because they were raised in different geographical areas.

Jessica was thirteen months old when she was adopted; Nicole was nineteen months. Coulter Adoptions told the Briggses that their daughter was not adopted earlier because she had been a sickly infant. By nineteen months she was healthy and stronger, ready for a new family. That's why she was in what Jessica called group five, not Jessica's own group three, six and a half months earlier. Even as a toddler, Nicole had been feisty and persistent. She didn't know her own limits, pushed boundaries, and took risks. She wasn't really a problem child, just a "handful."

Relations in the Briggs family often were strained. As teens, Nicole and Steven had frequently fought with their short-tempered father and with each other. Both children rebelled against their parents and against authority in general. They snuck out of the house at night to go drinking with their friends. Both had been caught smoking marijuana at parties. All teenagers rebel; Steven and Nicole took it to the next level. Suzanne said she did her best to keep the peace, with only sporadic success.

"Suzanne, did Nicole have any distinctive features that might be useful for identifying the remains we found as being hers? Did she ever break a bone or suffer any other significant injury as a child? Did she have any body piercings or tattoos that you know of?"

"She didn't have any visible tattoos when I saw her last. Her ears were pierced in multiple places. Those were the only piercings I knew about. Regarding injuries, Nicole fell out of a tree when she was nine and broke both bones in her lower right arm. Then, when she was about fifteen, she wrecked her bike, pedaling too fast, as usual. She pitched right over the handlebars after hitting a big pothole and broke an upper front tooth. She had it crowned when she was eighteen."

Jessica pulled the medical examiner's report from her purse. The skeletal remains found near Eugene had long-healed fractures in the radius and ulna of the right arm as well as a crown on one upper incisor. Both of these distinctive injuries were consistent with the incidents Suzanne had just described.

"I'm afraid those injuries exactly match features on the skeletal remains," Jessica said gently. "It sounds as though we have found your daughter, Suzanne."

Suzanne began to cry, shoulders shaking with silent sobs. Tears trickled through the hands that covered her face and dripped onto her lap. Jessica sat next to her and gently rubbed her back.

Suzanne eventually sniffled her sobs to an end. Jessica looked around the room and found a box of Kleenex. She handed several to Suzanne, who smiled her thanks as she wiped her eyes.

Jessica said, "To be completely certain this is Nicole, we'd like to be able to compare her dental X-rays to those of the remains. Do you remember who your family dentist was in Billings? If we could get the latest X-rays he had on file, maybe from when Nicole got the crown at age eighteen, that would let us make a definitive match."

Suzanne walked to the small desk in the kitchen corner and took an old address book from the top drawer. She flipped through it until she found the dentist's name and phone number. "I can call him to see if he's still practicing," she offered.

Jessica took Adam Longsdale's business card from her wallet and handed it to Suzanne. "If he does have the X-rays, please ask him to send them by overnight delivery, or by email if they're digital, to Detective Longsdale at this address."

Suzanne walked into the kitchen and picked up the phone. A few minutes later she returned to the living room and told Jessica, "Dr. Koenig does still practice in Billings. His office manager said she could pull the X-rays from his archive records tomorrow. She'll send them directly to Detective Longsdale. I didn't tell her why I needed them, but she could probably guess since they're going to a detective in Oregon."

Jessica told Suzanne about her meeting in Richland with Angela Montgomery, whom Suzanne remembered from Billings as Angela Stark. Jessica explained that Angela had pointed out many similarities between Nicole and Jessica. Suzanne confirmed Angela's details about Nicole's upbringing in Billings and added others. She was happy to hear that Angela was doing well; the two hadn't communicated since the Briggses had moved from Billings to Cheyenne.

Suzanne painted a rich picture of Nicole's upbringing and her personality. Like Jessica, Nicole suffered from respiratory allergies. She was adventuresome and outdoorsy, smart and energetic, but restless, in search of both excitement and herself. After she left Billings, Nicole moved from one town to another throughout the West. She worked at various jobs to earn just enough money for food and rent, with enough extra to let her indulge in the outdoors activities and partying she enjoyed so much. Until recent years, Nicole had contacted Suzanne and Mark only once or twice a year; she seldom visited. They didn't know much about what sort of woman she had become or where she had been living.

Suzanne said she hadn't heard anything at all from Nicole for more than five years. She had no idea what had happened to her. She had checked with some of her daughter's old friends after Nicole had been silent for some time. No one else had been in touch with her recently, either. She just disappeared.

As neither Mark nor Suzanne used a computer or a smart phone, they had no access to online social media. Jessica told Suzanne that Nicole's Facebook page had not been updated since May 25, five years earlier. She asked if that date held any particular significance, but Suzanne couldn't think of anything.

Jessica waited for the appropriate moment to inquire about Nicole's rape. When the time seemed right, she mentioned that Angela had told her about it. She asked Suzanne how the rape and pregnancy affected Nicole and her family. Suzanne looked sadly out the window and didn't say anything for a minute.

"We were all just devastated. We had been close to the Starks ever since the adoptions. We had no idea Brian harbored such anger against our lovely daughter. Mark was furious at Brian. After it was all over, he refused to ever speak to any of the Starks again. I don't blame him; I was just as angry. I was willing to try to move on. Not Mark. The whole thing left Nicole feeling isolated and unloved. A traumatic experience like that had to affect her emotions and her behavior. How could it not?"

"Forgive me if it's none of my business, but can you please tell me what happened to Mark?" Jessica inquired.

"The rape and abortion hit him very hard. He had always been something of a drinker. Afterward, his drinking worsened, and he became a full-fledged alcoholic. Mark and I moved to Cheyenne shortly after Nicole left Billings, just to start over. Steven had already gone off to college."

Suzanne got up and refreshed their iced teas. "Almost four years ago, Mark went out drinking at a bar till closing time. On his way home, he hit a concrete bridge abutment on the freeway. He died instantly. The police ruled it an accident, but I think it might have been suicide. He felt so guilty about not protecting his daughter, as well as being depressed over the breakup of the family friendships and Nicole's estrangement from us. A year later I bought this condo with the life insurance money and moved to Mesa."

Jessica told Suzanne how much she appreciated her frankness in sharing so many details about Nicole and the Briggs family. Suzanne showed Jessica some of Nicole's possessions she still had in the condo. Jessica felt closer and closer to her twin as she learned more about her. Suzanne brought out a large cardboard box from a closet and set it on the floor.

"These are the clothes I told you I had kept from when Nicole still lived with us."

Jessica dared not touch anything herself and risk contaminating it with her own DNA, which would invalidate any DNA tests. Sitting several feet away, she asked Suzanne to open the box without touching any of the items inside. Jessica could see several sweaters and other clothing encased in plastic bags.

"Suzanne, can you please look at those sweaters through the bags—again, without touching—and tell me if you can see any of Nicole's hairs on them?"

Suzanne peered closely at the uppermost bags. She said, "I do see some long black hairs. The wool in the sweaters traps hairs sometimes. I probably never sent these for cleaning, just left them in the bags."

Jessica was elated. "That's fantastic! Maybe we can get a DNA sample from those hairs. This might be exactly the evidence we need to prove everything we now believe about Nicole."

With her law-enforcement training, Jessica knew to protect the chain of custody for any evidence in a case. She called the Mesa Police Department and identified herself. She gave Adam's contact information to the Mesa detective so he could confirm that her request was legitimate. The Mesa detective called her back shortly and said he would send a technician to Suzanne's condo in the morning to process the clothing and send it to Adam.

Suzanne offered to take Jessica out for dinner in gratitude for all she was doing to bring closure to her daughter's life. As they sat at the table waiting for their meals to arrive, Jessica's phone pinged with an email from Adam. He had received the results of her mitochondrial DNA test. Her full mtDNA sequence—all 16,569 base pairs—exactly matched the DNA extracted from the Lorane County remains. "Wow, cool!" Jessica exclaimed.

"Good news?" Suzanne asked.

"Yes indeed. That email was from the detective I'm working with on Nicole's case. We got the results from the first DNA test. My mitochondrial DNA exactly matches that from the remains!"

"Does that prove that you and Nicole are twins? Do you still need some DNA from her old clothes?"

"There are different kinds of DNA," Jessica explained. "I just learned about all this myself. The kind we tested proves that Nicole—if she really is the victim—and I are related through some common maternal ancestor not too far back. I still need Nicole's hair samples to do a full DNA comparison and see just how closely related we are. But we are definitely cousins at the least, and we could well be siblings or even twins."

Suzanne and Jessica clinked their glasses of iced tea together to celebrate this latest link in the chain. Jessica could feel the pressure of Adam's timeline easing with each new bit of progress.

After dinner, Jessica told Suzanne, "This has been an intense day for both of us. Thank you very much for dinner and for all your time and hospitality. I'm sorry I had to bring you such unhappy news. I need to find a hotel now. My flight home tomorrow leaves midafternoon. Could I come back around nine in the morning to meet the police technician?"

Suzanne replied, "I wouldn't think of you going to a hotel tonight, Jessica. I have a spare bedroom and a second bathroom. You're more than welcome to stay with me. It's the least I can do for you. I can't tell you how much I appreciate all you're doing."

Jessica was happy to accept Suzanne's offer. Suzanne smiled, reminding Jessica of the way Sharon had often smiled at her. Jessica wondered if, for Suzanne, this shared night felt a little like being a mother again after many years.

*   *   *

Jessica awoke in a strange room once again. She just wasn't used to traveling as much as she had been recently; it was disorienting. She missed her own bed in her own house.

She looked around Suzanne's spare bedroom. Bright morning sunbeams prismed off the dresser's beveled-glass mirror and sprinkled rainbows on the wall. *Is that the dresser Nicole used in her bedroom growing up?* Jessica wondered. *Are those the pictures that hung in her house, the knickknacks and decorations she walked past every day?* She asked herself what it would have been like had the fate of the two twins been reversed, with Jessica adopted by the Briggses and Nicole growing up in Boise with David and Sharon. So many questions; so many possibilities; no answers.

The smell of the French toast and scrambled eggs that Suzanne was cooking for their breakfast finally pulled her out of her reverie and from the bed.

The police technician from the Mesa Police Department, a man named Miguel, arrived about nine thirty with a stack of large evidence bags. He put on nitrile gloves and carefully removed each item of clothing from the box Suzanne had used for storage. Miguel packaged each one just as he found it in the cardboard box in a separate evidence bag, sealed it, and labeled it. He gave Suzanne an itemized receipt for all of the pieces of clothing. Miguel told Jessica he would ship them to Detective Longsdale by overnight delivery.

Jessica and Suzanne sat quietly for a few moments. The act of removing Nicole's last items of clothing from the condo clearly sat heavily on Suzanne's shoulders. She sadly told Jessica, "The police said they'll probably return the clothing eventually. But now it really feels like Nicole is gone forever. I have almost nothing left of her."

"I'm so sorry, Suzanne," Jessica replied gently. "This has all been a shock for everybody. At least you still have your memories. I would give anything to have even one memory of my sister. Thank you for letting me get to know her a little through you."

Jessica stood to leave for the airport. Suzanne hugged her tightly, seeming not to want to break the last remaining connection to her own daughter. "Find out what happened to my baby," she pleaded. "I need to know."

"I promise I'll do my best, Suzanne. After all, Nicole and I were babies together."

Chapter 21

Tuesday, June 12

PORTLAND'S COMFORTABLE COOLNESS was a tonic to Jessica as she walked across the bridge from the airport terminal to the parking garage late Tuesday afternoon. *How do people stand the oppressive heat of Phoenix?* she marveled. Seventy-four degrees with moderate humidity was much more to her taste. She had emailed Adam before her flight took off and told him to expect both Nicole's dental X-rays from Dr. Koenig in Billings and her clothing, shipped by the Mesa Police Department.

When Jessica pulled into her driveway in Rosemount, she was delighted to see how tidy the lawn looked. She walked around the yard, admiring how neatly the mowing service had trimmed the grass along the pavement edges and around the landscape beds. They had even pruned the shrubbery. Their professional work put her own hasty mowing and trimming to shame. Regrettably, she couldn't use her parents' subsidies to keep the yard looking so fine indefinitely.

Which reminded her: she did need to request more funds from them to cover the cost of the Phoenix trip. She felt a surge of love and gratitude for her mom and dad. Not all parents would be so supportive, both emotionally and practically.

After dinner, Jessica called to check on Maria. However, Maria didn't seem very interested in yet another progress report on Jessica's grand quest for Truth and Justice. She sounded distracted and hurried. Jessica could hear people noises in the background over the phone. Maria had patience only for a brief update on the Mesa trip, and then she excused herself to get back to some friends who had come over to visit. Jessica noted the lack of an invitation to join the party. She realized unexpectedly that she felt neither disappointed nor annoyed, just surprised.

*   *   *

The next afternoon Adam phoned Jessica to thank her for obtaining the vital X-rays and clothing and to hear what else she discovered during her Mesa trip. He reported that the Lorane County Sheriff's Office had received both of the expected packages before noon on Wednesday. Adam had the X-rays delivered to the forensic odontologist who performed dental comparisons for several police departments in western Oregon. He had sent the bagged and tagged clothing items to the lab to look for any usable sources of DNA.

Jessica summarized everything she had learned to date about Nicole, including her rape and the possibility that Brian Stark was involved in her death. Adam offered to check Brian's police records. However tenuous, he was their sole possible suspect at the moment.

"The ducks keep lining up the same way, Adam," Jessica told him. "Suzanne corroborated everything Angela Montgomery told me earlier about Nicole Briggs. Like Angela, Suzanne was overwhelmed by the similarities between Nicole and me. I feel like I'm really getting to know her. I'll be astonished if we aren't twins."

"The dental X-rays and DNA samples should be all we need to confirm your conclusions. I requested an expedited analysis on the DNA and a comparison to the sample I took from you earlier. We should get the results in about a week. The dental X-ray results will be back within two days."

After a pause, Adam continued, "I have to say, Jessica, your investigative efforts have been impressive. You've convinced me there's an excellent chance you and Nicole are identical twins. I'm sorry I doubted your original reconstruction work. But it's my job to be skeptical of anything not backed up by solid evidence. Once a detective, always a detective."

"No problem," Jessica replied, hiding her enormous relief. "I'm glad we're back on the same page. Finding Nicole wasn't easy, but it's been incredibly rewarding to identify the victim and her family. Not to mention all I've learned about myself and my own background. I'm sad I never knew Nicole when she was alive. My life would have been so different."

Jessica added, "I'm on this case for the duration. Can I continue to work with you to help investigate? I know the sheriff's office has limited resources and, frankly, not a lot of interest in such an old case. But I need to know what happened to Nicole."

"We're happy to have the help. I'm still spending most of my time on the case in Forest City. That's bigger than it looked at first. Just remember: you are not law enforcement. I know you used to be and that you have the training. You're a civilian, though."

"I'm not planning on arresting anybody. But I have the time, and I'm super motivated. Honestly, beyond the personal angle, I've enjoyed putting my investigation experience to work again."

Adam cautioned, "Just be careful. We're still treating this as a homicide. Someone killed Nicole. That someone could still be around, and that someone does not want you to find them. Our next step is to locate anyone who might have known Nicole in the Eugene area."

"I had an idea about that. On a normal reconstruction project, we would publicize the sculpture through the media to try to reach someone who recognizes the victim. Now that we're all but certain Nicole is my twin, how about if we use some photographs of me, along with her Facebook picture, for the campaign instead of the facial reconstruction images?"

Adam contemplated her suggestion. "That's not the worst idea I ever heard. We'll have to be careful how we describe the pictures because they aren't of the victim herself. However, she resembles you enough that people might recognize her more easily from your photos than from the reconstruction."

"Is there any other way we could use our resemblance to help us solve the case?"

"Well, we could also run your own photos against the national missing-persons database to look for a match. I can work with the FBI field office in Portland on that. Could you please send me several photos of yourself from about four to eight years ago? We need clear facial shots, no hats or glasses."

"Sure, I'll get some to you as soon as we're done talking. Could I watch you run the search?"

Adam laughed. "It's not too exciting. In movies, you always see photos flickering by as the computer beeps away. Then when the facial-recognition software spots the terrorist, the picture turns red and flashes, and the computer beeps louder. It doesn't really work that way. I just submit digital photos to the database. Software there does the comparisons and reports any candidate matches it finds. It's boring unless we get a hit."

"Okay, I'll skip that, but I can help you prepare the materials for the public assistance appeal, if you like." Adam accepted her offer, and Jessica agreed to meet at his office right after lunch in two days.

Jessica was greatly relieved to be back in Adam's good graces, and with two days to spare from his convince-me deadline. Her reputation as a gifted forensic sculptor remained intact. She turned to her laptop, found four photos of herself that met Adam's specifications, and sent those to him.

*   *   *

The challenge now was how to find people who knew Nikki Briggs five or more years ago in a city of one hundred sixty thousand with a university enrolling more than twenty-three thousand students.

Jessica examined the list of friends on Nikki's old Facebook page. There weren't many, not even twenty. She messaged each one to ask if she could talk to them about Nikki.

Jessica was disappointed to receive responses from just four of Nikki's Facebook friends. Perhaps the others weren't inclined to respond to messages from someone they didn't know. All four were shocked when Jessica told them Nikki was dead. One of them used to live in Eugene and had connected with Nikki just as a Facebook friend-of-a-friend; they hadn't really known each other. Two others were older connections from towns where Nikki had lived prior to Eugene. Both offered to think about anyone who might have wanted to harm Nikki.

The one friend who still lived in Eugene agreed to speak to Jessica. Praveena Kapoor's Facebook page said she was a software developer at a health insurance company. Jessica called the phone number Praveena gave her. She brought Praveena up to speed on Nikki's death and her own involvement with the investigation.

"Can you please describe the relationship you had with Nikki?" Jessica asked.

"I've belonged to the Eugene chapter of the Cascaders Mountain Club for years. I met Nikki when she came to some of our rambles and hikes. Sometimes we'd go out for a drink afterward. I did some rock climbing with her too. She was fearless, but that's not always a good thing when you're on a cliff face or a mountain. You need to respect the rock."

"When was the last time you saw her?"

Praveena paused for a moment. "I don't remember exactly. Maybe four or five years ago? She suddenly stopped showing up at Cascaders events. I saw on her Facebook that she had a family emergency or something and had to leave town. I never saw her or heard from her again."

Jessica asked, "Do you know who any of her other friends were? Where she worked, where she lived, where she drank, what else she did for fun?"

"I don't know much," Praveena admitted. "We went out a few times together, but we weren't that close. If I thought about it, I could probably remember some bars we went to and maybe some other people she knew. If you ever get to Eugene, maybe we could connect sometime."

"Thanks, I'll definitely do that, Praveena. Can you think of any conflicts she might have had with other people that could have led to her death?"

"Not at all. Everybody seemed to like Nikki. She was friendly and fun. It's a tragedy about her being killed and buried like that. That shouldn't happen to anybody."

Jessica thanked Praveena and said she would get back in touch if she had more questions. Here was her first tangible link to someone who knew Nicole Briggs near the time she disappeared. Perhaps Praveena could introduce Jessica to others who had had personal connections to Nikki.

Chapter 22

Thursday, June 14

JESSICA AGAIN MADE the familiar drive to Eugene to meet with Adam. She surprised him by bringing two cups of real coffee, as Starbucks still had not opened the anticipated branch in the sheriff's office. The coffee almost made the detective crack a smile.

As he accepted the gift, Adam said, "I have good news, and I have good news. Which would you like to hear first?"

"I'll take the good news," she laughed, delighted that there was any news at all.

"The good news is that our forensic odontologist has positively identified the remains found off Redhawk Road as those of one Nicole Marie Briggs, based on antemortem and postmortem dental X-ray comparisons."

Before she could stop herself, Jessica threw her arms around Adam. "That is *great* news!"

Adam awkwardly returned her hug. Jessica disengaged, suddenly embarrassed by her reaction. She was torn between elation from confirming the identity and pain from knowing the victim was most likely her twin sister.

"I'm sorry," she apologized. "That wasn't very professional."

"No problem. I know what an emotional roller coaster this has been for you. I'm also excited we have a definitive identification.

I just don't look any different when I'm excited than I do the rest of the time." Jessica laughed. "You've done fine work, Jessica. Maybe you should go back into law enforcement."

Even more embarrassed now at the praise, Jessica said, "Thank you, Adam. Maybe I will. You said you had some good news too?"

"That's right. The lab did find long black hairs on the sweaters you got from Suzanne Briggs. Under the microscope they look to be head hairs from someone of Asian origin. Most of the hairs were naturally shed, which means they contain little or no nuclear DNA, just mitochondrial. However, some of the hairs do have intact roots. The lab is about 60 percent confident they can extract nuclear DNA from those to compare with yours. With some luck we should have test results in just a few days."

With an effort, Jessica restrained herself from hugging Adam again. His normally neutral expression stretched into an involuntary grin, mirroring Jessica's broad smile.

"I can hardly wait," she said. Though it was raining outside, it suddenly felt sunny and warm inside the sheriff's office.

"By the way, there were a couple bits of bad news too," Adam added. "I didn't find any matches with your photos in the missing-persons database. Some faces were close, but not close enough. Apparently Nikki was never reported as a missing person."

Did no one notice she had disappeared? Jessica wondered. *Did no one care about her?*

"Okay, that's unfortunate. What was the other bad news?"

"The DMV records showed Nicole's address of record as being in Bend. Maybe she had just moved to Eugene, or maybe she never updated her address with DMV when she moved here. So I don't know her last Eugene-area address yet. But we're just getting started with the hunt. We'll find someone who knows where she lived."

The rest of the afternoon was anticlimactic after the double shot of good news. Jessica and Adam worked together in a conference room to prepare a media package for distribution through numerous outlets. They used the photographs of Jessica in her late twenties, as well as the younger picture from Nicole's Facebook profile. Jessica used an image-processing program on the computer to add a mole on her own right cheek in the photos, just where Suzanne had indicated. The mole wasn't visible in Nicole's Facebook photo. In the media package they included photos of the three pieces of body jewelry found in the forest grave. Jessica also added the small nose stud and eyebrow ring to one of her own photos, making reasonable guesses where to place them.

The text that accompanied the photos said that Nicole Briggs was a probable homicide victim. It asked anyone who had known her within the past five to seven years to contact the Lorane County Sheriff's Office or the Eugene Police Department. Adam's write-up made it clear that some of the pictures were not of Nicole but rather of her identical twin sister. The text also pointed out that Nicole could have had a different hairstyle or color from those shown in the photos, as well as facial piercings, tattoos, or scars. She may or may not have worn glasses some or all of the time.

Adam and Jessica believed these materials were their best resource for calling the public's attention to this long-missing woman. Adam would have the package duplicated and distributed to media outlets as soon as he could, given his other work commitments.

Adam had also explored Brian Stark's criminal record. "This guy is what we police call a pain in the ass," he reported as he opened a thick file folder. "He's been arrested numerous times throughout the Northwest, mostly petty stuff. Stark seems to get into a lot of bar fights. He once spent seven days in jail in Lewiston, Idaho, after busting a beer bottle over another guy's head. I didn't find any warrants out for him at the moment. That's probably just a matter of time."

This wasn't what Jessica wanted to hear. "Do you know where he lives now? Could he be a possible suspect in Nicole's death?"

"His last arrest was eight months ago in Grants Pass, two and a half hours south of here. Could he be a killer? I don't know. We have no idea where he was when Nicole died, since we don't yet know just when that was. Stark is clearly violent, but there isn't any indication that he's gone from bar-fight asshole to stone-cold killer. Tell me right away if you hear anything from him or about him, though."

"I've been thinking about another issue," Adam went on. "Earlier today I suggested maybe you should get back into law enforcement. If you're going to be talking to people about this case, we should deputize you, make you official."

"Do you really think that's necessary?"

"Well, it might open some otherwise closed doors. Becoming a deputy would also provide some legal protection in case there's any problem or a citizen complaint. Do you mind being deputized?"

Jessica thought for a moment and then said, "I would be honored to be an official member of the team, Adam. I hope I get a cool badge. Don't worry, I'm still not going to arrest anybody."

Adam led Jessica down the hall and introduced her to the Lorane County sheriff, a serious-looking, middle-aged man wearing a regulation tan uniform and tinted glasses. His graying hairline was close to meeting up with the bald spot at the back of his head. The sheriff said he knew about her involvement with the case and was happy to have her help. He told Jessica how impressed he had been with her work on the facial reconstruction.

Adam stood silently nearby, chewing his ever-present gum, while the sheriff stood and swore Jessica in as a temporary Lorane County deputy sheriff. He took a badge from his desk drawer and handed it to her after they both signed the form Adam had already filled out.

When they returned to his office, Adam shook Jessica's hand. "Congratulations, deputy. Welcome to the force, even if it's just a temporary assignment."

"Happy to be aboard, sir," Jessica responded with a salute and her lopsided smile.

Adam said, "You're going to be interviewing various people around town as we follow up on leads and tips from the public. Let me give you some of my business cards. When you talk to some citizen, please give them my card along with your own and invite them to contact me if they have any recollections that might be useful." Jessica nodded her understanding and placed a rubber-banded stack of Adam's cards in her purse.

It was nearly six o'clock. Before heading back to Rosemount, Jessica asked if Adam was interested in catching some dinner. At his suggestion, they went to a local restaurant, Stella's Bakery & Bistro. Stella's was housed in a converted country-church building two miles from the sheriff's office. Jessica found it a little strange to see diners sitting at tables where pews clearly used to be arrayed under the high, vaulted ceiling. The kitchen occupied the space behind what was once the altar. The early-evening sunshine sent a kaleidoscope of colors through the church's original stained-glass windows, creating an unusual ambience for a restaurant.

As its name suggested, the bistro was filled with the entrancing aromas of fresh-baked goods. Jessica's nose followed the lure of cinnamon to the bakery display case, where she lusted after everything she saw. She settled for a grilled salmon burger on a whole grain bun with a side of sweet potato fries for dinner. Plus three giant cookies to go. She might get hungry on the drive home.

She and Adam enjoyed a pleasant conversation that had little to do with law enforcement, forensic facial reconstruction, or dead bodies. It was a refreshing respite from the past month's intensity. Jessica learned Adam had grown up in Syracuse, New York, and moved to Eugene to escape those nasty northeastern winters. He said he only missed New York for a few days in early October, when the air had that crisp autumn feel, the fall colors were spectacular, and lake-effect snow was still a future threat. Adam was married with two boys. He enjoyed his job, but he was not encouraging his sons to go into law enforcement. There had to be a less stressful way to earn a living, or maybe a hundred ways.

Before she left the restaurant's parking lot, Jessica phoned her parents to relate all of the week's excitement. They were greatly relieved to hear the time pressure looming over their overstressed daughter had been lifted. They were gratified to know they had contributed to building the web of threads that linked all those Chinese adoptees and their adoptive families. To think that Jessica—with some help from Adam—had not only located but also visited Nicole's mother! David and Sharon said they felt like they were related to Suzanne in some fashion, even if there was no true legal or blood relationship. Jessica marveled at how interconnected so many people's lives could be without them even knowing.

*   *   *

Jessica's mind wandered during the two-hour drive home. The epiphany that she had a twin naturally made her reflect on her own background. She had always matter-of-factly accepted the reality of her being adopted. Now she appreciated that her birth mother must have been overwhelmed with the prospect of caring for twins. This wasn't a true violation of China's one-child policy, which was really a one-birth policy. But something or someone must have made her give up both Jessica and Nicole—both Meilin and Chuntao—for adoption.

Where is my birth mother now? Did she have other children? Do Nicole and I have a brother or sister in China? Does she ever think of us? Does she regret losing us every day of her life, or were we just a nuisance to be disposed of? Jessica would never know. Nonetheless, simply being aware that Nicole existed made Jessica feel closer to her origins, giving her a link to the world beyond her adoptive family.

Jessica reached home about nine thirty, tired but encouraged by the progress. She emailed Angela, Maria, and BJ to tell them the police had confirmed Nicole's identity through the dental X-rays. Also they were on the cusp of knowing for certain if the two women were identical twins. Jessica was more anxious to get that news than she could ever remember being about anything.

Because Suzanne didn't use email, Jessica would have to give her the bad news about her daughter over the phone. She glanced at the clock and concluded it was too late to do that now; she would call in the morning. Suzanne would achieve the closure of knowing for sure what had happened to her daughter, but she still wouldn't know who killed her and why. Jessica had more work to do.

Chapter 23

Saturday, June 16

SINGLE AND CHILDLESS at thirty-four, Jessica had decided long ago that she was not the mothering kind. She just lacked that part of the brain that says, "Go forth and multiply." While she would no doubt miss certain experiences, she would never have to worry about getting a call like the one she was about to place to Suzanne Briggs.

Jessica dreaded telling Suzanne that Nicole's body had been positively identified. She was weary of sharing news of death with everyone she met who had some Nicole connection. Jessica sat at her desk, eyes closed, rehearsing how to break the news. There was no gentle way. She picked up her phone.

After the call, she breathed a sigh of relief. Suzanne had taken the news better than Jessica had feared. She had already accepted the likelihood that her daughter was dead, so this definitive answer was less shocking than it might have been otherwise. Suzanne said she would notify her son, Steven, and other relatives. Jessica promised to keep Suzanne informed as her investigation progressed, and also to report the DNA test results when those came in.

Now that the searches for the victim's identity and family were complete, Jessica could update her social media posts regarding the quest. She described the identification of Nicole's remains and asked anyone who had known Nicole in Eugene to contact her. Jessica didn't expect the people who followed her on social media to know anything about Nicole's life. If you cast a large enough net, though, sometimes you'll catch a fish.

*   *   *

Jessica spent much of Saturday strategizing how to explore Nicole's life—and death—in Eugene. Thus far she had only one solid entry point, Praveena Kapoor. Praveena could lead her to other members of the Cascaders Mountain Club in Eugene who might have known Nicole. A public appeal for assistance seemed like a good strategy, but it always yielded many false positives, leads that consumed time but went nowhere. The police would be screening those leads once Adam and Jessica distributed their publicity package to the media.

Jessica wondered if there was some way she could leverage what she knew about Nicole's personality and lifestyle to find other angles to pursue. She had read about some astonishing similarities between identical twins raised apart. Such cases were the subject of numerous research studies on the effects of "nature versus nurture."

She spent some time searching online to learn just how similar such twins could be. She discovered that twins separated at birth not only looked alike later in life but often shared many other characteristics as well: sexual orientation, health issues, habits like nail-biting (or playing with their hair when distracted, as she had already learned), and hobbies and interests. The similarities sometimes even extended to partner selection.

One article described two men who met randomly at a shared campsite while they were in separate groups paddling a wild and scenic stretch of Oregon's Rogue River. They observed that they both enjoyed kayaking the rivers, drank the same beer, enjoyed baseball to the extreme, and played in rock 'n' roll bands. They even bore a strong physical resemblance. One of the men knew he was adopted. Upon his return to civilization, the other one related this unusual encounter to his mother. She confessed, ashamed, that he did indeed have a twin brother. When the twins were born, the family simply could not care for both of them along with their six other children. They made the incredibly difficult decision to give one of the boys up for adoption. This chance meeting on the river revealed the close similarity between twins who had never known each other. That was the nature side of the equation.

Jessica also understood that a child's developmental environment and upbringing greatly affected her personality and health. Jessica came from a close-knit, financially stable family. Like her parents, she was warm and compassionate. In contrast, Nicole sounded more cynical and like more of a risk-taker. Her father drank; the family members fought. She and her brother were rebellious, drinking and partying from their teenage years. Jessica had already learned the Briggses were not as well off financially as the Sanfords, as Nicole had not had braces to straighten her teeth like Jessica had. Such differences reflect the impact of nurture—the context in which the child develops—upon the adult's behaviors, health, and appearance.

To get an idea of Nikki's likely lifestyle, Jessica reflected on her own hidden side. Her friends knew about Jessica's enthusiasm for outdoor activities. Some had accompanied her on mountain climbs in Oregon's Cascade Range and other adventures. However, not everybody knew she was bisexual, had some body art in rather private places, and enjoyed the club scene from time to time. She had been known to have one-night stands with both men and women.

Not even her close friends knew about her interest in having threesomes, though. What was more exciting than romping in bed with a man and a woman at the same time? Or on occasion, perhaps two men, or two women. She never invited her friends to participate in her threesomes; it was a greater thrill with strangers. When she got the urge, Jessica would visit a bar or dance club where she knew such opportunities were available. This was a dimension Jessica kept very much to herself.

Based on what Angela, Suzanne, and Praveena had told her, Jessica knew that Nikki reveled in the risk and the thrill of her wild side. Angela had said that Nikki sneaked into clubs when she was underage, going home with either a man or a woman as the mood struck her. Perhaps Nikki had gone home with the wrong person— or persons—one night in Eugene. Exploring Eugene's clubs and bars might be a starting point, especially if Praveena could tell her of some places Nikki had frequented.

Jessica contemplated the types of people she found appealing; perhaps Nikki was drawn to those same types. She found a website describing genetics studies that revealed how people were unconsciously attracted to those whose immune-system makeup was different from their own. This dissimilarity provided a reproductive advantage, because greater genetic diversity enhanced the process of natural selection that drove evolution.

Just in case there was anything to this theory of why opposites attract, Jessica mentally ran through the characteristics she found appealing. She favored tall, muscular Caucasian men. She was especially partial to blue-eyed blonds, although she wouldn't kick a man out of bed if he didn't qualify. You couldn't get much more of a contrast with her own attributes: a short Asian with black hair and brown eyes.

Jessica didn't have as much of a specific type when it came to women. Sometimes one caught her eye, sometimes another. Being stacked was a definite plus, and women with colorful tattoos were super-sexy. Was Nikki drawn to those same features? This was all a long shot, but all Jessica had at this stage were long shots.

The next phase of her investigation had to be in Eugene, assuming Nicole was living around there when she was killed. Jessica decided to spend some time trying to reconstruct her sister's final days in that city, with the ultimate goal of identifying, locating, and apprehending her killer, or killers.

A few minutes with her web browser suggested the Hideaway Inn as a reasonable place to stay in Eugene. The Hideaway was inexpensive and centrally located. Each unit had a kitchenette, so she could save money and time on meals. She made a reservation for one week, not knowing how long her mission might take.

*   *   *

Jessica walked into Maria's apartment for dinner late on Saturday afternoon with a chilled bottle of Riesling in hand. Maria looked to be feeling quite hale, other than still relying on crutches.

"How was your little party on Tuesday?" Jessica asked with a sarcastic edge in her voice.

"Oh, it was just a few of my friends from Great Northwestern Outfitters, nobody you know. I haven't seen them since I got hurt. It was fun. Too bad you couldn't come."

Jessica snorted. "I don't remember being invited." Maria did not react.

Maria had lined up the ingredients for dinner: tilapia fillets to be breaded and sautéed; russet baking potatoes; and a medley of fresh vegetables for steaming.

"Would you mind terribly assembling all this, Jess? I need a rest before dinner. I'm walking more every day to build my strength back, but I still get tired easily." Seeing Jessica's nod, Maria headed for the bedroom to lie down for a bit.

Jessica put the potatoes in the oven and poured herself a glass of the Riesling. She sipped as she caught up on email and flipped through some magazines from Maria's coffee table. The wine was delightful, just off-dry with an aromatic, fruity bouquet. The potatoes took long enough to bake that she needed a second glass of wine before preparing the fish and vegetables.

Maria woke up on her own just before seven and crutched into the kitchen.

"Mmm, that smells terrific. I've missed your cooking," she said. "And I'm glad I can finally drink wine again."

They both enjoyed the dinner. Plenty of leftovers remained. Jessica had no problem eating leftovers of something she enjoyed for days in a row. Maria had less tolerance for repetition. She could revisit the leftovers, but not until a day or two had passed.

Jessica washed the dishes as Maria finished her wine. As she cleaned, Jessica thought through her course of action once she got to Eugene. *Where to begin?*

Maria's voice interrupted her concentration. "Did you hear what I said, Jess?"

"Sorry, no. What was it?"

"I said, I've got a problem. All these medical bills are starting to come in now, like for my insurance deductible and co-pays. I don't have that much money saved, and I can't go back to work for weeks yet. I don't know what to do. Are you even listening to me?"

Jessica finished up the dishes and dried her hands. "Yeah, I'm listening. That really sucks, Maria. But look, I have to go to Eugene again to see if I can find anyone who knew Nikki and might know what happened to her. I leave tomorrow."

"Jesus Christ, I've had it! You've been in and out of here for weeks. Now you're not even paying attention when I'm trying to tell you really important shit. All you can talk about is Nikki, Nikki, Nikki. I'm fucking sick of it! You want to chase down this woman from five years ago? Fine, go to it. But you're going to need a new girlfriend when you come back."

Jessica stood in stunned silence at Maria's tirade. She had a point. Jessica *had* been neglecting Maria recently with her focus on the search. Maria was still in a bind, trapped on crutches for another month and now maybe headed for financial worries. Jessica simply could not turn her back on her twin sister, though. Whether Maria understood or not, Nicole was her priority right now.

"I hear you," Jessica replied calmly. "I'll take my things home tonight. I'm sorry it came down to this. But I'm going to Eugene tomorrow." Jessica removed Maria's apartment key from her key ring and set it on the dinette table without a word. She carried clothing, toiletries, and some other personal items out to her car.

Breaking up was always hard. This was the right step, though. Maria had been becoming increasingly challenging, even before the accident. The fun they had together no longer outweighed the stresses of the relationship.

Jessica drove home, leaving no vestige of herself at Maria's apartment besides cold tilapia. She felt slightly sad, but also liberated.

When she got home, Jessica emailed the Meals on Wheels coordinator at the Rosemount Senior Center. She apologetically told Kathleen she had to give up her route for a few weeks and described the quest that had been consuming her. She would let Kathleen know as soon as she was available to resume her commitment.

In just twenty minutes she received a response. To her surprise, Kathleen shared that she too was adopted. This had never come up in their conversations before. Kathleen understood the importance of the mission and wished Jessica the best of luck. Kathleen's understanding and encouragement soothed some of the guilt Jessica felt about bailing on her volunteer responsibility.

*   *   *

On Sunday Jessica packed for her trip to Eugene. She took enough clothing for a week. Eugene was only two hours from home. She could come back if necessary, but it wasn't as easy as just bopping across town. Plus the drive was boring. She made all the other arrangements required for her extended absence: asked her neighbors Matt and Kira to pick up the mail, paid those accumulated bills that weren't on autopay, and checked in with everyone who required checking in with, including her parents to let them know where she would be. Her father asked if she had enough money to cover her expenses in Eugene.

"Actually, this trip will put a big dent into my savings. I haven't done any work for a few weeks, either. I hate to ask, but might you be able to float me some more funds please, Dad?"

"Of course, honey. That's what we're here for. You have a house payment coming up soon, I imagine. Would $3,000 be enough for now?"

Jessica's warm glow of gratitude competed with her discomfort at not being entirely self-sufficient at her age. These were unusual circumstances, though.

"That would be fantastic, thank you so much. I cannot tell you how much your support means to me. Please tell Mom thanks too."

Jessica decided to take along her workout clothes. Her fitness center had a branch in Eugene she could use, and she could also do some running to stay in shape. Anticipating that she would be connecting with some Cascaders in Eugene, she stuffed hiking necessities into her day pack and put it in the car trunk. Finally she texted Praveena Kapoor that she would be in Eugene for the next week and looked forward to connecting with her.

Sunday afternoon Jessica drove to Eugene and checked in to the Hideaway Inn. The building was tired, but her room was clean, quiet, and reasonably equipped; it would do. There was a convenience store on the corner next to the motel, but Jessica was hungry. She found a Red Robin restaurant nearby. *Sometimes you just need a cheeseburger and fries*, she thought.

That night she turned on the television in the motel room and unplugged her mind. Fortunately the motel offered free HBO. It had been too long since she had vegged out in front of the screen for a few hours. She would need her brain in the coming week; no need to wear it out tonight.

Chapter 24

Monday, June 18

JESSICA WAS EAGER to solve this crime so she could return home to
Rosemount, sleep in her own bed, and get on with her life, albeit a
life that would never be quite the same. This reconstruction case had
revealed an entire new dimension of her reality. Helping to find
whoever had killed and buried her twin sister was all she could do
now to strengthen her ties to Nicole.

She decided to launch the next stage of her investigation at the
Lorane County Sheriff's Office, so she headed there first thing in
the morning. Adam was away working on another case. At Jessica's
request, he had pulled out all records the sheriff's office had on the
case. The deputy at the front desk led her to an interview room and
left her with the box of case materials to pore over.

Jessica began with the county medical examiner's report. She
had never read the full report before, just heard Adam's summary in
their first meeting nearly six weeks ago. The report held no sur-
prises, nothing new that would assist her. Cutting through the medical jargon, it boiled down to: this woman likely died from either the
big hole in her head or a broken neck.

She turned to the police report. She knew the broad strokes, but
the details regarding how the bones had been discovered were new
to her. Perhaps she could ask Professor Terry Engelman, whose dog

found the remains, to show her the burial site. Jessica wanted to build as complete a picture as possible of her twin's last hours.

Otherwise she already knew everything in the police report. Much of it was based on her own contributions to the case: the facial reconstruction, the skull X-ray comparison that established the likely twin relationship, the web of adoption connections that led to the victim's name and to her mother, the dental X-rays that finally confirmed the victim's identity.

Jessica had a thought. Even though the body was discovered in rural Lorane County, Nicole probably lived somewhere in Eugene. Maybe she had had some police interactions in Eugene that were on record. Given her taste for the wild side, it was not impossible. She left a note for Adam:

> Could you please check with Eugene PD to see if Nicole Marie Briggs had any run-ins with them? Citations, arrests, jaywalking, anything? Maybe also check with the university's PD. She could have got caught up in a party sweep on campus or something. Thanks. J.

Jessica walked back out to her car. She called Terry Engelman at his office and introduced herself.

"I'm working with the Lorane County Sheriff's Office on the case of the remains you discovered on your property on Redhawk Road in April," she said.

"Yes, Detective Longsdale told me about you. I check in with him periodically to see if there's been any progress on the case. You performed the forensic facial reconstruction, right? How did that work out?"

Jessica summarized the reconstruction's stunning outcome and how that had eventually led to identifying the victim's remains.

"That's an extraordinary story. This has to be a tough case for you, and such a shock to learn about your twin. How are you handling all of this, Jessica?"

"You know, you're the first person besides my mother who's asked me that. You're right, it *was* an incredible shock. I'm still trying to process it all. I've learned a lot about my own background I never would have known otherwise."

"Well, I appreciate the update, Jessica. Was there some other reason you called?"

"There was. This might seem like a strange request, but could you please show me where you found Nicole's remains? It's not just morbid curiosity. I'm here in Eugene trying to understand her life and her last days. I might as well start with the little we know for sure, which is where she was buried."

"That's not strange at all. Hang on a second." Terry paused, and Jessica heard papers rustling. "I don't have to teach any classes this afternoon. Would one o'clock work for you?"

"That's perfect. Thanks a lot, Dr. Engelman. Where should I meet you?"

"Call me Terry. If you can come to my office on the University of Oregon campus, I'll drive us over to my property and show you what happened."

He gave her directions to his office in Klamath Hall. Jessica thanked him and hung up. She mentally prepared herself for the emotions she would doubtless feel as she viewed the grave site.

Jessica's next called Silvia Miranova, who also had an office on campus. She wanted to touch base with the forensic anthropology professor.

"Jessica, how nice to hear from you," Silvia said. "Adam has been updating me on all the progress you've made. It's exciting that you were able to find so many people connected to the victim and get a positive ID on the remains. Congratulations!"

"Thanks, Silvia. I really appreciated your corroboration of my reconstruction. Even Adam believes Nicole and I were twins now. Would it be all right if I stopped by to say hello this afternoon?"

"Sure, it would be great to see you. I'm free any time after three thirty." She told Jessica how to find her office.

*   *   *

After a quick deli lunch of tuna salad on a pumpernickel bagel and a diet Mountain Dew, Jessica met Terry at his office in Klamath Hall. He led the way to his faded green Subaru Forester in the faculty parking lot.

"Sorry about all the dog hair," he apologized. "My year-old Labrador retriever, Chloe, thinks this is her car. She sits wherever she wants to. Sometimes she lets me drive."

It took twenty-five minutes to reach Terry's wooded property about ten miles southwest of Eugene. Terry carefully turned from Redhawk Road onto a narrow rutted lane. He drove past the decrepit fence with its crooked "Private Property No Trespassing This Means You" sign and stopped after thirty seconds of bumps and jostles. He told Jessica that he and his wife had postponed their plans for building their dream house on this private and peaceful lot. Although they didn't believe in ghosts, the knowledge of what had happened there might haunt them as long as they owned the land.

Jessica climbed out of Terry's car and looked around. The idyllic setting smelled like the world's largest air freshener. Tall fir trees stood in clusters, boughs swaying and moaning in the gentle breeze. She could hear no human noises other than their own, not even cars on a distant highway. She admired the spectacular view out over the Lorane Valley, with the low mountains of the Oregon Coast Range poking through the haze.

Terry led the way through the underbrush to the back corner of the plot, where Chloe had discovered the grave. Along the way he described that fateful day.

"Chloe and I came out here to play, like we usually do on the weekends. Being a retriever, she likes to chase things. My part of the game is to throw her blue rubber ball into the woods. Her part is to bring it back. But one time she brought back a piece of a rib bone instead of the ball."

Terry caught himself, looking embarrassed after so casually describing the random bit of bone that had belonged to the body of his guest's sister.

"Anyway," he continued as they walked further into the woods, "I went over to where the ball had landed and I saw bones sticking up out of the ground, in this little clearing over here on the left. When I saw a skull, I knew they were human remains, so I called the police right away."

As the case was still open, the area was marked off with yellow police crime scene tape wrapped around several trees. Jessica stood at the tape line with Terry and gazed into the shallow grave. She saw the signs of excavation where the police had scoured the ground for any clues to the identity of either the victim or the perpetrator.

The enormity of the scene was too much for Jessica. She began to cry, overwhelmed. This was the final resting place of her closest relative in the world. Terry gently put his arm around Jessica to comfort her. He didn't say anything.

The two walked back to the Subaru in silence. Terry drove them back toward the campus.

"Do you know how long the police will leave the yellow tape up?" Jessica asked. "I imagine it's difficult for you, the constant reminder that someone was buried on your property and the fact that you can't go into that area for now."

"I guess until the case is closed," Terry said. "But what if it's never closed? I know you and the police will do your best, but we all know not every cold case gets solved. At some point I imagine they'll decide it's no longer worth pursuing and give me my chunk of land back. It's okay with me, though. I do hope you learn what happened to your sister."

Shortly before four o'clock, Terry pulled back into his parking space and told Jessica goodbye. She thanked him for giving her this deeply emotional, and meaningful, experience.

Jessica walked toward Silvia's office. The University of Oregon campus was nicely treed with plenty of open green spaces. Jessica always enjoyed the distinctive feel of walking on a college campus.

Before she reached Silvia's building, her phone rang—she saw the caller was Adam.

"That was a good suggestion to check with the Eugene PD, Jessica. My contact there found one minor marijuana citation for Nicole, quantity for personal consumption from before it was legal for recreational use. One shoplifting bust, charges dropped. She also had six unpaid parking tickets over a span of five to seven years ago. Your sister was something of a scofflaw, my friend."

"That paper trail might be useful at some point. Thanks, Adam. Do you think the EPD has any jurisdiction here? Should they take over the case or help us with it?"

"We have no evidence she was connected to any crime inside the city limits. Therefore Lorane County still has sole jurisdiction. EPD did agree to cooperate with us if the right situation arises."

"Are you still planning to distribute the materials for the public campaign tomorrow? I'd be happy to help."

"Sure, come on over in the morning. I'll be in my office. I know you're really motivated for this, Jessica, but don't get your hopes too high. Crimes this old, with so little evidence, are nearly impossible to solve. We'll give it our best shot with the resources we have available. Just be realistic, please."

*   *   *

By the time she hung up with Adam, Jessica had reached Condon Hall, home of the Department of Anthropology. She found Silvia's office on the third floor. The two women greeted each other warmly. Silvia's office was lined with bookshelves filled with volumes on anthropology, archaeology, forensic science, chemistry, and biology. Her oversized desk bore mounds of papers in tidy stacks.

Jessica filled Silvia in on her reason for being in Eugene and her busy day so far. Silvia understood why her visit to the grave site was both necessary and poignant.

With some hesitation, Silvia cocked her head and said, "I'm not sure how you will react to this, Jessica, but I want to give you the option. If you like, I can drive you to the medical examiner's office and you can view Nicole Briggs's actual remains. It's up to you."

Jessica exhaled audibly. It was one thing to peer into an empty grave. It was quite another to view what used to be in that grave. She had put in many hours and traveled many miles during the past six weeks in search of her twin. Perhaps it was time to meet her in person. With some trepidation, Jessica replied simply, "Yes, please."

Silvia stood from behind her desk and limped around it, touching Jessica gently on the arm as she passed by. She took a cane from an umbrella stand near the door and walked carefully into the hall.

"Did you hurt your leg?" Jessica asked with concern.

"I was in a severe auto accident when I was twenty-seven. That's how I got the scars on my face and arm." Silvia raised her left arm to show Jessica the grooved scar she had noticed in their first meeting. "My leg was broken in several places. Usually it's not too bad, but sometimes it aches, like today. The cane helps."

Silvia walked with Jessica to her car and drove to the Lorane County Medical Examiner's Office, just ten minutes across town. She explained the purpose of her visit to the receptionist on duty, who knew Silvia from her forensic anthropology work. The receptionist led the two women to a back room labeled Osteology Room. The chilly room held a faint smell of musty earth. The receptionist removed a dark-blue cardboard box from one of the many gray metal shelves that lined the walls and placed it on a large table in the middle of the room. She stepped out quietly and closed the door.

Jessica shivered, wishing she had brought a jacket. Silvia handed her a pair of purple nitrile gloves and donned a pair herself. She looked over at Jessica.

"Are you sure you want to do this?" she asked.

Jessica met her eyes. After a moment, she nodded.

Silvia removed the lid from the box and stepped back. Jessica saw it was filled with yellowed bones, apparently a complete skeleton. She took a sharp breath involuntarily. Sitting in the middle of the box was an intact skull, the same skull for which she had an exact replica in her studio.

"Nikki," she breathed. "It's you."

Jessica stared at the remains for a full minute, absorbing the emotional impact of the moment. Her heart pounded. She reached out her hand and gently stroked the skull, imagining the terror Nicole must have felt in the moments before her death. Her fingers brushed against the triangular hole on the left side of her temple.

"Who could have done this to you?" Jessica whispered. "Why?"

Silvia stayed back, giving Jessica this priceless time alone with the twin sister she never met in life.

Finally Jessica nodded again and said, "Okay." Silvia gently replaced the lid on the box. Jessica turned to the older woman and hugged her.

"Thank you for this, Silvia," she said quietly through the lump in her throat. "It means more than I can say."

Chapter 25

Tuesday, June 19

ADAM AND JESSICA convened on Tuesday morning to launch the campaign to seek members of the public who had known Nicole Briggs. They started with the Eugene-area television affiliates for the four major networks, NBC, ABC, CBS, and FOX. The TV stations would probably only air brief segments during their local news broadcasts on a single day. That would generate a handful of exposures at morning and midday, in the evening, and late at night. Each airing could show just one or two photos and provide a very brief description of the case.

Adam asked the various stations' news departments to stagger their broadcasts about the case, spreading them over several days to increase the chance of viewers catching at least one of the spots. However, no news outlet wanted to get scooped on any story, no matter how small. None of the station personnel he spoke to could guarantee when they would run the segments.

The network affiliates all agreed to post detailed versions of the story on their websites, based on the media package Adam and Jessica had assembled. On their websites they could present multiple photos of the women, along with more extensive information about the case. Many people got their news online instead of from the TV, and online stories could persist for weeks, potentially reaching more people than the television broadcasts.

They also distributed the materials to several local newspapers. The *Eugene Times-Chronicle* had the largest circulation of any print media in the area. The *Willamette Valley Weekly* was a more specialized arts-and-entertainment-oriented paper. If Nicole had engaged with the arts community around Eugene, some readers of the *Valley Weekly* might know her. The *Springfield Update* was directed at residents of Springfield, the second-largest city in the Eugene metropolitan area with a population of some sixty thousand. Like the TV stations, newspapers could post longer articles on their websites and keep them visible indefinitely.

Finally Adam asked the city police departments in Eugene, Springfield, and Cottage Grove, as well as county sheriffs' departments throughout west-central Oregon, to post the full media package on their websites. That would spread the word broadly in case Nicole had spent much time outside the Eugene area.

As it had been around five years since Nicole disappeared, neither the Lorane County Sheriff's Office nor the Eugene Police Department expected to receive many tips. They could anticipate some excited pronouncements from people who saw space aliens—and maybe Nicole—behind every tree. There would be well-intended though fruitless pointers to Asian women who only vaguely resembled Nicole/Jessica. Each call demanded follow-up though. You never knew when one of them would turn out to be the key.

*   *   *

Just before noon, Adam received a call from Mary Brighthaven, a producer at KEUO-TV, Eugene's NBC affiliate. Mary said she found Nicole Briggs's story tragic and Jessica Sanford's investigation inspiring. She wanted to produce a story about the case to air on their local news broadcasts and asked if Adam could help arrange an interview.

Adam turned to Jessica, who was still in his office. "You'll want to hear this," he said. He put his phone on speaker. "Mary, could you please repeat for Jessica what you just said to me?"

Mary reiterated her request and asked if the two of them were available for an interview that afternoon. KEUO wanted to air the story within a few days to augment the brief public service spots Adam and Jessica had already set up.

Jessica looked at Adam nervously. She had been interviewed before regarding her reconstructions, yet she wasn't totally comfortable in front of a camera. Her afternoon was open though. The story could provide great visibility, possibly drawing out others who remembered Nicole. She nodded her agreement.

Adam spoke into the phone. "That sounds good, Mary. How about two o'clock? Should we come to your studio?"

Mary said, "Excellent! I think this will be a terrific story. If it's all right with you, I'd like to shoot it at the sheriff's office to get the atmosphere I'm going for. We can be there about two thirty to set up. Our feature reporter, Jacqui Randazzo, will handle the interview. We should only need about two hours in all. Does that work for both of you?"

"It does. We'll be here and ready to show some visual aids, like the facial reconstruction Jessica performed that was the key to identifying the victim. Thanks for your call, Mary. We're trying hard to discover who killed Nicole Briggs. This story just might help." He turned off the speakerphone.

Jessica let out her breath. "Oh my," she said with more than a hint of panic. "I don't know if I'm ready for this. I didn't bring along clothes for a TV interview."

"Don't worry so much, Jessica," Adam replied soothingly. "You've done this sort of thing before. You'll do fine. Your clothes are fine. It will all be fine."

"But this gives me hardly any time to think about what I want to say!"

"Don't sweat it. All you have to do is answer the reporter's questions and tell your story. It's a friendly interview, and it's a hell of a story. With your passion for the case, the tenacity you showed in your investigation, and the visuals from your laptop, this will be a snap. Enjoy it! Not everybody gets to be on TV."

Jessica felt a little calmer. She began arranging the key files to be ready to show during the interview. Adam was right; she knew how to do this. And if it would help them find Nicole's killer she couldn't say no. Adam ordered them lunch from a sandwich shop so they could continue working until the TV people arrived.

*   *   *

Jessica's phone rang while they were eating. She saw the call was from Praveena Kapoor, the only one of Nikki's Facebook friends who still lived in Eugene.

"Hi, Jessica. I hope you're making progress in Eugene. Would you like to come to a ramble with the Cascaders tonight? Every Tuesday we do a low-key hike for a couple of hours. Tonight we're going through Alton Baker Park. This is more social than cardio. The park is flat, but it's quite pretty. You could meet some other Cascaders who might remember Nikki."

"Sure, thanks for the invitation. When and where should I meet you all?"

Praveena suggested she join the group by six o'clock in the park's community garden parking lot, on the north bank of the Willamette River that runs through Eugene.

Jessica smiled at Adam. "I feel like we're gaining momentum now," she said. "This might not be as impossible as we feared."

Mary Brighthaven and Jacqui Randazzo arrived just before two thirty, along with a cameraman. Just as Adam had promised, Jessica did a fine job.

Jacqui had a warm, sympathetic manner. She began taping the interview with Adam, who recapped how the remains were discovered and the highlights of Silvia's anthropological analysis. Jessica then described her work on the reconstruction and the shock of seeing her own face looking out from the computer screen. Jacqui skillfully walked Jessica through the steps in her investigation. Adam summarized how the dental X-rays provided the final proof of the victim's identity. He pointed out that they were still awaiting the DNA test results to prove whether Jessica and Nicole were indeed identical twins or if they were related in some different way.

When the taping was completed a little before five, both Mary and Jacqui said they were delighted at how the session had gone. Mary said, "That was fantastic, both of you. We're planning for this to be our second story on the six o'clock news on Thursday unless we're invaded by Martians or something between now and then. Thank you both for participating on such short notice."

"It was our pleasure," Adam said. "Anything that might help solve this case is fine with me."

*   *   *

Jessica had just enough time to drive back to the Hideaway Inn, inhale some dinner, change into hiking clothes, and race to Alton Baker Park. She parked near a cluster of people carrying water bottles. As she got out of the car, an athletic-looking, dark-skinned Indian woman waved and walked toward her.

"Hi, Jessica, I'm Praveena," she said as they shook hands. Praveena had a broad face with full lips and thick eyebrows. "My God, you do look amazingly like I remember Nikki. I'm glad you could come tonight."

A short, blond woman wearing hiking shorts and a tank top got out of her car several spaces away. She stared at Praveena and Jessica. Leaving the car door open, she ran across the lot calling, "Nikki! You're back!" As she drew closer, arms outstretched for a hug, she halted in confusion.

Jessica smiled wistfully as the blond woman dropped her arms, puzzlement wrinkling her brow. "I'm sorry to startle you. I'm not Nikki. I'm her twin sister, Jessica."

"Oh, I'm so sorry. You look just like Nikki."

Jessica was getting used to that reaction by now. It reminded her of a friend in college who had an identical twin who lived in another city. Jessica met him once when he came to visit his brother. Even when she was expecting it, it was startling to see a duplicate of someone she knew well. She had kept looking from one to the other, comparing and contrasting their features, wondering what the one she didn't know was like. She felt odd being on the other side of that situation now.

The blond woman said, "I didn't realize she had a twin sister. I'm Stephanie. Nikki and I used to go on rambles all the time, but I haven't seen her for years. Where is she? Is she coming tonight?"

A gentle sadness washed over Jessica. She said, "It's very nice to meet you, Stephanie. I'm afraid I have some bad news though. Nikki is dead."

Stephanie slumped against Jessica's car, and Jessica put an arm around her for support.

Jessica continued, "She didn't even know she had a twin sister. I didn't know it myself until recently. It's a long story. I'm working with the Lorane County Sheriff's Office on the case. I'm afraid it appears to be a homicide."

"How awful," Stephanie said, voice cracking. "Nikki was so much fun. Why would someone want to kill her?"

"We don't know yet. That's why I'm here tonight. I'm hoping to meet people who knew her to get some clues that might help us discover what happened. Maybe you can help us. We can talk as we walk, okay? I don't want to hold up the group."

Praveena introduced Jessica to the other ramblers as they walked briskly through the beautiful park. Many other people were enjoying the comfortable June evening there as well, running and biking on the trails or paddling on the canoe canal. Others just absorbed the colors and smells of the well-manicured landscaping, the flower beds in full bloom, and the newly-mown lawns. Families with small children threw bread to the ducks in the pond. Whenever Jessica saw that, she wondered why people thought bread was part of a duck's natural diet.

Jessica explained to the group why she was in Eugene and asked if anyone else remembered Nikki Briggs. A few did, vaguely. She learned Nikki was not an official member of the Cascaders. She had gotten to know several of the regulars and sometimes participated in their activities. No one remembered anyone in particular who hung out with Nikki, nor anyone with whom she had had any apparent conflict. She came to their events for a while, and then she didn't anymore.

Stephanie and Praveena were among the Cascaders who would often go out for a drink or two after a ramble. *Half the fun of adult athletics is drinking afterward,* Jessica mused. They remembered some bars and nightclubs where Nikki liked to go with them, because those were still their regular post-event meeting locations. The places they mentioned were Dark Horse, the Main Street Pub, Manhattan Bar, Ruby Slippers, The Grog, and Bogie's Gin Joint. Jessica wrote those names on a small notepad she had brought along. Visiting such establishments would be a good starting point for her search.

As they approached the parking lot where they began, Jessica thanked the others for letting her join them and pick their brains. She passed out her business card and Adam's and asked everyone to contact her if they thought of any other information that might be helpful to the investigation.

Jessica spoke with Praveena and Stephanie for a few minutes after all the others had gone. She asked if they knew where Nikki had worked around Eugene.

Stephanie said, "I don't think Nikki ever had a steady job here. One day I saw her working as a barista at the Use Your Bean coffee shop by the U of O. She looked cute in her apron." She smiled as she remembered. "She did some waitressing too, I think maybe at the Paradise Sidewalk Café. And once I noticed she had paint splotches on her hands when we went on a ramble. She said she was doing some house painting for a friend because she needed the money. I don't know who the friend was."

Praveena invited Jessica to join some Cascaders for a hike on Saturday. The hiking group was more hardcore than the lower-key ramblers. The ramblers were more interested in the friendly Tuesday evening get-togethers than in raising pulses and burning calories. Praveena recalled that Nikki was into the more energetic activities, so Saturday's hike could draw more people who knew her than the ramble had. The hike would be up Spencer Butte, a serious climb compared to the easy walk in Alton Baker Park. Jessica promised to be there. She needed the exercise as well as the diversion.

*   *   *

Jessica's mother phoned shortly after she returned to the Hideaway Inn. "Hi, Jessie. Dad and I just wanted to know how things are going for you in Eugene."

"There's not much to report yet, Mom. It's a slow process. But I am going to be on TV later this week." She described her interview and how she and Adam had launched the media campaign. Jessica also told Sharon about her sobering visits to Nicole's grave site and the medical examiner's office.

"So far we've just been trying to find some threads to start pulling on to see if there's anything useful on the other end. We're working very hard at it. I'll be here as long as it takes to get some answers about Nicole."

"Try not to wear yourself out, honey. I know how seriously you take things and how important it is to you that they come out just perfectly."

"I just have high standards. If I do something, I want to do it as well as I possibly can. What's wrong with that?"

"Nothing, unless it makes you crazy or burns you out. Do you remember the final art project your senior year of high school? You lost points for turning it in late because you didn't want to hand in something if it wasn't perfect. Sometimes perfect is the enemy of good. Sometimes good enough is, well, good enough."

"I hear you, Mom," Jessica replied. "I haven't gotten into this far enough yet to see whether we're going to hit pay dirt or not. We're grasping at straws until we start getting some calls from the public. I'll keep you posted."

Jessica had to admit her mother had a point. Perfectionism had always been one of her less attractive features. She wouldn't apologize for it though. True, perfectionists could be hard on the people around them. Maria certainly hadn't appreciated Jessica's fine-tuning attempts. However, this case demanded everything Jessica could put into it. She owed it to Nicole's memory and to Suzanne Briggs. If solving this case required that she be a perfectionist, so be it.

Chapter 26

Wednesday, June 20

JESSICA DRESSED FOR a run, and before she warmed up with some calisthenics and stretching, she flipped through the early-morning local TV programs. She caught the publicity spot about Nicole on channel 8, where the announcer said they had first aired the story during their news report the previous evening. Jessica found it odd to see her photo on TV, standing in for a twin sister she had never met. If all went well, all four channels would broadcast the same spots throughout the day on their local news reports. She planned to check out the channels' websites later to see just what they had posted about the story.

Before she hit the sidewalk, Jessica scanned the newspapers in the motel's lobby. All had printed largely the same story based on the media information package she and Adam had assembled. All of them had printed the shot of the real Nicole from her Facebook page along with at least one photo of Jessica from a different angle.

Jessica enjoyed running outdoors in the morning coolness. A run was a good way to become familiar with her temporary neighborhood. Her route took her along the shaded city sidewalks through quiet neighborhoods of single-family homes, apartment buildings, and convenience stores. The forecast was unusually warm for late June, but the temperature before eight in the morning was perfect for working up a sweat without dehydrating. She could remember years in Portland when she was still wearing long sleeves for Fourth of July fireworks. The extra warmth that came from being a little farther south right now was fine with her.

She wrapped up her twenty-five-minute run with a hundred-yard sprint back to her motel. Jessica walked around the block to cool down and catch her breath before going inside to get dressed and eat breakfast.

The quiet Hideaway Inn had proven to be a good choice. The kitchenette was well-stocked with dishes, cookware, cups and glasses, and cutlery. She had picked up some essentials at a local supermarket: two boxes of cereal, milk, orange juice (real orange juice, not that frozen concentrated stuff), fresh fruit, whole-wheat bread, almond butter, and some cherry preserves. Those supplies would keep her in breakfasts and lunches for a few days, provided she could have something more interesting for supper. Fast and cheap: a perfect combination.

*   *   *

Adam called Jessica just before ten in the morning. "I don't know if you saw any of the segments on TV. All four stations are airing them now in their news blocks. We're starting to get some calls. One of our deputies is doing a first-cut screening on them so you and I don't chase our tails too much."

"I did see one before I went out for a run. Do any of the calls sound promising yet?"

"Not yet. It's still early. These public campaigns have a common pattern. We get a bunch of worthless calls right away. Some come from kooks who get off on wasting our time and others from people who are clearly delusional or mentally ill. Some people look for any excuse to talk to the police, for reasons I've never understood."

"How long does it usually take to start getting useful leads?" Jessica asked. She hadn't participated directly in a public-appeal campaign before, so the details were all new to her.

Adam said, "The junk usually quiets down after a day or two, and then we start getting some prospects worth looking into. Sometimes we never get any useful calls at all. This is the oldest case we've publicized like this. We just have to be patient. How is your own search going? Did you get anything from the Cascaders?"

Jessica perked up. "I did. On the ramble last night I met some people who knew Nicole, although not well. She sometimes went drinking with them afterward. They gave me the names of several bars and clubs they used to visit. I'll start checking those out today. Which brings me to a slightly delicate point." Jessica told Adam about the research she had done on the similarities of identical twins raised apart. She described her theory that Nikki might have been attracted to the same types of people that she was. Maybe she could use that information to focus her search for people Nikki might have met, perhaps to her detriment.

"I never told you, Adam, but I'm bisexual. I have a girlfriend in Portland—well, I did until last weekend anyway. We just broke up. I learned from Angela Montgomery that Nikki was also bi. I'm assuming she liked to hook up with both men and women, maybe even together, whom she met at a bar or a nightclub. I have some ideas of the types of men and women she might have liked."

"Your personal life makes no difference to me," Adam replied. "If your theory helps us find her killer, I'm down with it."

"I don't know Eugene very well yet. Do you know of bars and nightclubs that might be appealing for someone looking for those sorts of rather transient relationships? I could check out any places that particularly cater to the hookup scene."

"I'll check with my contacts in the EPD and get you a list. I'll also keep you updated as we look into leads that come out of the publicity campaign."

Jessica sat down with her laptop to look at the online media outlets where the public-appeal materials should be up. She also wanted to build her own list of some drinking establishments to visit today, beginning with the six from the Cascaders. She began to sketch out an itinerary to make the tedious quest more efficient. A university city the size of Eugene offered a lot of places to drink.

*   *   *

Jessica's phone rang. She glanced at the caller ID, but the caller's number wasn't shown. She answered the phone and heard nothing. No one responded to her multiple hellos. After a few seconds she shrugged and hung up.

Ten seconds later the phone rang again.

"Hello?" she answered. Nothing. "Is anyone there? Can you hear me? I can't hear you."

No response, not even breathing. She hung up again. Cellular signals were notoriously fickle.

Ten seconds later her phone rang. She picked up but didn't say anything. Nobody there. Either something was wrong with her phone or something was wrong with the caller's phone—or some jerk was playing a not-amusing trick on her. She waited a full twenty seconds in silence. The call disconnected.

Ten seconds later her phone rang. She snatched it up.

"What do you want, asshole?" she shouted. "Say something or leave me the fuck alone."

A tentative voice asked, "Nikki? Is that you?"

A chill ran down Jessica's spine. "No, this is Jessica. Who are you?"

"Nikki, this is Brian. Do you remember me?"

The chill deepened. This had to be Brian Stark, Angela's older brother who had raped Nikki back in Billings eighteen years earlier.

"Brian, this is not Nikki. My name is Jessica. How did you get this number?"

"From your brother, Steven. We've been in touch ever since I left Billings. Your mother gave him your number in case he wanted to talk to you. He didn't, but I do."

This didn't sound like the picture of an angry and violent Brian Stark that Angela and Adam had painted for her. This sounded like a confused, perhaps delusional, man.

"As I told you, I am not Nikki. Steven is not my brother. I'm afraid Nikki is dead. What do you want, Brian? Where are you?"

"Don't you worry about where I am. No one knows where I am. Why do you keep saying your name is Jessica? If you're not Nikki, why do you sound so much like her?"

"I am Nikki's twin sister. I didn't even know about Nikki until a few weeks ago. Do you know what happened to her?"

"Oh, yes, I know all about what happened to Nikki. But do you, *Jessica*? Do you know just what happened to Nikki?"

Now Jessica was getting scared. Was this man playing a game with her? Was he mentally ill? Was he a sociopath, trying to get under her skin? She wasn't sure how to handle any of those scenarios. She decided to play it straight with him for now.

"I don't know exactly what happened to her, but I'm trying to find out. Can you tell me, Brian? Did you hurt Nikki?"

"She said I hurt her, but I didn't. It was her fault. She wanted it. Then the bitch blamed me. She ruined my life. I found her, though. It took years, but I found her. If you're her twin, like you say you are, you're probably just as much of a man-hater as Nikki. I can find you too."

The call disconnected.

Jessica set the phone down with a shaking hand. Brian clearly harbored rage toward Nikki, even after all these years. Perhaps Brian *did* kill Nikki. Maybe her own safety also was at risk. Brian had blocked his caller ID, so she didn't know what number he had called from. He could be in Eugene, around the corner and ready to strike, or halfway across the country, making idle threats. She had no clue.

She called Adam and described the frightening call. He had dealt with threatening phone calls before in his nearly two decades on the force. They were almost always just for harassment and intimidation; the caller rarely followed through with physical harm.

Occasionally they did, though, so he took the call seriously. Adam said he would ask her cell phone carrier for information about the source of Brian's call. He would also send Jessica the mugshots from Brian's recent arrests so she would know what he looked like.

Jessica phoned Angela in Richland to tell her about Brian's call. Angela said she was shocked that Brian had learned about Jessica, obtained her phone number, and placed the intimidating calls.

"How did he even know how to reach you?" Angela wondered.

"Brian said he got my name and phone number from Nikki's brother, Steven. I think their mother must have told Steven about me. I have to say, Angela, his behavior shook me up. Does Brian have any history of mental illness?"

"Not as far as I know. He always was short-tempered and unpredictable, but that's not necessarily a sign of mental illness. The way you describe his call doesn't sound like something I'd expect from him though."

"How worried should I be about him? Is he dangerous?"

"I don't think Brian would actually hurt you. However, people do change. Remember, I don't know him well now."

Angela's comments weren't much comfort to Jessica. She looked across her motel room to make sure the door was locked, deadbolt in position, and security chain hooked. Brian apparently was still fixated on Nikki, so it didn't help that Jessica looked just like her twin. Angela said she didn't know where Brian was now and that Jessica should be careful in Eugene. She offered to send some pictures of Brian so Jessica could keep an eye out for him.

Jessica's pulse gradually drifted back toward its normal sixty beats per minute. She might want to ask Adam about carrying a weapon. She had qualified on handguns when she worked for the Boise Police Department several years earlier. She also still had a valid concealed-carry permit, although she had never owned nor carried a pistol. As she was now an authorized deputy sheriff in Lorane County, she could legally carry a firearm. That might be a little extreme at this stage, she thought.

She decided to continue with her investigation but to pay more careful attention to the people around her as she walked through the city. She'd look for anyone who seemed to be following her and be wary of anyone who appeared excessively interested in the case. Jessica smiled wryly to herself as she remembered the old saying that you're not paranoid if they really *are* out to get you.

*   *   *

In the middle of the afternoon, Jessica gathered her courage and stepped out into the warm sunshine to begin visiting drinking establishments. Three of the places where the Cascaders used to congregate were located around the University of Oregon campus, two were in downtown Eugene, and the sixth, the Ruby Slippers Club, was on the south side of the city.

She decided to start near the university. Jessica charted a walking path that would take her past Dark Horse, The Grog, and Bogie's Gin Joint. The area contained other bars besides those three. She might as well check all of the ones she encountered along the way. She found a parking space and put three hours on the meter.

Jessica walked into Dark Horse first. The club should have been called Dark Room. She could hardly see after stepping inside from the bright sunlight, even after removing her sunglasses. As her eyes adapted to the dimness, she saw that only a handful of patrons were present at this time of the afternoon. Some sat on stools at the bar, and a few more were shooting pool in the back. She spotted one bartender and a single waitress. Both looked to be no older than twenty-five. That wouldn't help, as they would have been too young to work in an establishment serving alcohol five years earlier, when Nikki might have been a patron.

She hadn't considered that constraint before. Not only did she need to identify likely establishments, she needed to speak with people there who were old enough to have potentially been on staff several years ago. She made a note to return to Dark Horse later in the evening to try to reach more experienced staff.

Jessica walked down the sidewalk toward The Grog, three blocks away. The area she passed through was a typical university campus–town district. She walked past an assortment of small businesses, bookstores, bars, and restaurants that catered mainly to students, along with two legal cannabis shops. She didn't know if Nikki had been into drugs at all, other than the old marijuana citation Adam had reported. No one so far had said anything about Nikki having serious drug issues; that might be worth keeping in mind.

The Grog was busier than Dark Horse. Jessica squeezed past the patrons crowded around the bar and approached the bartender, a red-haired man with a soul patch and big black plugs in both ear lobes. When he saw Jessica, he said, "Hey, I saw you on TV last night. You're looking for your twin sister or something, right?"

"Right," Jessica replied. "I'm glad somebody watches the news. I'm Jessica Sanford, working with the Lorane County Sheriff's Office. We're trying to find anybody who might have seen my sister, Nicole Briggs, also known as Nikki, around five or six years ago."

"That was before my time. We do have a waitress who's been here quite a while. Let me ask her."

He called over to a woman in her mid-forties wearing an apron and carrying a tray piled high with empty glasses. She walked over to the bar and set down the tray. Her dyed-blond hair was pulled back into a bun.

"Linda, this is Jessica. She's trying to find her sister. You've worked here a long time, right?"

"Seven years now," Linda replied in a voice that said she had waitressed enough for a lifetime. "Do you have a picture of your sister?"

"Actually we're identical twins, so she looked almost exactly like me. Do you remember seeing someone who looked like me in The Grog anytime around five or six years ago? I know it's a long shot to remember back that far."

"Nothing wrong with my memory, hon," Linda replied. "It's just that we get hundreds of people in here, and it's different people every year because of the university. I get to know some of the regulars. Most of them come and go, though."

She studied Jessica's face. "There aren't a lot of Asian women around here who drink much. I remember seeing a few." She thought for a moment. "One of them could have looked like you. I can't say for sure. Sorry."

Jessica thanked Linda and the bartender for their time. She could see this was going to be a tedious process. A lot of bars, a lot of patrons, a lot of time gone by. Maybe she'd get lucky. Or maybe she would just wear out her shoes walking around Eugene. She moved on down the street, sweat trickling down her forehead in the afternoon heat. This was a good time for a frozen-yogurt break.

Chapter 27

Wednesday, June 20

JESSICA SPENT HOURS Wednesday afternoon and evening walking the sidewalks of Eugene, wandering from bar to nightclub to bar. She asked bartenders, owners, waiters, and waitresses if they remembered ever seeing her in their establishments before.

This question generated some peculiar facial expressions. *Wouldn't you know if you had been in here before?* people seemed to be thinking. She explained that she did not have amnesia but rather was searching for anyone who might have seen her missing identical-twin sister. A few people had seen the spots about Nicole's case on the local news channels, online, or in the newspaper. Jessica got sympathy from those people, but no useful information.

After five years of turnover in both staff and clientele, no one remembered one particular short Chinese woman who might have come in for a drink from time to time. If they did recall someone fitting that description, they certainly didn't remember whom she might have arrived with, spoken to, danced with, drunk with, or left with. Jessica left a trail of business cards behind her like Hansel and Gretel's bread crumbs.

Despite all of walking on Wednesday, by Thursday morning Jessica felt the need for some vigorous exercise. She couldn't start working the drinking establishments again until afternoon anyway.

Her Portland fitness-center membership got her into a facility located just a mile from her motel. An hour on the weight-machine circuit and cardio machines left Jessica drenched in sweat and happy about it. No matter how tired she was at the start, a good workout always revitalized her, boosting her energy for the rest of the day.

After she returned to the Hideaway Inn and cleaned up, Jessica sat down with her laptop. This search in Eugene was going to take some time. The exploration involved picking up countless rocks and looking for Nikki connections hiding underneath. She needed to organize her records of where she went, whom she spoke to, and what she learned.

Jessica was one of those uncommon people whose mind was equally adept at logic and art. Some people would say she used both sides of her brain. Her law-enforcement training and experience had taught her to be systematic and analytical, complementing her natural creative and artistic talents. She could paint or sculpt to meet the needs of an ad agency or a television show; she could also work a spreadsheet.

She set up a record-keeping scheme to track the establishments she had already visited and those she still planned to check out, along with the names of people to whom she had spoken at each. She also began to list possible suspects. As yet there was just one name on that list: Brian Stark. Jessica created a third list to record the name, phone number, and email address of anyone else with a Nikki connection, however tenuous. That list started with Praveena Kapoor and Stephanie from the Cascaders. She would have to ask Praveena for Stephanie's last name and contact information.

*   *   *

After her workout, Jessica called Adam to ask if any useful phone calls had come in yet.

"I'm just pulling up at a warehouse district on the south side of Eugene to interview a man named Philip Ray Goselin," Adam said. "He claims he knew Nikki, so that's encouraging. How about if I meet you for coffee afterward and I can fill you in on both the interview and the other calls we've received so far?"

"That would be great. There's a Starbucks two blocks from my motel. It's a real Starbucks, not that imaginary one you keep claiming is going to open up in the sheriff's office. I'll meet you there around eleven."

Forty-five minutes later, Jessica saw Adam walk into Starbucks, and she waved from her table. He waggled his fingers in greeting and walked to the counter to place his order.

The coffee shop wasn't busy at that hour of the morning, so his drink came out quickly. He carried it over to Jessica's table and sat opposite her. She offered him the last piece of her ginger-peach scone, but he looked askance at her.

"Cops eat donuts, not scones. Did you not read the manual, Deputy Sanford?"

"Sorry, boss." She shrugged. "Productive morning?" she asked, a bit too eagerly.

"Yeah, I think so. Let me catch you up on things." He pulled out his notebook. "As of this morning, our office had received twenty-four calls, with another seventeen coming in to Eugene PD. The call screeners eliminated twenty-three as being from our usual array of cranks, crackpots, and conspiracy theorists. I've followed up on fourteen of the other calls. Most didn't fit the timeframe of what we know about Nicole's disappearance, or their description of the woman they were thinking of wasn't close enough."

Jessica's face fell. This was not an auspicious beginning. "What about the guy you just talked to? Another nut?"

"No, he seems legit. This Philip Ray Goselin is thirty-five, looks like a bodybuilder with a shaved head and a little goatee. He drives a forklift around these warehouses, loading and unloading stuff all day. He said he had a 'little thing' with an Asian woman named Nikki five or six years ago. He met her at a nightclub downtown, either The Midnight or maybe Ruby Slippers. He never knew her last name, but he said she sure looked like the pictures we sent out."

"What exactly did he mean by 'a little thing'?"

"He said it was just the usual for the club scene. They were attracted to each other, they danced and drank, and she went home with him. This woman told him she liked muscular men. I don't know what he looked like back then, but he's muscular as hell now. He saw her a few times later in the clubs, sometimes with another woman, a white woman."

Jessica sat up and leaned forward toward Adam. "Wow, that sounds like it could be our Nikki, if she's anything like me. Did Goselin remember the other woman's name?"

"No, he was mostly interested in Nikki. The three of them did all go home together once, but he didn't remember the second woman's name. I asked him if Nikki had any other unusual sexual tastes besides being bi—no offense—but he didn't know about anything. He did say they all smoked a little weed. No surprise there. As far as he knew, Nikki wasn't into any other drugs. But he really didn't know her that well. They just hooked up sometimes."

"Boy, it does sound like Nikki was quite the party girl. Could he add anything to her physical description that we didn't know?"

Adam sipped some coffee and looked down at his notebook again. "Everything he said corroborated what we know. She was short, had a mole on the cheek like Suzanne told you about her daughter. She did have some blue or purple streaks dyed into her black hair. And also some tattoos, a butterfly on the side of her neck and he thought maybe barbed wire around one upper arm. He's quite certain the woman he knew was Nicole Briggs."

"Well, that's about the most solid information we've received so far, even if it doesn't get us much closer to whoever killed her. It's good to see the publicity campaign is reaching some of the right people, at least. Could Goselin be a possible suspect?"

"I don't think so. He wasn't evasive at all, and I didn't detect any signs of lying. If he had been involved with Nicole's death, he'd have to be incredibly stupid to call us. He didn't seem stupid to me."

Jessica mused, "The Ruby Slippers club is already on our list of places to check out. I'll visit The Midnight today and see if anybody there remembers anything." She told Adam about the files she had set up to log information as she accumulated it.

Adam said, "I'm almost done assembling the list of some other bars and nightclubs that are supposed to be good for a quick hookup involving any gender combinations. I'll email that to you after lunch."

They both finished their coffee and got up to leave. Adam headed back to his office, and Jessica returned to the Hideaway Inn. She had a lot of ground to cover later in the day.

*   *   *

Jessica fixed some lunch in her motel room and cleared one pile of papers from the little kitchenette table. She might have to take a break from the almond butter and cherry preserves sandwiches. She enjoyed them, but they were getting old. Maybe tomorrow she would eat lunch at an actual restaurant. She planned to spend the afternoon and evening continuing her footslog through Eugene's drinking establishments. Before she could leave for that exploration, Adam called again.

"Jessica, I just received the results from the DNA tests I requested last week. Are you ready for this?"

She sat down, her heart racing. This was what she had been waiting for, the answer to the most central question facing her: *Who exactly was Nicole Briggs to me?*

"I'm ready. What does it say?"

"I'll send you the full report, but here are the highlights. The mitochondrial DNA from the hairs we found on Nicole's sweaters exactly matches your mitochondrial DNA, and it exactly matches the mitochondrial DNA extracted from the skeletal remains. We already expected that. And here's the clincher. The nuclear DNA comparison showed over 99.99 percent similarity between you and

Nicole. There's no way to get that close a DNA match except with identical twins."

He paused, and then added, "You and Nicole Briggs are twins."

Jessica felt lightheaded. She had just received the most significant information about herself she could imagine. It was incredible to think she and Nicole had begun their lives together and then split into two people who would never know each other after their first few months. Thirty-four years later, she knew Nicole again, after a fashion.

But Nicole would never experience the same flood of emotions Jessica was experiencing now. Nicole went through her life thinking she was alone, just one more unwanted Chinese girl who had the good fortune to be adopted into an American family. If only Nicole and Jessica could have known each other earlier. How different their lives could have been! A wave of love and sadness for the Nicole she never knew washed over her.

"Are you still there, Jessica?" Adam finally asked. "I just emailed you the report."

"Yes, I'm here. I feel like—actually, I don't know what I feel like. I've been waiting to hear this news for so long. It's not a huge surprise after everything else we've learned, but still, the reality is a lot to process. I need to call some people."

"There's more information in the report I just sent you. People often think identical twins have exactly the same DNA, but that's not quite right. You and Nicole probably picked up a few different mutations during your lives that changed your DNA very slightly. For all intents and purposes, though, your DNA sample is the same as Nicole's. Congratulations on the great work you've done on this case, Jessica. And thank you on behalf of all of us in the Lorane County Sheriff's Office."

Still stunned by the implications, Jessica mumbled her thanks and hung up. She drank almost an entire bottle of iced tea as she stared absently into space, trying to collect herself enough to share this information with others who were eager to hear it.

First Jessica called her parents. They were thrilled to learn she had reached such an important milestone in her personal journey, even though the homicide case was still far from solved.

She sent a quick text to BJ:

DNA proves Nicole and I are identical twins! I'm blown away. Details later when I have time to talk.

Next she phoned Suzanne Briggs in Arizona.

"Suzanne, I just got the final DNA results from Adam, the detective. My own DNA is almost an exact match to the DNA we got from Nicole's sweater! Now we know for sure she was my identical twin. I figured you'd want to know right away."

"Thank you for telling me, Jessica," Suzanne replied calmly. "I must say, I'm not at all surprised. The similarities between the two of you just couldn't have been a coincidence. I feel more at peace now knowing what happened to Nicole, horrible as it was. I'm so glad I met you!"

"Me too. I'm grateful to you for opening your home—and your heart—to me." Jessica felt a flush of warmth toward the woman who had brought her sister from the Chinese orphanage to a new life in America.

"Have you made any progress on finding out what happened to Nicole in Eugene?"

Jessica brought Suzanne up to date on her attempts in Eugene to reconstruct Nicole's last months of life. She cautioned, "I don't want you to get your hopes too high about us solving this case, Suzanne. Adam and I are doing all we can to find people who knew her. I'm even a sheriff's deputy now, so I'm officially on the case. We're making some headway, but the end is not yet in sight. It's still early. I'll certainly call again if we get any definitive information."

Finally Jessica called Krysta Kendricks at the Coulter Adoption Agency in Boise. Without Krysta's offer to circumvent Coulter policy, it would have been nearly impossible for Jessica to identify Nicole. Jessica didn't want to compromise Krysta by speaking to her at work. She merely said she had some news and asked Krysta to call her back that evening. In retrospect, Jessica felt a little guilty about not keeping Krysta better informed about her progress. That had just slipped her mind with everything else going on.

It occurred to Jessica that Loren McDaniel, the lead adoption agent in Coulter's Boise office, might be interested to know that a Coulter adoptee had been identified as both a homicide victim and another adoptee's identical twin. However, Loren might then begin to wonder just how Jessica had figured all that out. She had carefully covered her tracks so only she and Krysta knew the little secret of the leaked information about the other groups. That pot was best left unstirred—Loren wasn't going to get any explanations from her.

*   *   *

At last Jessica could get back to scouring bars and clubs for anyone who remembered Nikki Briggs. On Wednesday she had covered some establishments near the University of Oregon. Today she headed for downtown. She had yet to visit the Main Street Pub and Manhattan Bar, two of the places the Cascaders patronized.

Philip Ray Goselin had told Adam he might have connected with Nikki at Ruby Slippers or The Midnight. The Midnight was downtown too. The list from the EPD named several places in the same area. She plotted a route to cover as many places with as few steps as she could. She collected her notepad, water bottle, and sun hat and drove downtown.

Jessica walked for hours. She spoke with dozens of people, wrote down names, took extensive notes, and got nowhere. She stuck her head into every bar she encountered. She quickly ruled out the ones catering to hardcore neighborhood drinkers, bikers, and other specialized clienteles. As she learned more about Nikki, Jessica felt she was acquiring a sense for the places Nikki might have found appealing. They were the kinds of places to which Jessica herself might be drawn were she seeking a good time rather than a killer. She visited some clubs more than once, hours apart, to reach out to employees working different shifts. She didn't want to miss any possible connection.

Jessica returned to the Hideaway Inn shortly before 10:00 p.m., footsore and frustrated. Her day had yielded interesting observations, puzzled looks, and sympathetic comments, but not a single tangible lead. *So this is what it's like to be an investigator again,* she thought wryly. She had forgotten about the repetitive monotony that characterized most real police investigative work. You had to just keep grinding, hoping to get lucky while knowing you might not.

Some people she spoke to actually had seen Nikki, years ago. None of them knew her well enough or remembered enough specifics to be helpful, though. As Jessica pieced together fragments of information about Nikki's life and behavior, she better understood why her sister had a butterfly tattooed on her neck. She was just that elusive, flitting from town to town, from club to club, from man to woman to man.

In that way, the two sisters were quite different. Jessica enjoyed adventure all right, and yet she also valued stability. Jessica reminded herself that she was five years older now than Nikki was when she died. Would Nikki have matured in the same way and become less volatile, less of a risk-taker by now? *Perhaps,* Jessica thought, *but probably not.* They were two different people, despite their outward resemblance.

*   *   *

Walking through nearly twenty alcohol-serving establishments had made Jessica thirsty for something stronger than tea. However, not interested in going out after hanging around bars all day, she picked up a bottle of Merlot from the supermarket near her motel. Their bakery department also was irresistible. She couldn't say no to a giant slice of their signature cake: one layer of yellow cake and one of chocolate, coated with chocolate ganache icing.

Jessica found a corkscrew in the silverware drawer of the motel room's kitchenette. She poured a glass of the Merlot, stretched out on the bed with the cake and a fork, and triggered the TV remote just in time to catch the late-night local news. She flipped to NBC on channel 16.

After the opener on the local crisis du jour, the news anchor introduced the next story, the hunt for the killer or killers of local woman Nicole Briggs, whose remains had been found in a forest grave outside Eugene. Jessica recognized reporter Jacqui Randazzo from the interview just two days earlier. She was almost getting used to seeing her own face on television and computer screens.

Mary Brighthaven, the producer, had edited the piece deftly. The story built on the brief public-assistance spots that had aired earlier. It was hard not to be captivated by the poignant story. As well as being an engaging human-interest piece, perhaps this story would touch someone else who would remember Nicole Briggs.

Chapter 28

Thursday, June 21

SIX MILES AWAY from the Hideaway Inn, Joy Sprague watched the same story. She ate cookie dough ice cream from the carton as she stood in the kitchen of her apartment in Springfield, just east of Eugene. Ten seconds into the story, the ice cream carton and spoon dropped to the floor.

The last time Joy had seen the face on the TV screen was just before she wrapped it in a bedsheet more than five years earlier. She remembered blood slowly soaking through the sheet as she waited for her boyfriend, Randy Thornton, to return to the apartment and carry the body out to his truck.

The last time she had seen that body, she and Randy were shoveling dirt onto it as it lay in a grave dug into a clearing between fir trees in the woods above the Lorane Valley.

The last time she had seen Randy was nearly three years ago.

The last time she had thought about that face was last week.

Joy had returned just hours earlier from a trip driving a truck for her employer, Cascade Food Distributors, on a three-day loop throughout western Oregon. She was tired when she got home, wanting nothing more than some dinner, some beer, and the ice cream that now lay melting at her feet. She had turned on the TV for idle company before going to bed.

Joy hadn't seen a Eugene television station or newspaper since she pulled the truck away from the loading dock the previous Tuesday morning. The local news show she was watching now was her first glimmer that someone had discovered the body she and Randy had hastily buried five years earlier.

Joy picked up the ice cream carton and spoon and put them in the kitchen sink, swiping half-heartedly at the messy floor with a dish towel. She sank onto a chair at the kitchen table, heart in her throat. *Holy shit*, she thought, *this could be bad*. She hadn't been paying close attention, so she had missed the beginning of the story. It caught her focus only when she recognized the face on the screen.

Her instinctive reaction was that the woman they had buried was still alive. In three seconds she realized that was ridiculous. The woman wrapped in the sheet was stone-cold dead when she went into the ground. Then she listened more carefully and understood that the story was about the identical twin of the dead woman. The twin had discovered the name that went with the remains and was now searching for whomever had killed her.

Joy had thought that harrowing incident was far in her past. She and Randy never expected anyone to find the body, let alone identify who had fallen onto the nightstand in their apartment all those years ago and punched a hole in her own head. Randy and Joy were not the killers the police sought though. There were no "killers" of Nicole Briggs. Her death was an accident, not a homicide.

Okay, maybe she and Randy weren't *totally* innocent. They had covered up the accident, fearing the trouble they could get into if anyone discovered a bloodied dead woman with multiple injuries in their apartment. That was a minor thing, though, just trying to keep them out of jail for something they hadn't done. They weren't murderers! But now Nicole's sister was poking around, trying to find out what happened to her. That was a problem.

Much as Joy hated to do it, she had better get in touch with that asshole Randy so they could figure this out. She had ditched him after getting fed up with his cheating. It was one thing to go out clubbing and come home with a new friend for some three-way fun and games. It was another to go out clubbing on your own and not come home until the next day or the day after that. Week after week. She had finally kicked his ass out of their apartment on Sumner Street in Eugene. After she began working for Cascade Food Distributors, Joy had moved to this much nicer place in Springfield.

Randy had moved back to his hometown of Eureka, about a hundred miles south of the Oregon border on the California coast. Eureka was almost far enough away to satisfy her.

Fortunately, she still had Randy's number in her phone, though she wasn't sure why. She called him.

"Joy?" Randy answered with surprise. "I never expected to hear from you again."

"Under normal circumstances, you wouldn't. Something has come up that affects both of us. Remember the package that we delivered to the Lorane Valley five years ago?"

Randy didn't say anything for a moment. "You mean that sheet thing?" he asked cautiously.

"You got it." Randy wasn't the brightest bulb in the chandelier, but at least he had figured out her code and recognized it was something they didn't want to talk about too openly. "We should discuss this on old-style telephones," she said. "Do you have one available?"

"There's one outside the lobby of a motel right near here."

"Go there now," Joy instructed. "There's a pay phone by the gas station down the block from my apartment. Call my cell back in five minutes and I'll give you the number."

Six minutes later, Randy called Joy at the pay phone. "What's with the cloak and dagger?" he asked.

"We've got a problem." Joy quietly told him about the story she saw on the TV. "Somebody must have found that chick's body. I never imagined anyone could have identified her, but somehow they did. I can't believe it. We were so smart getting rid of her. What do you think we should do?"

"Did they say if they had any suspects?"

"Not yet, I don't think. But did we miss something? Is there any way in the world they could figure out it was us?"

Randy said, "I think you're overreacting. There was nothing in the ground except the girl and the sheet, right? We tossed all her clothes and jewelry."

"Apparently we missed some body jewelry. They said they found a navel piece, an eyebrow ring, and something else. Other than that, it was just her and the sheet."

"See, they've got nothing. How could they possibly tie us back to her?"

Joy wasn't convinced. "Maybe we weren't as smart as we thought. Could any of our DNA have been on the sheet? We had a pretty good fight. She clawed my arm, remember? She could have had skin from my arm under her fingernails. I saw on that *Bones* show once how they got the killer's DNA from under some dead girl's fingernails."

"Even if they got some DNA, how could they tell it was from you? Besides, she was out there for five years. There couldn't have been anything left of her. She wouldn't have fingernails, let alone your skin beneath them."

"Hell, I don't know how fast bodies rot in the woods. What makes you a fucking genius scientist all of a sudden? Plus, if you remember, we used her own cell phone to send out texts and post on her Facebook page. Could they use cell records to see where her phone was the night she died? And I Googled how to get blood out of the carpet. I can't believe I used my own phone for that." Joy paced as far as the pay phone's handset would let her as she and Randy talked, promising herself a shot or three of tequila as soon as she returned to the apartment.

"Joy, Joy, take it easy. None of that makes any sense. It was five years ago. They probably don't keep cell phone and Google search records that long. What we *would* have to worry about is if anybody saw the three of us leaving Ruby Slippers together."

"Oh, geez, do you think there were any security cameras there? I never thought about that before."

"Look, if they had that kind of evidence, they could have caught us a long time ago, as soon as someone reported her missing. So I'm not too worried."

"What about fingerprints? Do you think they could get your fingerprints from when you moved her car? Now that they know who she was, they can probably find her car. But even if they got your prints, they wouldn't have anything to match them against, so you're safe."

"Umm, that could be a problem," Randy said hesitantly. "I got busted down here last year for a pot-grow operation. It wasn't mine," he added hastily, "but I was there when they busted it. I got arrested along with the growers. They took my fingerprints and a DNA sample. So if the cops find any evidence like my DNA on the sheet, I'm screwed."

Joy was very nervous. They couldn't know what evidence and clues the twin sister and the police were digging up. If there was any way for the cops to tie the dead woman to them, they could be headed for prison.

Joy suggested Randy drive up from Eureka and meet her so they could plan what to do. Being unemployed at the moment, Randy had the time available. Joy had to make another delivery run on Saturday, but then she had a few days off. They agreed Randy would make the five-hour drive to Springfield on Sunday.

Joy walked back to her apartment and properly cleaned up the melted ice cream from the kitchen floor. She pulled up the TV station's website on her phone to see if there was more information. Sure enough, she found an extended article with more pictures of Nicole and her nosy sister, Jessica Sanford.

Joy had tried for five years to forget that incident and move on with her life. Now it was back. She finally understood the old expression: you can run, but you can't hide.

Chapter 29

Friday, June 22

JESSICA DID NOT sleep well Thursday night. The noise of an unusual late-June rain plinking onto the old building's metal roof woke her several times. It sounded to her like someone throwing BBs onto a sheet of tin all night long. She had friends in Portland with a ridiculously expensive home on which some idiot had installed a metal roof. She couldn't comprehend how anyone could sleep in that house during Portland's long rainy season.

Jessica liked total silence when she slept, which was why she often wore ear plugs. The Hideaway Inn was pleasantly quiet, being located on a primarily residential street without much traffic, so she hadn't thought to use her ear plugs last night. She would check the forecast before going to bed tonight, though.

Adam called her at about eight thirty in the morning to update her on the phone calls coming in to the police switchboards in response to the publicity campaign. The kooks had all crawled back into their holes; the legitimate calls had slowed to a trickle. One recent call merited a follow-up. It came from a Meredith Smith, who was positive she had known Nicole in the relevant time frame. Adam needed to get back to Forest City today to work his other case, so Jessica took the woman's contact information.

Jessica asked Adam, "Did you learn anything more about that phone call from Brian Stark? He hasn't called again, but frankly, he rattled me."

"I described the situation to a security officer at your cell phone carrier. He said they could only release phone records with a court order. A paralegal in the office said she didn't think Stark's threat was overt enough for a judge to issue a court order. It was frightening, I know, but he didn't directly threaten you with physical harm. Unless the calls continue or escalate, there's nothing we can do."

Disappointed and still nervous, Jessica said, "I understand. I got the mug shots you sent, thanks. Brian's sister also sent me some photos. I've been keeping an eye out for him, but I hate looking over my shoulder all the time. He did sound more like a nut than a killer, but killers sometimes start out as nuts."

*   *   *

Jessica called Meredith Smith. She agreed to meet with Jessica later in the morning at her art gallery in downtown Eugene, Art of the Heart, to share what she remembered about Nikki Briggs.

Jessica still had a few places to check on her list of bars and nightclubs. She couldn't do that until later in the day, though. The bars that were open at eleven in the morning were not the kinds that would appeal to Nikki's sense of fun. Before heading downtown, Jessica updated the spreadsheets she had set up for her search and picked up some more groceries from the nearby supermarket.

Art of the Heart was sandwiched between a pizza parlor and an insurance office. Jessica scanned the walls and shelves as she walked in. The gallery offered an eclectic mix of abstract and photo-realistic paintings, ceramics, and art glass. Although she had never done any work in the medium herself, Jessica loved art glass. She paused on her way in to admire some glasswork, fascinated by how the artists could blend the colors, a thousand shades of blue in a single piece. *Someday,* she thought, *I'm going to learn how to do this myself.*

The only other person in the gallery was a rather overweight woman around fifty in a billowing red muumuu who was standing at a table near the middle of the room. Jessica walked over and introduced herself to Meredith Smith. Meredith had a motherly air about her, with gold-flecked brown eyes that exuded intelligence and warmth. Her long braided brown hair was streaked with silver. As with everyone else Jessica met who had known Nikki, Meredith commented on how similar the two women looked.

Meredith said that Nikki had wandered into her gallery one day several years ago just to browse. Nikki clearly had a good eye for art. The two women became friends. Meredith had seen some drawings Nikki had done and was impressed by her ability. She offered to hang them in her gallery to see if they would sell, but Nikki declined. She said she drew only for her own amusement.

"When did you last see Nikki?" Jessica asked.

"It was just over five years ago. I had hired her to help me paint the interior of my house. She was always tight on funds. That didn't seem to bother her, but everybody needs money. I had offered her a part-time job in the gallery, but she wasn't interested. The last time I saw her was at my house, the third or fourth day we were painting."

"Do you recall the date?"

"Not exactly," Meredith said, "but I'm certain it was a Friday. My sister always comes to visit for my birthday, June 4. We were trying to finish the painting before she got here. I hired Nikki so I wouldn't have to do it all myself. So this would have been no more than two weekends before June 4, five years ago."

Jessica pulled up the calendar app on her phone and scrolled back five years. The Friday before June 4 that year was May 31. The previous Friday was May 24. Jessica made a note of this possibly significant information.

She asked Meredith, "Do you remember what happened on that last day you saw her?"

"We had been painting all afternoon. We knocked off in early evening and cleaned up. I remember Nikki looking at her phone and suddenly jumping up. She said she had to run because she was going out to some club that night. I never saw her again. I had to finish the painting myself."

"Did you think about reporting her to the police as a missing person?"

"It never even occurred to me, Jessica. She sent me a text the next day saying she had a friend with some emergency and had to leave town. So her departure seemed legitimate, if abrupt. That was Nikki, though. She flitted around a lot. I didn't even consider that something bad might have happened to her."

"Do you by any chance remember which club she was planning to go to?"

"I'm not certain," Meredith answered. "She used to go out to clubs a lot. She loved to dance. I do remember her talking about Ruby Slippers. I'm not sure if she was going there that particular night. I don't go to nightclubs myself, so I don't keep up with that scene at all."

Jessica thanked Meredith for her time and for all the valuable information. She handed Meredith the usual pair of business cards and asked her to call if she remembered anything else. Jessica walked out of Art of the Heart, but she made it only a few feet down the sidewalk before the aroma of pepperoni and tomato sauce sucked her in through the adjacent doorway.

As she ate her pizza, Jessica felt confident she was beginning to assemble a picture of Nikki's last few days of life. Several people now had mentioned Ruby Slippers. That was the only club that had come up more than once in the interviews. Jessica consulted her shrinking list of drinking establishments yet to investigate. She sketched out a sequence to cover most of those on the way to Ruby Slippers, on the south edge of Eugene's downtown area.

*   *   *

At about a quarter to eight, Jessica walked into the Ruby Slippers Club. A few patrons were already present. Pop music played over the sound system at a tolerable volume as the band set up. From her own clubbing experiences, Jessica knew the real Friday night action, with its pounding live music, light show, and dancing throngs, was still an hour or so away. As she had in the other establishments, Jessica began at the bar.

The bartender, a husky man with short brown hair and a full beard, was bent over the dishwasher behind the bar. When he looked up at her, he did a double take. He quickly recovered and said, "Wow, I haven't seen you in forever. Where have you been?"

His reaction startled Jessica. A few of the bartenders she had spoken to recognized her from the publicity campaign, but this man actually thought he knew her.

"My name is Jessica Sanford," she said. "Do you think we've met before?"

"Yeah, of course. You used to come in here all the time, years ago. Don't you remember? I'm Peter van Tassel. But I'm confused. I thought your name was Nikki or Vicky, something like that. Do I remember wrong, or did you change your name?"

As she had so many times this week, Jessica handed him a pair of business cards and explained who she was and what she was doing. Peter had not seen the TV coverage of the case, nor read about it in the newspapers or online. He said he never watched the news because it was all so damned depressing. That's why he had thought it was Nikki who had walked into his bar.

"I'm so sorry to hear that Nikki's dead. She always looked like she was having a good time when she was in here. She was funny too. We laughed a lot whenever we had a chance to talk."

"It sounds as though you knew Nikki quite well. Could we talk for a few minutes about her? It's really important."

Peter signaled another employee to cover the bar for him. He led Jessica to a quiet table in the back.

Peter said he was a part owner of Ruby Slippers. He had been there for close to ten years. Nikki used to come into the club quite often. They would chat when it wasn't too busy. Peter felt like they were buddies, although he never saw her outside the club. Being a professional bartender, he even remembered her favorite drink: Stoli vanilla vodka, neat. Jessica started at that and opened her eyes wide.

"My favorite hard drink is Stoli vanilla with soda!" she exclaimed. "Neat is too intense for me." She told Peter that although she had never met Nikki other than as infants, she was learning a lot about how similar the two women were from others who knew her. The vodka connection was a new insight.

Peter raised his hand and caught a waitress's eye. "Could you please bring a Stoli vanilla with soda for my new friend? And I'll take a draft Heineken, seeing as how I'm off-duty at the moment."

Jessica smiled her thanks. She said to Peter, "As we've been talking with people who knew Nikki, Ruby Slippers kept coming up as a club she liked. We're not sure exactly when she disappeared. It seems to be late May, five years ago."

"Do you think somebody from Ruby Slippers might have killed her?" Peter asked guardedly.

"That's one possibility we're exploring."

Peter got slightly defensive. "We run a clean club here. We rarely have any problems, except the occasional idiot who's had too much to drink and takes a swing at somebody. Our bouncers handle anybody who looks like they might be trouble."

"We aren't ruling anything out yet. Do you remember anyone who Nikki might have met, come in with, or maybe even left with? Anyone she talked with regularly? She might have favored big guys, muscular guys. She also liked women, so it's possible she hooked up with a man-woman couple from time to time."

The waitress returned with their drinks. Jessica sampled the vodka and soda. "Perfect," she told the waitress with a smile.

Peter sipped some of his beer. He said, "Well, it's a nightclub. People come here to connect, so she could have met anybody. This place is hopping in late May. Students are finishing classes, some are graduating, everybody's partying. You might ask Jeannie. She's been a regular here for several years and probably knew Nikki."

He walked over and spoke to a woman who had just seated herself on a barstool. She nodded, stood, and they both walked to Jessica's table. Peter introduced Jeannie McIntyre and brought her up to date on Jessica's exploration. Jeannie was about forty years old, large-breasted and curvy. Even in the club's low light, Jessica could see Jeannie's striking ice-blue eyes and the extensive tattoos along her arms and around one shoulder. Peter left so the two women could speak privately.

Jeannie did indeed remember Nikki. They had had an on-again, off-again sexual relationship. Jeannie swore she had nothing to do with Nikki's disappearance. "We were friends and sometimes lovers, but we never had any kind of a conflict. I can't imagine why someone would want to hurt her. She was a cool lady."

Jessica asked if she could think of anyone else who might know what happened to Nikki, or anyone she had clashed with. Jeannie thought for a moment.

"She had some hassle with one bouncer. I don't remember his name, but Peter will. At first she was friendly with him. Nikki told me they had dated some, but he slapped her around once. She didn't put up with that shit from anybody."

Peter returned to their table with a fresh drink for Jessica, on the house, he said.

Jeannie asked him, "You remember that really big bouncer you had a few years ago, the Ducks football player? Nikki had some problem with him. What was his name?"

"That was DeWayne Clinton. They had a loud argument once inside the club. I had to break it up. I got complaints from some other patrons and a couple of waitresses that he came on too strong and wouldn't take no for an answer. I finally had to let him go. We can't have staff scared of the bouncer."

Jessica wrote the name down. "Do you know what happened to Clinton afterward?"

Peter said, "I think he was a senior at the university when I hired him, so he probably graduated and left Eugene. Most of the football players I hire as bouncers work out fine, but that guy was just an asshole. He was a good defensive tackle for the Ducks, though. Big dude. He might have tried to go pro, but I never saw him in an NFL game."

Jessica added this information to her notes. She could look Clinton up online to see if he made it to the pros and where he might be now.

Neither Peter nor Jeannie could think of anything else that might be helpful. They had her card and would call if anything else came to mind. Jessica thanked them both for their time—and Peter for the free drinks—and headed back to the motel for the rest of the night.

*   *   *

This eventful day called for one more glass of Merlot back at the motel and maybe some more of that cake. Jessica searched online for a football player named DeWayne Clinton. He did attend an NFL training camp after graduating but didn't make the team. He played in an arena league for a short time. His football career apparently didn't turn out as planned. Unfortunately Clinton had died in an automobile accident eighteen months ago. Even if he was involved with Nikki's death, there was no way to learn that now.

At around 9:45 p.m., Jessica received a call from Peter van Tassel. She could hear club noises in the background. Peter said he remembered one couple who used to go to Ruby Slippers occasionally and sometimes left with a second woman late in the evening. One of those women could have been Nikki on some occasion; he wasn't sure. The guy was pretty large and good-looking, with blond hair. The woman was a knockout redhead, major-league stacked, covered with tattoos. Peter hadn't seen the couple for several years. He thought the woman's name might be Joy, which fit because she was clearly a party girl. "Joy" could have been just a nickname. He didn't know the man's name. Eugene was a college town; people came and went all the time.

Jessica added everything she had learned that busy day to her tracking records. Anyone who had known Nikki was a potential suspect at this point. Practically speaking, though, she couldn't think of any reason to suspect people like Peter van Tassel, Meredith Smith, Jeannie McIntyre, or Philip Ray Goselin of harming her. They had all been forthcoming regarding their connections to Nikki and seemed genuinely surprised to learn of her death.

The information she and Adam had gathered was painting a picture of Nikki's last days. Ruby Slippers was a recurrent element. Nikki had apparently disappeared sometime in late May or early June, five years earlier. Her final Facebook post was dated May 25. They had yet to meet anyone who had had contact with her later than that. She added the deceased DeWayne Clinton to the list of possible suspects, despite the fact that she didn't have any notion of how they could investigate him further.

Jessica's brain was full. She wanted a good night's sleep before hiking with the Cascaders in the morning. She put in her ear plugs and turned up the volume on the alarm clock, just in case the fickle Oregon skies decided to dump more water on the motel's metal roof during the night.

Chapter 30

Saturday, June 23

JESSICA ENJOYED THE indulgence of sleeping in on Saturdays. Not today, though. She needed to be at Spencer Butte south of Eugene by nine o'clock for the hike with the Cascaders Mountain Club. The alarm clock sounded at 7:00 a.m., a disgusting time to awaken on a weekend. At least it looked like a fine day for a hike. Iron-gray clouds hung overhead when Jessica got up, but the forecast promised clearing by midmorning, with a high near eighty degrees.

She gave Adam time to ingest at least one cup of coffee before calling him. Jessica related what she had learned on Friday about Nikki's connection to Ruby Slippers. Based on the information they both had collected, there was a good chance Ruby Slippers was the last public place Nikki was seen.

"Adam, do you think there would be any footage from street security cameras around Ruby Slippers we could search to try to spot Nikki?"

"Unfortunately, no. Back then we only kept security-camera recordings for thirty days. Now storage is much cheaper so we can keep it longer, but that wasn't the case five years ago."

"Would Ruby Slippers itself have any recordings?"

"I'm sure they have security cameras—all the clubs do—but commercial establishments usually overwrite their recordings after a few weeks. Besides, those clubs are so dark and have so many flashing lights that it's nearly impossible to recognize anyone on a video recording, either tape or digital."

Disappointed but not surprised, Jessica told Adam goodbye and got ready for the hike. She drove to Spencer Butte, the highest point visible looking south from Eugene, where she spotted a group of about twenty hikers forming in the parking lot by the main trail. She recognized Praveena and some others from Tuesday's ramble.

Praveena walked over and greeted her. She introduced Jessica to the hikers she hadn't met before. There were too many names to remember. The news of Nikki's death and Jessica's quest had spread throughout the Cascaders community. Most of the hikers knew she was joining them that morning. They were eager to help Jessica if they could.

Jessica studied the path the group was heading for. The summit of this ancient volcanic formation stood some 700 feet above the multiple trailheads at the butte's base. It looked like the trail they were planning to take would yield an energetic hike. *Perfect*, she thought, *just what I need today.*

Before the group set off for the summit, Praveena warned her guest to watch out for poison oak. The stuff was everywhere around the hiking trails. The best strategy was to avoid brushing up against any greenery with bare skin. Oh, yes, there could be rattle-snakes too. Good to know, Jessica thought.

As they headed up the trail, Jessica talked with the other hikers. They had some mutual friends in the Portland Cascaders chapter, particularly among people who were also into mountain and rock climbing. Jessica's enthusiasm for the more extreme outdoor sports had dropped considerably after Maria's accident. Hiking and biking would suffice for her now.

Jessica asked if Praveena knew where Nikki had lived. She did not, but she remembered that another hiker had given Nikki a ride to an event one time. Praveena called to Sanjay Seshagiri, a young, lanky Indian man with wavy black hair and a mustache who took long strides to catch up with the women ahead of him.

Jessica said, "Sanjay, Praveena said you might know where Nikki lived when she used to hang out with the Cascaders."

"Yes, she asked me for a lift once because we were just a few blocks apart. I don't live there anymore, but I can tell you where her apartment was."

He gave Jessica the address of his old apartment building and described how to find Jessica's building from there. He didn't remember the street number, just that it was in the 1800 or 1900 block on Jasper Street. Jessica felt confident she could recognize the building from his description.

The trail wound through the woods as the hikers ascended the peak. The climb provided an invigorating workout. Jessica loved the rich forest smells, the mélange of earthy undergrowth, damp leaves, and fir trees. Oregon had such a variety of forests. Those on the west slope of the Cascade Range had different vegetation from the forests you would encounter driving down the east slope, which were distinct yet again from those in the central part of the state.

The group reached the Spencer Butte summit before noon. As forecast, the skies had cleared to yield a gorgeous day. Spencer Butte had no trees at its summit to block the spectacular view. The city of Eugene spread out before them to the north. Several snow-capped volcanoes were visible in the Cascade Range. Oregon's volcanic history had produced a plethora of terrain types, ranging from the Columbia River Gorge's basalt cliffs to volcanic peaks both massive and modest and to the extensive lava fields around Bend, nearly a hundred miles due east from where Jessica now stood.

After enjoying the scenery and eating lunch at the summit, the group hiked back down to the parking lot. Jessica thanked Praveena and the others for letting her tag along and for the recollections about Nikki that several of them had shared. Each bit of information was a tile in the mosaic that was Nikki's life—and her death.

Jessica drove back to the Hideaway Inn to clean up. She wanted to check out Nikki's old residence that afternoon.

*   *   *

Jessica entered the address Sanjay had given her for his former apartment building into the mapping app on her phone. To her surprise, it was less than half a mile from the Hideaway Inn. She decided to drive anyway in case it took her a while to find Nikki's building. Her feet had been working hard, tramping all around Eugene and both up and down Spencer Butte. Sanjay's description led her easily to the building where he had picked up Nikki that time. A sign in front identified the Coronado Apartments, 1847 Jasper Street.

Jessica pulled into the building's parking lot. The two-story gray building held about eighteen apartments. Jessica noticed a large dumpster in the alley next to the building. She followed the signs to the manager's unit, where she found the building manager, Cynthia Liebermann. Cynthia was a thin, pale woman of thirty-one with a face full of freckles. Her spray of frizzy copper-colored hair was held back with twin barrettes above black-framed plastic glasses. Jessica introduced herself and explained why she was there.

Cynthia said, "Yes, I saw that story on TV. I've only been the manager here for two years, so it was before my time. It must be weird to know your sister used to live in one of these apartments." She took off her glasses and rubbed one lens with her shirttail, peering to see if she got the spot off.

"It's a peculiar feeling," Jessica acknowledged. "I'm staying at the Hideaway Inn while I'm in Eugene. I had no idea it was this close to Nicole's apartment. It's almost like she was guiding me to this part of town. I'm sure it was just a coincidence."

"Since I wasn't here then, I can't tell you anything about Nicole. You could try the apartment manager before me, Marco Sabatini. I had to call him a few times with questions, and I've still got his phone number."

Cynthia looked up Marco's number, and Jessica entered it into her phone. She walked back to the parking lot and called him. When Marco answered, she described who she was and the information she was seeking. Marco said he still lived in Eugene. He was available, not doing anything important. He invited Jessica to meet him at the apartment building he managed now so they could talk.

Ten minutes later, Jessica found his unit and knocked on the orange door. She could hear Marco yelling on the phone, something about he'd fix it when he got around to it, just wait your turn, goddammit. Marco yanked the door open and glared out. When he recognized Jessica his face relaxed momentarily. Then he stepped back in surprise.

"Man, you look just like her. That's freaky as hell. Good thing you warned me you were coming or I would've thought Nikki had come back to get her shit." Jessica had no idea what he meant.

Thirty-eight years old, Marco stood five feet nine, with a wiry build, tanning-bed complexion, and curly, dark hair. He invited Jessica inside, offered her a chair, and paced nervously around the apartment. His cheap cologne permeated the space. The roar of a NASCAR race emanated from the big flat-screen TV in the corner. Marco muted the audio at his visitor's request.

Jessica explained, "As I mentioned on the phone, my twin sister, Nicole Briggs, disappeared about five years ago. We recently identified her remains as a probable homicide victim. Her last known address was in the apartment building you used to manage at 1847 Jasper Street. I would appreciate anything you can tell me about Nikki that might help us with our investigation, including which apartment she rented."

"This is all new to me," Marco replied. "I had no idea she was dead. I do remember Nikki just disappeared. She never canceled her lease or notified us like she was supposed to."

"Would somebody still have records so we could check the date of her last rent payment?"

"The current apartment manager should have that information available. Do you want me to call and check?"

"If you don't mind. I just spoke to her, Cynthia Liebermann. She's probably still home."

Marco dialed the office number for the Coronado Apartments from memory. He asked Cynthia to check on the payment records. She said she needed a few minutes to find them in the computer. Marco waited, and then he covered the phone and told Jessica that Cynthia had reported that the last rent payment from Nicole Briggs for apartment 12 was received on May 11, five years earlier. "Is that all?" he asked Jessica, and when she nodded, he hung up. Jessica made a note of this fresh information.

"That sounds right," he said. "She was always late on her rent. I got tired of banging on her door trying to collect. To be honest, Nikki was a difficult tenant, but very cute." Jessica smiled to herself at the unintentional compliment.

"So she never paid the June rent?"

"No, I remember now." As Marco searched his memory, he idly stroked the narrow beard and mustache that looked painted onto his angular jaw. "I didn't get the rent for June. I waited a week or so into June because I knew she was always late. She didn't answer her door. I tried to reach her by phone, email, and text. I even taped notes on her door. She never got back to me. None of the other tenants had seen her or her car around the building for a while, either."

"What do you do in a situation like that?" Jessica asked.

"There's a process. We give the tenants a little leeway. Around the middle of June, I began sending her past due notices, but she never responded. Finally I gave her notice that I wanted to access her apartment. She still didn't respond, so I let myself in."

"You can do that, just go into a tenant's apartment?"

"Yes, if we give notice. I did. It looked like she had just bugged out. Most of her clothes and personal stuff were gone. But she could have just been out of town for a while, so we have to wait before we can do anything. Eventually I sent her a certified letter saying she'd be evicted if she didn't pay her back rent."

"You still didn't hear from her?"

"Not a peep, so the building's owner got a court order to evict her. The court approved the eviction because she didn't appear at the hearing. I collected the rest of her stuff—there wasn't much—and put it in some trash bags in a storage locker. Only then could I rent the apartment to somebody else. It's a pain in the ass when someone just takes off. We lost several months of rent, thanks to your sister."

Jessica restrained herself from retorting. Marco seemed tightly wound and short tempered. *Why is he in a people job if he hates dealing with people so much?* she wondered. Jessica was happy she owned a house and no longer had to deal with absentee landlords, unhelpful apartment managers, and only thin walls between her and noisy neighbors.

"How long did you leave her personal property in storage?"

"I forget exactly how long we had to keep it back then. The laws keep changing. Nobody ever claimed it. After a few months it becomes abandoned property. I threw the bags in the dumpster."

Marco remembered this old incident remarkably clearly, Jessica thought. He must have had other tenants bail on him. Either he had a great memory, or something about Nikki had stuck in his angry little brain. Perhaps there had been something personal between the two of them. Jessica thanked Marco for his time and headed back to her motel.

Jessica now had one more data point corroborating the date of Nicole's disappearance as mid to late May, as well as knowing where she had lived. Could she have been taken from her apartment by force or coercion? Could she have been killed right in the apartment, for that matter? Even if she had, there couldn't possibly be any evidence left after the countless number of people who must have passed through it in five years.

Jessica called Adam to report that she now knew Nicole's last address, in case he thought there was any value in examining the premises. Adam said he would pass the address along to the media outlets that still had the story on their websites so they could make an update. Maybe someone who used to live there—or even still did—would remember something.

Jessica had been in Eugene for close to a week now. She needed to go home to catch up on the backlog of her life, and she wanted to purge the smell of bars and nightclubs from her nose and her clothes. Jessica packed her belongings in the car, including the remaining food items from the kitchenette. The clerk at the Hideaway Inn's front desk set her up with a new reservation for a second week, beginning on Monday. Jessica left Eugene around 5:00 p.m. and stopped in Salem, halfway to Portland, for something to eat. She was too tired to think of cooking at home.

The sight of her house was most welcome when she pulled into the driveway just before eight o'clock. Jessica had just enough energy left to carry her bags into the house and collect her mail from the neighbors. She took off her clothes and shoes, dropped them on the floor, and climbed under the covers of her very own bed.

*   *   *

What luxury! To awaken as late as she wished in a familiar room, with sunshine seeping around the bedroom blinds and no commitments for the day. Jessica indulged herself with two cups of coffee and a leisurely exploration of *The Oregonian* newspaper's Sunday edition. She was pleased to have more breakfast options than the two kinds of cereal she had been living on at the motel. She ran some laundry and processed her backlog of emails and calls.

Her mail included a check for $3,000 from her parents. A glance at the clock suggested they should be home from church by now, so that was her first call of the day. Sharon and David were eager to learn how the investigation was coming along. They were excited to hear she was homing in on the date of Nicole's disappearance and identifying some potential suspects. Her parents cautioned her to be careful, though. If someone had killed once, they might kill again. Jessica elected not to tell them about Brian Stark's intimidating phone call. They would only worry more.

With some trepidation, Jessica called Maria, who seemed to have little interest in talking with her. She was still recovering. An old friend had become a good helper and a supportive companion, so she was doing just fine right now, thank you very much, goodbye. Jessica knew her relationship with Maria was truly at an end. She felt a sense of freedom along with the sense of loss. Connections among people are dynamic: they come, and they go.

Next she gave BJ a call.

"It's great to hear from you, Jess. I've been wondering how you were doing in Eugene but didn't want to interrupt. I figured you were super busy. What are you doing today?"

"Just getting caught up on stuff and hanging loose. It's a relief not to have anything particular I need to do today. I want to tell you all about what's been going on, though. Can you come over for dinner?" Jessica wasn't up for a bike ride, but she craved a friendly face. She had had enough physical activity to suit her for a while.

"Sure can. How about if I bring some food along for us around six thirty?"

"Excellent, surprise me. You know what I like. I can't wait to see you!"

*   *   *

Jessica heard BJ's car door slam. She opened the front door just as BJ walked up carrying bags from Jessica's favorite barbecue restaurant, a bottle of Zinfandel tucked under one arm. Jessica rescued the wine first and then took one of BJ's bags.

"Perfect!" Jessica said. "Zinfandel, barbecue, and I all get along very well together."

The kitchen filled with the smoky aromas of baby back ribs, pulled pork, and sliced barbecued turkey. BJ pulled containers of baked beans and coleslaw out of a bag, along with some cornbread and spicy barbecue sauce.

"This is fantastic, BJ. Thanks a lot for getting all this. Let me get some money for you."

"No charge. I'm a full-service friend, Jessica. You should know that by now." Jessica gave her a big hug. BJ was the sort of friend who made everything easier. BJ was picking up a tan; she must have been working in her garden or out training for her Seattle-to-Portland bike ride.

BJ caught Jessica up on family doings as the women filled plates and carried them out to the table on the patio. She listened attentively as Jessica summarized her busy week in Eugene. BJ was impressed by how many bars and nightclubs Jessica had explored.

"It's a good thing those weren't all wine bars you were scouting out," she teased. "You wouldn't have made it past the second one."

Jessica toasted her friend's insight with the Zinfandel. After they ate, she showed BJ the files she had set up to track her investigation records.

"Impressive," BJ observed. "Do you feel like you're getting close to finding out who killed Nikki?"

"Yes and no. That's the thing, BJ. We have these clues that point to Ruby Slippers as the club where Nikki hung out the most, and maybe the last place she was seen. We know approximately when she disappeared, around the last week in May, and we've identified some possible suspects."

"So what's the problem?" BJ asked.

"The problem is that we still have nothing solid that points us either to the specific location where she died or to who might have done it. We don't have a likely suspect, just suppositions. There's no way we could convict anybody based on what we know so far."

"Why not?"

"There's just no physical evidence and no eyewitnesses. The killer could be a man, could be a woman, could be both. Maybe it was a random thing, having nothing to do with the clubs or Nikki's lifestyle at all. It could have been an accident, first-degree murder, or anything in between. I'm starting to fear we might not solve this. Five years is a long time in a homicide case."

"You know, Jess, even if you can't totally solve the crime, you've made a real breakthrough," BJ pointed out. "You discovered a brand new twin sister, you found her family, and you brought closure for her mother. That ain't nothing, even if it ain't everything."

The women sat in silence, sipping their wine while Jessica contemplated the possibility that Nicole Briggs's killer—or killers— might get off scot-free. Despite all the effort she, Adam, Silvia, and others had put into this case, despite the leads, there was currently nothing that would be admissible in a court of law. The thought was discouraging.

This brief interlude at home was refreshing and restful, but Jessica had to drive back to Eugene in the morning. Much as she hated to lose them, she sent the barbecue leftovers home with BJ.

Chapter 31

Sunday, June 24

LATE SUNDAY AFTERNOON, Randy Thornton pulled into a parking space near Joy Sprague's apartment building in Springfield. He climbed out of his pickup and stretched his legs and back. The five-hour drive from Eureka was among the most scenic in the country. He had taken Highway 101 along the Northern California coast through Redwood National Park, cutting east at Crescent City to cross the border into Oregon. The heavy showers near the coast had transformed into sunbeams by the time he reached Eugene.

Randy took an overnight bag from his truck, climbed the stairs to the second floor, and rang Joy's doorbell. She opened the door and urgently motioned for him to come in. Joy looked around furtively, as though anyone in the vicinity might have seen the two of them together years ago, leaving Ruby Slippers with Nicole Briggs. No one had, of course.

Randy looked at Joy. Her hair was much shorter than when he had seen her last and not as brilliantly red. She looked thinner and well-toned, like she had been exercising regularly. "You look good," he began cautiously.

"Don't even start," she said. "You're only here because we've got a big fucking problem that we both have to deal with. Afterward we go right back to how we were last week. I'm here, and you're far, far away."

Randy thought that maybe she was still a little bitter about their breakup.

Joy looked at the overnight bag in Randy's hand. "You don't think you're staying here with me, do you?"

Randy was a little embarrassed. "I didn't know. I'm not working now, so I don't exactly have money for a hotel. I brought a sleeping bag. Can I crash on your floor or couch, please? I won't come near you, I promise."

Joy looked at him skeptically and then conceded the couch was available. He set his bag in the corner of the living room and sat on said couch.

"Have you seen anything more about Nikki in the news?" Randy asked.

"After we talked, I looked around online and found a longer story." Joy showed Randy a TV station's website on her laptop. "Apparently she had a twin sister nobody knew about, named Jessica. She just happens to be someone who rebuilds faces on unidentified skulls to try to find out who the dead person is. A forensic sculptor, it's called. And wouldn't you know, she got this case when the bones we buried came out of the grave I told you was too goddamn shallow. So they identified our girl, and now this Jessica is trying to find whoever killed and buried her sister."

"Does the article say if they have any suspects yet?"

"Not yet. That's the only good news here. The cops have been trying to get anybody who knew Nicole to come forward. I haven't seen any updates about that so I don't know if they're getting anywhere. All I know is, if they do, we're in trouble."

Randy exhaled with relief. "We got away with it for five years. Maybe it's not hopeless. I still don't think we left much evidence behind. Just in case, though, maybe we'd better get sister Jessica under control."

"Brilliant idea," Joy replied. "And where do you suppose we might find Jessica, Sherlock?"

"You don't have to get nasty about it. I'm just trying to help. The story said she lives outside Portland. If she's been in Eugene working with the police and poking around, she can't be driving two hours here and back each day. She must be staying someplace here in town."

"Should we call every hotel, motel, and Airbnb in town until we find her?"

Randy suggested, "Maybe we need to do a little investigation of our own and see if Jessica has stumbled onto anything that could identify us. For instance, do you think anyone has figured out where Nikki lived?"

"I don't remember seeing anything about that when I read the article earlier." Joy scanned down the web page with the story. "Uh-oh, here it is: 1847 Jasper Street. They added that since the last time I looked. It still doesn't say anything about suspects, though."

"It's bad they found her apartment, but it might be good for us. Jessica must have talked to someone there. How about if we pretend we want to rent an apartment and see if we can get anything out of the manager about Jessica?"

Joy didn't say anything, apparently mulling it over. She realized it was risky to be seen where anyone might remember them from years earlier. She looked at Randy's face and then scanned his body, making him feel self-conscious. She said, "You know, you've changed. Your beard's bushier, and, um, you maybe picked up a couple of pounds. And I've changed my hair. If I just put on long sleeves to cover my tattoos, I doubt that anybody who saw us late at night long ago could recognize either of us." She agreed with Randy's suggestion.

*   *   *

A little past ten on Monday morning, Joy drove Randy over to the Coronado Apartments in her Mustang. She didn't want to take

Randy's truck, as that was the vehicle they had driven to the building when they cleaned out Nikki's apartment that fateful night. They had concocted a plan for approaching the apartment manager. Joy parked around the corner from the building and walked up to the apartment manager's unit. She wore a lightweight long-sleeved top and sunglasses, and Randy had on a baseball cap. It was a thin disguise, but they had agreed they didn't look much like they did five years earlier.

When the manager answered her doorbell, Randy said, "Good morning. We're moving to Eugene from Medford soon. We drove up this morning to look for an apartment and saw your vacancy sign. Could you show us what you have available, please?"

"Sure. Thanks for stopping by. I'm Cynthia Liebermann, the building manager."

"I'm Greg and this is Michelle. Nice to meet you."

Cynthia got her keys and led the way upstairs to apartment 16. Joy felt a chill as they walked past Nikki's old unit, number 12, on the way to number 16.

"Is this the only unit you have available right now?" Randy asked.

"We have four others, all single-bedroom just like this one. This is a good time to be apartment hunting. Most students are gone now, so I can give you a discount on the summer months."

Cynthia showed Joy and Randy around the empty apartment, which was laid out exactly as Joy remembered Nikki's unit. The couple pretended to be interested in the apartment, opening closets and cupboards and asking about rent, utilities, other tenants, and the security deposit.

Randy said, "This looks like the kind of place we're looking for. We just started hunting, so we'd like to scout out some others before we sign a lease. Can you suggest a motel around here that would be a good place for us to stay overnight?"

"I live here, so I don't pay much attention to motels or hotels," Cynthia said. "But a couple of days ago a woman who stopped by said she was staying at the Hideaway Inn, only half a mile away. I can look up the address for you."

Joy felt a flush of excitement. Chatty Cynthia had just saved her and Randy a lot of time, and perhaps much more than that. "That would be helpful, thanks, Cynthia," Joy said. "Did that woman say anything in particular about the Hideaway?"

"Just that it was close by. It was so strange why she stopped here, though. She's investigating her twin sister's death. The sister used to live in this apartment building several years ago. Isn't that just too weird?"

"Very weird," Joy agreed. "Is this a high-crime area? No offense, but we don't want to live someplace where we get nervous about walking to the car."

"Not at all. I've never heard of any serious crime around here in the two years I've managed the building. This was a long time ago. Her sister just disappeared. It was probably some freak thing."

Randy asked Cynthia, "Did that woman say if the police were making any progress on the case? That's pretty scary, someone just disappearing like that."

"She didn't say either way. I saw a story about it on the news last week, but I had no idea the sister had lived here. I hope that one thing doesn't put you off this building, Greg. It's a nice place, with good tenants."

Randy said, "If it was just that one time, I'm not too worried. We do want to look at some other places before committing. Can you give us your card so we can call you if we want to follow up?"

Randy, Joy, and Cynthia walked back to Cynthia's apartment. She pulled out a business card for them and wrote the Hideaway Inn's address on the back. Cynthia took another card and asked for their names and phone number.

Randy hastily said, "That's okay, we'll get in touch with you if we need more information. Thanks for your time, Cynthia."

"My pleasure, Greg. It was nice to meet you both." They shook hands and Cynthia closed the door to her unit.

"Greg" and "Michelle" walked around the corner and got into Joy's car.

"Jackpot!" Randy said exultantly. "I believe our next stop is the Hideaway Inn."

They drove to the address Cynthia had given them and parked on the tree-lined street, seventy-five feet from the parking lot entrance. The motel was a white, U-shaped building with fifteen units and an office on a single level, occupying half a block in an otherwise residential neighborhood. A convenience store sat adjacent to it on the corner. The motel's parking lot contained seven cars. The No Vacancy sign was lit, indicating that it was fully booked for the night.

Joy took out her phone and looked up the motel's phone number. A young man's voice answered her call.

"Hideaway Inn, Devon speaking. How may I help you?"

"I'd like to speak to a guest, Jessica Sanford, please."

"One moment, please." Joy heard computer keys clicking in the background. "It looks like she hasn't checked in yet. May I take a message for her?"

"No thanks. I'll try again later." She hung up.

Joy said to Randy, "He said she hasn't checked in yet. But that's weird, because Cynthia at the apartment building said she was already staying at the Hideaway Inn."

"Maybe she checked out for the weekend. It sounds like she's supposed to be coming back, right?"

"Yeah, that's what the kid at the motel implied. You're probably right. Maybe she went back to Portland for a little while."

Randy asked, "So now what?"

"Now we wait. She could be anywhere in Oregon right now. If she's supposed to check in at some point today, it seems like our best bet is to sit here and wait for her to show up. Unless you have a better idea?"

"No, that sounds okay. We're going to need some lunch, though. Plus I have to pee like crazy. I've never done a stakeout before. How do the cops do it on TV?"

Joy said, "We'll take turns. Why don't you go over to the convenience store, take your very important leak, and get us something to eat. When you come back, I'll go to the bathroom and then buy some snacks. We don't want the cashier to see us together, and we can't be going in and out of there all day."

Joy watched as Randy walked over to the convenience store to take care of business. When he returned, Joy did the same. Then they sat in the car and got ready for a wait. Joy hoped it wouldn't take too long.

Chapter 32

ADAM GREETED JESSICA as she walked into the sheriff's office late Monday morning. The building was right on her way to the Hideaway Inn, so she had decided to check in with him in person for a status update.

"The incoming calls have slowed to a trickle," said Adam. "I'd be quite surprised if the media campaign yields any new leads at this point."

"How about calls into the Eugene PD? Anything promising there?" Jessica asked.

"My contact there told me they got a call from a Robert Chung, who said he used to date Nicole Briggs. Do you want to check that lead out?"

"Sure, I can handle it today," Jessica replied. Adam passed along Robert's phone number, email, and home address. "Are there any other updates I should know about?"

Adam said he had stopped by Nicole's old apartment building. Three tenants had rented unit 12 in the five years since Nicole had lived there. Adam had walked through the currently-vacant apartment and looked around, then concluded there was no point in testing for fingerprints or other trace evidence after all this time. Although the lack of evidence and clues was not surprising, Jessica was increasingly frustrated at how difficult it was to get traction on a lead that might actually take them somewhere useful.

Jessica called Robert Chung from her car. He had to work until 5:30 p.m. but would be happy to talk with Jessica later in the evening at his house. Jessica agreed to meet him at seven.

After stopping for lunch and more food supplies for her week-long stay, Jessica reached the Hideaway Inn about two. She picked up her key from Devon at the front desk. Because he knew she was returning, Devon had thoughtfully kept the same unit available for her and arranged for early check-in. Devon reported that someone had called for her but didn't leave a message. She felt a chill. Could Brian Stark have found her? She reassured herself that that seemed highly unlikely. She couldn't think of anyone else who might try to reach her at the motel. *Oh well, nothing to be done about it.* She moved back into her home away from home.

*   *   *

Randy poked Joy in the side repeatedly. "It's her," he hissed. "I think that's Jessica!"

Joy jerked awake from her doze. Several empty potato-chip bags crinkled underfoot as she stirred.

"Stop poking me!" Joy blinked rapidly a few times and looked to where Randy was pointing. They watched Jessica unload her car and close the door to room 4 behind her. "Yeah, that must be her. There aren't too many Asian women around here. I can't see her face well enough from this angle to be sure."

"She's short like Nikki was," Randy observed. "I think we found her."

"Excellent. Now we wait until she comes out and follow her to see what she's up to. We haven't talked yet about what we're going to do with her."

"Let's see where she goes first. Maybe she's just fumbling around and doesn't know anything important. Maybe we won't have to do anything."

"You're an optimist, Randy. Just in case, we should come up with a plan before we miss our chance."

Joy added, "I thought of something else. Convenience stores have security cameras everywhere. Let's be careful where we park so if we do have to take care of Jessica the cops don't see videos of us sitting out here for hours."

Randy studied the convenience store on the corner. "I see two cameras. Maybe there are more. I don't think they can see our car. I wore my hat when I walked in there earlier."

Joy said, "Tomorrow maybe we should use both cars and park in different places where we can see the motel lot. That would make it easier to follow her without her noticing, no matter which way she goes."

They hunkered down to wait until Jessica came out. It took less than an hour. Joy started the car and waited to see which way Jessica turned out of the lot.

Jessica wanted to check out several places in Eugene where her sister had worked, according to some of her friends. She drove to the west side of the university campus and walked into the bustling coffee shop called Use Your Bean. She closed her eyes for a second and basked in the aromas. She was floating into coffee heaven.

When she reached the head of the line, Jessica asked the harried woman behind the counter if she remembered Nicole working there as a barista several years earlier. Sorry, no, she had just bought the place recently and didn't know anything about the old employees. Jessica asked for the previous owner's name, but the next customer already had the busy owner's attention. Jessica decided to stop back later when it might be less frenetic. She settled for a large, iced, white-chocolate mocha for now.

As she sucked sweet, cold coffee through a straw, she walked several more blocks to the Paradise Sidewalk Café, where Stephanie said Nicole had waitressed for a time. The manager on duty hadn't known Nicole, but she referred Jessica to an older woman who had worked there a long time.

"Yeah, I remember Nikki," the woman told Jessica. "I just saw on the news she had died. That's too bad. She didn't work here long. She wasn't a very good waitress, either. Nikki pretty much kept to herself."

"Did you know anything about friends she had, things she liked to do for fun, clubs she went to?"

The woman snorted. "Oh, she did like the clubs. Sometimes she'd come in really late, hungover. She wasn't very reliable. But I don't know where she partied. One day she quit without any notice, just bailed on us. I haven't seen her since then."

*   *   *

Joy sat at a little metal table in the shade outside an ice cream shop, licking a cone of chocolate-vanilla swirl as she stared from behind big sunglasses at the entrance to the Paradise Sidewalk Café. Randy had stayed in the Mustang as Joy followed Jessica discreetly from across the street. Truth be told, Joy was rather enjoying the secret-agent act, as long as her quarry didn't spot her shadowers.

When she saw Jessica walk out of the cafe, Joy waited a few seconds and then stood to continue her surveillance. Jessica headed back to her car. Joy finished the cone, wiped her fingers with a napkin, and dropped the napkin in a trash can on the street corner. She got into the Mustang and reported her observations to Randy. The two followed Jessica at a safe distance as she drove back to the Hideaway Inn.

*   *   *

Early in the evening, Jessica returned to the Coronado Apartments where Nicole had lived. She was hoping to catch some tenants at home around dinnertime. She stopped by the manager's office; Cynthia was in.

"Hi again, Cynthia. I'm Jessica Sanford, from last Saturday."

"Sure, I remember. What can I do for you, Jessica?"

"I didn't mention it when I was here before, but I am at the moment a Lorane County sheriff's deputy, assisting with the investigation of the death of my sister, who used to live in this building." She displayed her slightly tarnished deputy's badge. "I'm here tonight to look for any long-term tenants who might remember Nicole. I would appreciate your cooperation with this."

Cynthia hesitated. "I hate to bother all the tenants. I guess it's okay if it's an official police investigation."

"Thanks a lot, Cynthia. Can you please give me a list of the empty apartments so I don't waste any time on those?"

Jessica thanked Cynthia for the list and began canvassing the rows of apartments. Some people weren't home. Most who were had only lived there a short time. A tired-looking woman in her late twenties opened the tenth door she knocked on. Even the limp dishwater-blond hair straggling around her pale face looked tired.

Jessica introduced herself and said she was investigating a homicide. She asked the woman how long she had lived in the apartment building.

"Almost six years," she replied, swallowing a big spoonful of strawberry yogurt from the container in her hand.

"Excellent, you're just who I'm looking for. May I ask your name, please?"

"I'm Lee-Anne Christiansen. Come on in; I'm just finishing dinner. You look familiar to me. Have we met before?"

"No, we haven't, but you might have met my twin sister, Nicole Briggs. She lived here several years ago, in apartment 12. Did you know Nicole?"

"Ah, that's why you look familiar." Lee-Anne said she had seen Nikki around the building from time to time and chatted with her occasionally. She hadn't seen or heard any news about the case. She had been practically living in her lab at the university for the past several weeks, trying to finish up her PhD research in microbiology and write her doctoral thesis.

"Do you know of any conflict Nikki might have had with anyone in the building, anyone who might have wanted to do her harm?" Jessica asked.

Lee-Anne finished her yogurt and pushed her glasses back into place. "I know she did not get along well with the apartment manager back then. His name was Marco. I can't remember his last name, something Italian. I saw them yelling at each other in the parking lot at least twice. Once I thought I heard some threats. I was afraid it might turn violent so I called the police."

"What happened when the police came?"

"The cop spoke with both of them and everybody calmed down. They were both still here when he left, so I don't think anyone was arrested."

Jessica made a note to ask Adam to check with the Eugene Police Department for the specifics on this incident.

"Do you have any idea what the problem was between Nikki and Marco?"

"I don't know if it was something about the rent, or if they had a personal relationship issue, or what. Marco was a lousy apartment manager. He hated dealing with everybody's problems. He took forever to get my toilet fixed once. He was gone a lot too. He used to brag about picking up women in bars, or going to the Indian casinos to gamble. I was happy when Cynthia took over."

"Do you remember when this altercation took place?"

Lee-Anne stared into space for a few seconds as she thought back. "I was still taking graduate classes then, hadn't started my lab research yet. So it must have been in spring quarter, five years ago."

Jessica made another note: that was not long before Nicole's disappearance. Maybe Marco Sabatini was more than just a building manager with a bad attitude.

*   *   *

Randy and Joy slunk lower in their car seats when they saw Jessica's Honda pull out of the Coronado Apartments parking lot. They had followed her cautiously from the motel, becoming increasingly nervous as they saw where she was heading. They had parked at a spot where they could see Jessica's car when it left the lot. The apartment manager, Cynthia, could recognize them, so they didn't dare try to follow Jessica as she walked around the building. They didn't know whom she spoke to or what she might have learned. Randy said, "Jessica is getting way too close for my comfort."

Chapter 33

Monday, June 25

JESSICA RANG ROBERT Chung's doorbell a few minutes before 7:00 p.m. Robert was a nice-looking man of Chinese descent with a lean, athletic build. Robert invited Jessica to come inside and sit in the living room. His two-story house on the west side of Eugene was cute and cozy, decorated simply but tastefully. Jessica estimated him to be around her age, mid-thirties—about the same age Nicole would have been as well.

"I want to thank you again for contacting the police and taking the time to meet with me tonight, Robert," Jessica began. "We've been trying to find people who knew Nicole Briggs in the hope that someone might lead us to discover what happened to her."

"I'm happy to try to help," Robert replied in a soft voice. "Can I get you something to drink, wine or coffee or some pop, perhaps?" Jessica accepted his offer of coffee.

"What kind would you like? I have a Keurig and a variety of coffee pods."

"Surprise me. I like almost any coffee."

She looked around the living room while Robert was in the kitchen. A stack of cycling magazines sat on the coffee table. The fireplace mantelpiece displayed several photographs of Robert with what looked to be his parents and some siblings, all Chinese. He brought her a steaming cup, along with a plate of molasses cookies.

"How did you know I like cookies?" Jessica asked with a smile as she took one.

"Just a guess. Nicole liked sweets. I thought you might also. Then again, who doesn't?" He cocked his head and stared at Jessica with a sad smile. "You remind me so much of her. I'm glad I was prepared for that or it would have been quite a shock to see you."

"I've been getting that a lot the past few weeks. I've considered getting a big name tag that says 'I'm Jessica, not Nicole.'" They both laughed at that image. "The detective who's leading this case, Adam Longsdale, told me you used to date Nicole. Could you please tell me how you knew her and what your relationship was like?"

"I manage a sporting-goods store near the university campus. Nicole came in one day to look at mountain bikes. They were all out of her price range, unfortunately. I found her attractive and interesting. She said she was a barista at Use Your Bean. I had always gone to Starbucks, but I started going there instead. Nicole made great lattes. We flirted a bit, and eventually I asked her out."

"About how long did you two date?" Jessica asked.

"Only about three months. I really liked Nicole. All her other friends called her Nikki, but she looked like a Nicole to me, so that's what I called her. We had fun and got along well. Sometimes I would borrow a bike from the store for her and we'd ride together."

"How serious was your relationship?"

"I would have liked for it to become serious. I was falling in love with Nicole, but I knew I wasn't exactly her type. She liked to go out dancing and partying. I enjoy that scene up to a point; then I've had enough. I didn't mind her going to clubs with her friends without me sometimes. Eventually I felt left out, and I knew the relationship wasn't going to last."

Jessica asked, "Do you remember approximately when you two were dating?"

"I met her in January, almost five and a half years ago. We started dating a few weeks later. In late May, Nicole went dark on me. She didn't return my phone calls, texts, or emails. The last thing I saw from her was a Facebook post saying she had to leave town to help a friend, I don't know who, with some kind of problem. I kept checking her page for a long time. That old message is still the most recent post, though."

"Did you hear anything from Nicole after that?"

"Never. I tried for a while to contact her and finally gave up. I figured she used the emergency as an opportunity to break up with me and move on with her life. That hit me pretty hard. When I learned last week her body had been found I was shocked. I sure hope the police find who did this and arrest them."

Robert offered Jessica something else to drink. She chose wine this time. He brought two glasses of Chardonnay from the kitchen.

Jessica asked, "How would you describe Nicole's state of mind? Was she happy, angry, bored, depressed?"

Robert looked pensively out the window. "Nicole liked to give the impression of being fun loving. Something was missing inside her, I could tell. She kept other people at arm's length, except for the casual partying." He studied his hands, clasped in his lap, and then looked Jessica in the eyes.

"She really was a loner at heart, not one for relationships. She once said to me, 'I don't need anybody else.' It was like something had been taken from her as a child and could never be replaced. Maybe it was because she was adopted. I was sad that I couldn't plug the hole for her."

Robert still had some pictures of Nicole on his phone. He sat next to Jessica on the couch and showed them to her. Jessica hadn't seen any recent photos of Nicole, just the childhood ones from Angela Montgomery and the one on her Facebook page, when she was about twenty-five. As Jessica scrolled through the photos, she was struck again by how much Nicole and she looked alike—and by their subtle differences. Nicole seemed so alive in the photos, so happy and energetic.

Robert played a video from his phone. For the first time—for the only time—Jessica heard her sister's voice. Despite her efforts to maintain her professionalism, Jessica began to cry, listening to the sister to whom she could never say "I love you."

Robert didn't seem to know how to react. Hesitantly he put his arm around Jessica to comfort her. Jessica rested her head on his shoulder. Robert leaned in, bringing them into closer contact.

Jessica realized that Robert must be hurting too. Having a woman you liked dump you was one thing. Learning that she had died in a brutal fashion and you would never see her again was quite another.

Comforting led to an embrace, which led to a kiss. Before either of them fully realized what was happening, they were upstairs in Robert's bedroom. They both needed the therapeutic release.

Jessica drove back to her motel about eleven o'clock, a torrent of thoughts racing through her head. Yes, it was unprofessional for her to sleep with Robert. It just happened, as these things some-times do. No, it wouldn't happen again. Yes, it was very pleasant at the time. No, Robert couldn't have hurt her sister. She had felt the tenderness he had for Nicole, and it was real.

She smiled to herself. *Yes, I might be interested in seeing Robert again after this case is finished, if I wouldn't just be a Nicole surrogate.* He seemed to be a genuinely nice man. She could use one of those in her life.

*   *   *

Randy wondered why Jessica was taking so long in Robert's house. When the light went on in the bedroom upstairs, he figured it out. He and Joy had followed her to Robert's neighborhood and parked halfway down the block. Randy was getting tired of this stakeout stuff. How did detectives do it? Sitting in cars for hours, munching on junk food all day, peeing hurriedly when they had the opportunity, trying to make sure they didn't miss the subject's departure. Cop shows on television never depicted the tedious reality of trying to surreptitiously follow a suspect.

Randy also was finding it strange to spend so much time close to Joy. Until this all happened, they hadn't spoken since their ugly breakup almost three years earlier. He could feel Joy's smoldering resentment at his presence, yet this was a problem they needed to solve together. She smelled just as good as he remembered, which aroused memories of all the fun they had had in their playpen. Randy pushed those thoughts out of his mind so he could focus on dealing with Jessica.

Joy and Randy had spent the time waiting in the car discussing exactly what they should do about Nikki's sister. She was snooping around in dangerous places. They could only hope she wasn't close to assembling the puzzle. They decided to watch her for another day or two and see where she went. If she got too close to the truth, she would have to go.

"Have to go" was fine in the abstract, but Joy and Randy weren't sure just how that might work in practice. They had identified four elements to getting Jessica out of the picture. First was to snatch her and get her under their control. That had to be done in a way that didn't draw attention. People came and went regularly at the motel, so that wasn't an option. Jessica was driving all around town meeting people. It wasn't obvious how to set a trap where they could quickly and quietly subdue her. They didn't have a syringe loaded with a magic knockout potion they could stick in her neck, like the bad guys in the movies all seemed to carry.

The second step would be to transport Jessica someplace where they could take care of business. No suitable place came to mind. Joy's apartment was out. That could leave too many evidence trails: witnesses, DNA, everything. They had no other secret lair available, no cabin hidden in the woods. Renting a storage locker was one possibility, provided they could pay cash.

The next step would be to actually do the deed. Yes, Joy and Randy had participated in the accidental death of Nicole Briggs. But it wasn't their fault! All they did was protect themselves by burying the evidence. If Jessica had to go, one or both of them needed to do it. They didn't have a gun (but maybe Jessica did, Joy pointed out—that risk was worth remembering). What was the best tool: a hammer, a knife, a rope, an axe? They had none of those available. Even if they did, could either of them really wield it? These were not easy questions.

Finally there was the matter of disposal. Their grand plan to eradicate Nicole Briggs from the face of the earth had obviously been imperfect. Her reappearance was now a royal pain in their collective asses. They would need to do a better job this time.

All they could agree upon was the need for the deed.

After following Jessica home, the two returned to Joy's apartment. They would get up early to observe their quarry for another day. Using two cars would make it easier to monitor Jessica's movements without being noticed. That would also let them pick up the materials they needed.

Chapter 34

Tuesday, June 26

FLOATING IN SEMISLEEP before her 7:30 a.m. alarm went off, Jessica snapped her eyes open with a fresh idea. Her investigation had revealed that everyone's last known communications with Nicole were in late May, five years past. She got out of bed and called Adam to ask him to check the dates on her scofflaw sister's unpaid parking tickets to see if any were from around that time. An early riser himself, he was already in the office.

She heard Adam clicking on his computer keyboard. "Let's see, there were six unpaid tickets. Wow, you're right, the latest one was on Saturday, May 25. Good thinking; I'm glad we deputized you."

"What was the citation for?"

"It was a residential permit violation. Visitors may only park up to two hours in certain residential parking zones unless they have a guest permit. This citation was issued at 11:53 a.m. on May 25."

"Where was her car parked at the time?"

"At 353 East Sixteenth Avenue. That area's full of apartment buildings, mostly renting to university students."

"This might be important. Could we meet there this morning and look around?" Adam agreed to meet Jessica at that address at 10:00 a.m.

"I want to tell you about something else, Adam." She related what Lee-Anne Christiansen had told her about Nicole's clashes with Marco Sabatini. Adam said he would see if Sabatini had a police record. He would also contact the Eugene PD regarding their intervention in the argument Lee-Anne described. Sabatini just might be a suspect in Nicole's death.

Jessica looked out the window. The day was cool and gloomy, with intermittent rain showers forecast, including the one going on right now. She considered taking a run. The quiet weekend at home had soothed her sore feet and replenished her energy. A wet, chilly run didn't sound appealing, though. She could wait until tomorrow.

*   *   *

Joy and Randy had been parked outside the Hideaway Inn since before seven in the morning, Randy in his Silverado pickup and Joy in her Mustang. Their vehicles pointed in opposite directions. The previous evening they had each downloaded a cell phone app that let them use their phones as walkie-talkies so they could stay in touch during the day's operations.

Randy was getting cramped sitting in his vehicle and antsy that Jessica was still in her room. Neither he nor Joy had slept much; Randy was barely awake.

Joy walkie-talkied Randy to suggest he go buy some of the items they needed. She would keep her eyes on the motel. He could also get rid of the coffee he had been drinking all morning and pick up some more. "But make it quick," Joy urged. "She could come out any minute now."

Randy headed for a Home Depot store he had pinned on his phone's mapping app the previous night. Fortunately the store opened very early, 6:00 a.m. on weekdays. His top priority there was to race into the men's room. Then he paid cash for a roll of duct tape and a claw hammer. He went for the cheap hammer; titanium didn't seem necessary for the job he had in mind. One advantage of shopping at a huge chain store, he thought, was that the cashiers were unlikely to remember any of the dozens of customers they served each day.

Randy bought a cup of coffee from a walk-up cart in the same shopping plaza and drove back toward the motel. His phone had remained silent so he assumed Jessica was still in her room.

Before Randy returned, Joy saw Jessica's Honda turn out of the motel's parking lot. She called Randy over the walkie-talkie app, urgency in her voice. "She just pulled out. She's heading west, not east like she did yesterday. How far away are you?"

"About two blocks. I can see your Mustang. Good thing it's bright blue. I'll pull in behind you. Don't lose her!"

All three vehicles headed west, with Joy's Mustang half a block behind Jessica in her silver Accord and Randy's truck in trail half a block farther back. The shadowers followed as Jessica made a couple of turns. Randy got caught at one red light, but Joy noticed that in her mirror and told him they were still going straight. He gunned the truck and caught up to the women.

Joy realized they had turned onto Sumner Street, where she and Randy used to live. A tingling of apprehension crawled up her back.

"Do you see where we are? I've got a bad feeling about this," she called to Randy.

Jessica turned right onto East Sixteenth Avenue and slowed as though she were searching for an address. A man standing by a streetlight waved at Jessica. The Honda's brake lights flashed, and the turn signal blinked. As the man raised his arm to wave, Joy thought she saw a badge glint from his belt.

"Oh, shit! I think that's a cop. We've gotta get out of here. Meet me at the Home Depot lot."

Joy had to stop while Jessica parallel parked. She kept her hands on the steering wheel and her head facing forward, swiveling her eyes to the side to try to study the man standing by the streetlight. She thought he had "cop" written all over him. Then again, as tense as Joy felt, anybody could look like a cop to her today.

Randy and Joy rendezvoused in the parking lot of the Home Depot that Randy had just visited. She climbed into his truck.

"You know where we were, don't you?" Joy spoke rapidly in a high-pitched voice. "That's right about where Nikki parked when we drove to our apartment that night! Something's going on there. Do you think that guy looked like a cop? He looked like a cop to me."

"Take it easy," Randy urged. "They didn't see us. I turned off a block early when I saw you waiting for her to park. There's no way they would know we were together. You're just a woman driving a Mustang. They probably didn't even notice you."

"How did they know to look there, though? It can't just be a coincidence, can it?"

"I don't know. Maybe there's something we forgot about that led them to that neighborhood, or even to us."

"Well, there's nothing we can do about that now," Joy said with determination. "They're practically knocking on our old apartment door. If we're going to do anything with Jessica, we'd better do it soon. Did you get everything we need?"

"I didn't want to look too suspicious by buying everything at once, so I just got the hammer and the duct tape. How about if you go into Home Depot and buy the clothesline and rubber gloves? I'll go to Walmart for pillowcases and a plastic tarp."

"Okay. Afterward can you go to that self-storage place we found in northwest Eugene and rent us a locker for a month, maybe a ten-by-ten? That should be big enough. Be sure to pay cash. Meet me back at the motel. I'll call you if she takes off again."

They exited Randy's truck and walked in opposite directions across the plaza.

*   *   *

Jessica and Adam looked around the area. 353 East Sixteenth Avenue was an old house next to a twelve-unit apartment building.

"Nicole's Honda Civic was parked right about here when it was ticketed," Adam said. "We know she lived a couple miles away, so why was her car here? Maybe she drove here with somebody or to meet somebody and then spent the night and didn't know about the guest parking permit. Maybe she just ignored the ticket like she ignored all her other parking tickets. She could have been perfectly fine when she left here."

"Or," Jessica observed, "she might never have left here alive."

"Maybe, but if the car was still in the same spot the next day, it would have gotten another residential permit violation. If the parking enforcement people saw a car that hadn't moved and was accumulating tickets, they would have it towed."

"Good point. So we can narrow the time frame of Nicole's disappearance to between Friday evening, May 24, and Sunday morning, May 26. Someone must have moved the car between about noon on the twenty-fifth and sometime on the twenty-sixth. Is it possible to find out who owns the car now from the ticket?"

"Let me check the computer in my car." A fresh shower broke out, spattering on the sidewalk and street around them while Adam brought up the citation record. He went into a DMV application to look up the license plate.

"That plate is not currently issued. In Eugene, we don't write the car's vehicle identification number on a parking ticket, just the plate number, so there's no info about the car on the ticket."

"Could you get the VIN from DMV records?"

"I could. Then I could see if the car's registered in Oregon with different plates. If not, we'd have to check with all the other states to see if any of them have that vehicle registered. Then we'd have to trace its ownership history back to try to figure out how it got from Nicole to whoever owns it today. That would take a while, assuming the car still exists at all."

Unraveling the history of Nicole's car didn't sound promising. Even if they could locate it, there was no point in looking for fingerprints or other trace evidence after five years and countless occupants. Maybe whoever bought the car back then could describe the seller.

However, Jessica thought back to when she had sold the last car she owned to a man just two years earlier. All she remembered about him was that he was white, in his twenties, and around five feet eight inches tall with an average build and dark hair. That description only fit a few hundred thousand Americans. Besides, whoever was involved in Nicole's death might have disposed of the car as well. The Civic could have been in a chop shop on Sunday and in bits by Monday, for all they knew. Tracing the car wasn't likely to reveal a suspect.

Adam and Jessica pulled their jacket hoods over their heads and walked around the neighborhood. Oregonians rarely used umbrellas. A hat and a jacket with a hood normally sufficed. It's just water, Jessica would always say to people who asked her how she could stand all the rain in Oregon.

They agreed that their best guess was that Nicole Briggs died somewhere in this area. The location made sense. Whoever buried the body could have easily driven south to Lorane Highway heading out of town and then to the isolated Redhawk Road. A reasonable quest for suspects would start with the residents in this area at the time Nicole disappeared.

Such a search would be feasible if it had been a fresh case. They could canvass the neighborhood for anyone who saw anything, heard anything, or knew anything. However, within a few blocks of Nicole's last parking spot stood more than twenty apartment buildings, many homes subdivided into rental units, and numerous single-family residences. Eugene was, after all, a college town, with short-term renters and frequent resident turnover, plus some "unofficial" residents.

It would require astronomical effort to identify everyone who lived in these blocks five years ago, discover where they were now, and suss out any connection they might have had to Nicole. Even if they could do all that now, the chance of locating evidence sufficient to identify suspects, build a case, and secure a conviction was microscopic. Not zero. But close enough.

Jessica and Adam completed their circuit through the residential neighborhood and returned to their vehicles, very near to where Nicole had parked that fateful weekend. They sat in Adam's car, the intensifying rain drumming on the roof.

Adam broke the silence. "As much as I hate to say it, Lorane County couldn't possibly devote the resources to track down all those residents and reconstruct what they were doing here five years ago. It's a really old, really cold case." Jessica had come to the same realization, although she had not wanted to say it aloud. But an idea began to dawn as Adam continued, saying "You've done a great investigative job, Jessica. Everyone in the office is impressed, and we're grateful for your contributions. I just don't see where we can go from here, though."

"Wait," Jessica said excitedly. "We're inside the city limits now, right? So wouldn't this case transfer to the EPD's jurisdiction? The remains were found in rural Lorane County, yes, but all the evidence indicates the initial crime took place around here."

"We don't know that for sure, Jessica. Here's one scenario. Nicole meets somebody in a bar. They drive over here, maybe in Nicole's car, maybe in two cars. They could be going to the other person's house or apartment, or they could be going to a party. All voluntary: no harm, no foul. Then they go for a drive in the countryside. Could be two people, could be ten in a bus; we don't know. Maybe they go out to Redhawk Road, have a big party and a bonfire, somebody kills Nicole out there for some unknown reason and then buries her. In that case, it's still Lorane County's jurisdiction."

Jessica sighed. "I see your point. All we have is suspicions. We can't prove where a crime took place. We can't even prove *that* a crime took place, other than the obvious cover-up. So, what next?"

"It's still possible something will turn up that suggests new suspects. You can pursue this to whatever extent you wish. All I'm saying is that the sheriff's office and the EPD do not have the resources—or frankly the motivation—to try to locate all the old residents of this neighborhood. This really is one of the best leads we have. But it's a blind alley. There's just not enough to build a case. I'm sorry, Jessica."

Discouraged and disheartened, Jessica said she was going back to the Hideaway Inn. She would sort through all the information they had accumulated. Perhaps she would see something fresh to bring to his attention. Perhaps the phone call from the public that would break the case was right around the corner. Or perhaps there was just no point in continuing. She would touch base with him later in the day.

Chapter 35

Tuesday, June 26

THE SKY THREATENED more precipitation when Jessica returned to her room at the Hideaway. Instead of raindrops, she heard a rare rumble of thunder. Hailstones begin to plink onto the motel's metal roof, amplifying to a roar as the ice pellets poured from the sky. For two full minutes it sounded like she was inside a giant snare drum. The hailstorm passed as abruptly as it had arisen, leaving the parking lot a winter wonderland for about ten minutes.

Jessica fixed herself a quick lunch and then spent the next hour and a half scouring the notes she had accumulated regarding people she had interviewed, phone calls from the public, and possible suspects. Her original hope had been to reconstruct the last weeks of Nicole's life. In the end, that reconstruction was Swiss cheese. She had learned a lot about her twin sister's life. She just hadn't learned much about her death.

Jessica reflected on all the people who might have had some motivation to kill Nicole. Brian Stark was their first possible suspect. He had a history of violence and had raped Nicole years earlier. His phone call to Jessica made him sound somewhere between delusional and deranged. He appeared unpredictable and dangerous, and nobody knew where he was.

Jessica called Adam. "I haven't heard anything else from Brian Stark since that scary phone call last week. I just had an idea, though. Could you please check the records you found for him to see if he had any police problems around the time we now know Nicole disappeared?"

"Sure, hang on a second." Jessica waited, listening to Adam riffling through papers. "Here it is. We're talking about May 24 through May 26, five years ago. I'll be damned. At that time he was in jail in Lewiston, Idaho, for the beer-bottle fight I told you about. He got seven days for that assault. He served the sentence from May 23 through 29. So it looks like we can rule him out as a suspect in her death."

"That's good to know, even if it doesn't help us solve the case. Did you have a chance to check on the police incident with Marco Sabatini and Nicole?"

"I just heard back from the EPD on that." Jessica heard Adam's fingers clicking on his keyboard. "The call was for a disturbance on April 9. There was just a bunch of shouting going on between them, no violence. Sabatini complained that Nicole was late with her rent, again. Nicole said she would pay her goddamn rent as soon as Sabatini got rid of the goddamn mice in her goddamn apartment. The responding officer calmed them both down and they went back to their corners. No citations, no arrests."

"How about his police record?"

"Nothing serious. He had been in some fights, usually when he'd been drinking and gambling. I guess he wasn't good at either of those. How did he seem to you?"

"Like he had a temper that could go off easily. Before he opened the door I heard him yelling at somebody on the phone, sounded like another tenant he wasn't happy with. I think he's in the wrong business. I doubt he killed Nicole, though, unless there's something there we don't know yet."

"I agree. He probably didn't do it, but let's keep him on the list."

"I'm still working through my notes and records. I'll get back to you later today when I figure out just where we stand."

Her suspect list was dwindling. The old bouncer from Ruby Slippers, DeWayne Clinton, was still on the list. He had definitely pissed off Nicole; she might have done the same to him. Having died in an auto accident, he wasn't available to interview. Of the people she had met so far, no one else who knew Nicole appeared to have any possible motive for harming her.

She kept coming back to the Ruby Slippers Club, the common denominator numerous people had mentioned. The bartender there, Peter van Tassel, had speculated that Nicole might have connected with this mysterious couple he sometimes saw leave with other women. That was very thin. He hadn't actually seen the three of them together, he didn't know the couples' names other than maybe "Joy," and there was no way to determine their identities after all this time. Another red herring.

Unfortunately Adam was right. Based on everything they had learned so far, it did not look as though Jessica, the Lorane County Sheriff's Office, or the Eugene Police Department was going to solve this case anytime soon. Jessica recognized the logic from law enforcement's perspective. All of her candidates for knowing Nicole's fate either didn't seem to be involved, could not be identified or located, or were dead. More pressing—and more solvable— cases would understandably get higher priority.

Jessica began to despair of ever being able to reconstruct Nicole's final days. She placed one more call. "Adam, I just can't quit now. There must be something else we can try. I promised Nicole and Suzanne," she pleaded.

"You know, Jessica, in a perfect world, the police would solve every case, and every perp would get what he deserves," Adam said kindly. "You might have noticed we don't live in a perfect world. I had to learn long ago to just swallow the defeat and the disappointment sometimes. I hate it, but that's just the way it is."

Jessica did not respond. She had failed on this all-important case. Never before had she felt so impotent, so frustrated at the lack of justice for a wronged victim. She silently apologized to Nicole for being unable to solve the mystery of her death.

Finally she said, "I understand. We're not going to get there, not with what we have now. Are you getting any more calls at all from citizens?"

"No, the publicity campaign has pretty much wound down."

"Okay," she said resignedly. "I'm going to drive back home to Portland later today. If you get anything new, please tell me. You know how important this case has been to me. It tears me up that we can't solve it."

Adam said, "I know the feeling. I've been there before, many times. Solving cold cases is damnably hard. We've done better than I ever expected at the beginning, but sometimes we lose."

Jessica knew Adam was right, but that was little comfort to an investigator who had found only dead ends. She sighed and said, "I'll stop by your office on my way home later today and return the badge. Is there anything else we need to do to undeputize me?"

"Just a signature on a form when you stop by. The badge will still be there for you the next time you need it. It's been a pleasure working with you, Jessica. I've never had a collaborator so passionate about a case, or so persistent and tenacious. I hope we can work together again, preferably on something we can solve."

After Adam and Jessica hung up, she walked to the convenience store next door and bought a bottle of iced tea. As she sipped, she continued walking around the block, thinking about possible paths forward. She noticed a few hailstones from the recent downpour still melting away in the shaded patches of grass.

Jessica struggled to accept that she might never know who killed Nicole Briggs and buried her in the woods. She wasn't looking forward to telling her parents, BJ, Nicole's mother, Angela, and all the other people who cared about this case. But she had some other commitments to meet, friends to catch up with, and work to do. She had spent enough of her time and her parents' money on this quest. It was time to go back to Rosemount and pick up her life where she had left off weeks earlier.

She would never be the same, though. The realization that she had shared life, however briefly, with an identical twin would affect her forever. She would always feel a connection of love she had never known before.

Maybe Nikki's quest for thrills had ultimately put her in that cold forest grave, just as Maria's zest for danger had landed her in the hospital. In the future, Jessica was going to be more careful about whom she got involved with and how she spent her free time. She could have enough fun without pushing the limits of safety and good judgment. It was too late for Nikki to learn that lesson; it wasn't for Jessica.

When she reached the Hideaway Inn after her circuit around the block, Jessica packed up her belongings and loaded them in the car. She walked to the motel office and told the clerk she would be checking out earlier than planned, so please cancel the rest of her one-week reservation. Yes, she realized they had to charge her for tonight because she was leaving way after checkout time. Whatever.

Chapter 36

Tuesday, June 26

RANDY AND JOY had patiently maintained their two-vehicle vigil outside the Hideaway Inn. They perked up when Jessica returned after meeting with the cop near their old apartment building. When Jessica walked into her motel room, they figured they had a little time before the next act began. Joy joined Randy in his truck to finalize their plans. They didn't want to do that over the air with their walkie-talkie app.

"Whatever we're going to do, we have to do it today. I need to leave on another delivery route for work tomorrow morning, and it would look suspicious if I canceled at the last minute. Do we have everything we need?" Joy asked.

"I'm pretty sure. Pillowcase, hammer, rope, duct tape, hunting knife, gloves, tarp. Also I found a BB pistol at Walmart to make sure we can get her attention."

"Are you sure you can do this? It's a big step."

"Yeah, I think so. I never told you, but when I was hanging around with those pot growers in California, we had to deal with some intruders one night. Me and two other guys kicked the shit out of those assholes. They were hurt bad, really bad. I have to say, I got a rush from it. They deserved it. You gotta admit, Jessica deserves it too. If we don't get rid of her, we're about one inch from getting our asses sent to prison. So yes, I'm ready."

"I still don't see exactly how we're going to grab her."

"Let's play it by ear," Randy suggested. "It depends on where she goes when she leaves. We can maybe rear-end her car with my truck if she goes someplace that's kind of isolated, then grab her when she gets out. Or maybe pretend we have some problem and ask her for help, and then get her. I'm not sure. We'll have to see what she does."

Joy returned to her own car. They settled in to wait some more. They watched Jessica load her items into her car, walk to the motel office, and then return to her car.

*   *   *

Jessica pulled the Honda out of the motel's parking lot to leave Eugene for the final time. She first headed south, back to Ruby Slippers. As far as she knew, that was the last place Nicole was seen alive by anyone other than her killer. It seemed like the right place to say good-bye to both Nicole and Eugene. It wasn't busy late on a Tuesday afternoon. People were starting to trickle in for an after-work drink with their friends. Jessica didn't recognize the bartender on duty or any of the patrons she saw.

Jessica sat at a small table by herself and ordered a Stoli vanilla vodka—neat—from the waitress. She silently toasted Nicole's memory before taking a sip of the fiery liquid.

A stocky, bearded man with thinning, curly blond hair and an intricate dragon tattoo on his forearm walked into the club. He took a seat at the bar and ordered a beer. A few minutes later a heavily tattooed, buxom woman with short, dark-red hair walked in. She sat at a table near the entrance.

As Jessica sipped her drink, she looked around Ruby Slippers. It was a nice nightclub, she'd give it that. Good-sized dance floor, plenty of room for the band, a big retro-style bar that might have been resurrected from an old saloon or something. Maybe the last party

Nicole ever attended had started just feet from where she was sitting. The very thought gave her chills.

As she finished her vodka shot and got ready to leave for home, the blond man sitting at the bar stood up and walked over to her table. He smiled and said, "Hi, I'm Randy. I know it's an old line, but haven't I seen you in here before?"

Acknowledgments

THE RECONSTRUCTION **IS** my first work of fiction, but I've written enough books to know how vital it is to get review input from others. No matter how experienced a writer you are, having other people review and edit what you write will always make it better.

First, thanks to my ever-patient wife, Chris, who endured months of ceaseless chatter about Jessica and Nikki, and who read every word, often two or three times.

I'm especially grateful to Joy Beatty, Tanya Charbury, Richard Mavis, and Anne Millbrooke for their detailed comments on the entire manuscript. Thanks also for the additional helpful input from Mary Baillargeon, Adriana Beal, Bob Beatty, Joanne Beatty, Jim Brosseau, Sharon Buhlinger, Tam Dougherty, Diana Grace, Lea Loiselle, Scott Meyers, Thea Rasins, Kathi Schroeder, Dick Schubert, Alice Tarachow, and Ruth Wiegers.

Thanks much to several people who shared their knowledge on various specific topics: Loran Lamb-Mullin, David Reichle, Alice Tarachow, and Bruce Wiegers. Any differences between what they told me and how the information appears in the book falls under the forgiving category of artistic license.

I consulted numerous print and online sources while I was researching topics like forensic facial reconstruction, skull–photo superimposition, Chinese adoption, DNA analysis, and other topics. Lisa Bailey's book *Ask a Forensic Artist: Skulls, Suspects, and the Art of Solving Crime* (Honeybee Media 2014) is an engaging read for anyone interested in this topic. To see some fascinating videos of computer-based forensic facial reconstruction in progress, I suggest you visit http://bit.ly/2tY0c9g. The AFRAM software I described is not real, but it's patterned after the examples illustrated at that website. Thanks to Amy R. Michael for uploading a chapter titled "Human Identification Using Skull–Photo Superimposition and Forensic Image Comparison" by Norman J. Sauer, Amy R. Michael, and Todd W. Fenton from *A Companion to Forensic Anthropology*, edited by Dennis C. Dirkmaat (Wiley-Blackwell 2015).

I'm grateful to Laura Garwood of Indigo for her excellent copy editing and to Vinnie Kinsella for the cover design. They both added a great deal of value and were fun to work with. Thanks also to Chris Zambito and Anne Millbrooke for their careful proofreading.

About the Author

Karl Wiegers has a PhD in organic chemistry. He spent the first half of his career at Kodak as a research scientist, software developer, software manager, and process improvement leader. Since 1997, Karl has been Principal Consultant at Process Impact, a software-development consulting and training company. Karl is the author of seven books on software development and management, as well as a memoir of life lessons. *The Reconstruction* is his first novel. Karl lives in Happy Valley, Oregon, with his wife, Chris, and five guitars. You can contact Karl at either www.thereconstructionbook.com or www.karlwiegers.com.

Made in United States
North Haven, CT
24 December 2021